SAVING THE DREAM

by

Lois Carroll

Lois Carroll

WHISKEY CREEK PRESS
www.whiskeycreekpress.com

Published by
WHISKEY CREEK PRESS

Whiskey Creek Press
PO Box 51052
Casper, WY 82605-1052
www.whiskeycreekpress.com

ISBN 978-1-61160-345-3

Credits
Editor: Marsha Briscoe

Printed in the United States of America

Dedication

In admiration of the sturdy pioneers and native Americans who first lived under the broad blue sky of North Dakota

Chapter 1

Early Summer in Dakota Territory 1866

A shrill wail rose over the roar of the perpetual wind that bent the tall northern prairie grass to its will. The eerie and unexpected sound sent a shiver down Ingor Oleson's spine. He pulled up his reins and listened intently. Standing in his stirrups, he searched in all directions to identify the source. He saw nothing out of the ordinary and yet he knew the cry was no bird or animal that he'd ever heard before.

Had it been the damned wind howling? Spurring his horse on at a walk, he scanned the trees in the stand as it thickened around him, giving him better cover. Not one of them was growing up straight, not with the north wind constantly pushing against them. He often had to lean over to avoid drooping or broken branches.

He pulled his hat down more snugly and reined his horse even deeper into the tree cover that extended along the Sheyenne River that he was following northeast. His thirsty packhorse followed more closely now, smelling the water ahead of them. A cool drink would bring some relief from the constant dry wind to Ingor's dry throat, too, and maybe he could scare up a rabbit for dinner.

But just as he found cover behind the scrawny tree trunks, he heard the high wail again. This time the cry sounded shorter but higher than before. What was it? A man screaming for help in this empty wilderness? Or an injured animal he hadn't heard before? Whatever it was, it was making him feel uneasy and he didn't like it. Sound traveled long distances across the prairie, but he had a hunch the source was not all that far off. Not knowing what it was made him more wary of getting closer. The last thing he wanted to do was ride into a band of Dakota Sioux whooping it up.

Stopping at the riverbank where his horses could drink, he searched for signs of anyone who had passed that way. All he saw were signs of the receding floodwaters and the new tree leaves wagging in the breeze. They grew greener and thicker each day now that summer had finally come to the northern prairie.

The birds above him were chirping and flitting from branch to branch. Nothing seemed wrong or out of place to them, but Ingor's keen senses told him differently. Following his senses had kept him alive for nearly two years since he had made his way to the Dakota Territory, but he had learned what could happen when a man didn't pay attention to his surroundings. Pushing away the terrifying memories that still haunted him, he took just a minute to slide to the ground, scooped some water into his mouth for a fast drink, and filled his tin canteen. That should last him until he reached his cabin late that night near the Red River of the North.

He still remembered the first time he'd crossed that north-flowing river after his long lonely trek all the way from Norway. His parents dead, the farm unable to support all the sons, Ingor bore the burden of being the oldest and left for a better life in the United States first. His brother Lars followed last year and had settled a day's ride to the west with his wife, her brother, and a new son. Working together when they could, the brothers would make a life that had to be better than that which they left.

Making it to the Territory, Ingor had picked up a handful of the rich black soil and saw the hearty tall grass growing so thick a horse could hardly get through it, and he knew he was home at last.

But life since then certainly hadn't been easy. He still wondered how the trees and wildlife in the area could live through the wild winter blizzards that swept across the vast wide-open spaces. Storms that often lasted for days carried the temperature way, way down for long enough to freeze the ground solid to six feet deep. And it would freeze a man or animal in no time at all if they weren't careful, as it had almost frozen him his first winter here.

If Ingor had learned anything, he'd learned to be careful. But maybe since getting caught in a killer storm that was almost his end, he was overdoing it now. Maybe the wails he'd heard were just the cry of a hawk, and he was worrying for nothing.

Maybe, but he didn't think so.

He gazed through the twisted branches at the high puffy white clouds racing each other across the bright blue, unending sky. It couldn't have been thunder that he'd heard. There was no storm in sight and besides, the pitch had been way too high.

The leather of his saddle creaked as he mounted Thor, named after the Viking Thunder God, and patted his neck. The horse blew, letting Ingor know he was anxious to get on home.

"You not like sound either, huh, Thor? For a while there, I thought it was human." He shook his head. "I hope not. That would mean the Sioux move east, and I don't like that idea. Aw, maybe I'm just hearing things." He chuckled. "Hell, now I'm talking to my horse in Norwegian as if he would answer me." He patted the horse's neck. "I don't suppose that farmer I bought you from in Pennsylvania taught you Norwegian, did he, fella?"

Ingor clucked Thor into a steady walk and checked to be certain the packhorse was following. Seeing her reins were still tied tightly to his saddle, he leaned down to rub his leg that had ached everyday of the seven months since a trap had closed over his calf. He couldn't believe that he'd been so careless. But now the rows of bumpy scars where the iron teeth had chewed on his flesh and the healing bone that had broken were constant reminders to be on his guard.

If it hadn't been for his brother Lars, his pretty bride Lissa, and her younger brother Wally finding him, he never would have lived. Arriving at his cabin after crossing the country in a Conestoga wagon, they had saved his life and his leg. Now his calf predicted the weather for him, and he could tell that despite the mostly blue sky, there was a storm coming. Probably be here overnight, he thought. He wanted to get back to the cabin before that.

"Yaahoooo!"

At the new deeper sound, Ingor reined in Thor and leaned low in the saddle. "Now that was a man shouting up there beyond the trees. But who would be that stupid?" he said in a low voice to calm the horses and keep them quiet. He stroked Thor's neck and listened but heard no other shouts. "Is he white or Indian? Some poor settler in trouble?" he wondered out loud. "We'd better go a little closer and check it out. We're too close to home to want trouble to follow us there."

Turning Thor to follow a deer path just inside the edge of the tree line, he could see something moving out in the high grass beyond the trees. "There they are, Thor, but they're too far away to see who they are or what they're doing."

Ingor knew for damn sure that he didn't want whoever it was to see him before Ingor knew what he was up against. He worked his way to the edge of the trees and waited until he could make out that there were two white men on horses, shouting.

"Damn. Those fellas carry on like they're drunk in the middle of the day."

Ingor was not looking for trouble and just wanted to get

home to his cabin. He had to pack up the furs that he never took to Winnipeg in the spring on account of his leg needing time to heal. Now, he needed to sell them all fast, and then get back to work on oiling and repairing all his traps for the coming winter season. He only took animals then when their fur was the thickest.

Pulling off his hat, he wiped his forehead on his homespun shirtsleeve. "Why are those two men crazy enough to make noise that calls attention to them in Indian Territory?" he asked Thor quietly.

He could count on one hand the number of trappers and traders who lived between Canada and Fort Abercrombie to the southeast. Every one of them knew enough to be quiet so as not to attract the attention of any Indian parties roaming around looking around for trouble. There had been enough of that with deadly results.

Parties of young bucks had been scaring up trouble ever since the Army started rounding up Indians and relocating them to where they didn't want to go, namely off land that the white man wanted. It didn't matter that the Indians had lived there for centuries.

Ingor couldn't imagine why there wasn't plenty of room for everyone out on the endless open prairie—white and Indian alike. But the Great White Fathers, as his Sioux friend Red Moon called the men running the federal government, didn't agree. And lately they were getting more insistent that the Indian do things the way white man did, and that they get out of the land that the white man wanted as they moved west.

Ingor had made sure his brother and his family knew to keep an eye out for small bands that were roaming the area, set on getting even. He didn't think Chief Red Moon was looking for trouble, although Ingor knew he had announced that he wasn't about to follow government orders to move out either. He wanted to live his life as his people had for generations and tried to peacefully avoid the army.

"Come on! Move," the closer man in the prairie grass shouted angrily.

Stopping, Ingor checked the revolver holstered on his hip and the rifle in the long leather holder within easy reach at his knee on his saddle. They were both clean and loaded, but not knowing who was out there, he hoped he wouldn't have to use them. If he started shooting at Indians, it was a sure bet that he wouldn't live long enough to tell anyone about it. But he didn't think the noisy fools were Indians. They didn't yell orders in English that clear.

Not out here alone anymore, he had to think of his brother and his family. Ingor was on his way home after spending a couple of months helping Lars, Lissa and Wally build a sod house on land farther to the west. They'd picked out a section on the James River where they were going to claim their homestead.

After sharing his small cabin with them all winter while they cared for him, Ingor was happy to help them get a place of their own built. The work behind the sod-cutting plow had been harder than riding his trap line, but other than the delayed trip to Winnipeg to sell his furs, he had little better to do in the summer when furs were too thin for harvesting.

Two men's voices could be heard now. Thor snorted nervously and Ingor tapped his flanks with his heels to pace him at a walk again. The voices sounded louder and raucous. If that meant a party of Indians had gotten a hold of some firewater and they discovered him, he would wish he had some of his furs with him to bargain himself free. The alternative could get real ugly.

Torn between retreating until the men shouting went on their way or moving closer to see just what exactly they were doing, he gave his injured calf one more quick massage as he listened. Perhaps the voices were more settlers coming west, but he couldn't take the chance riding out in the open to see. Not much chance of it being settlers though, with no covered wagon in sight.

Unable to pick out any other words in their shouts, he even wondered if they could be an army patrol. He didn't want to take any chances of getting between the Army and any Indians because he didn't want to have to take up with either side. He wanted peace on the prairie.

He'd always gotten along fine with the Indians. He traded regularly with Chief Red Moon and his small band of about ninety Sioux, despite the Sioux reputation of being fierce fighters. They'd even saved his life his first winter here, and he didn't want that friendly relationship to change now.

Shifting in his saddle, he tightened his grip on the reins when he thought how proud any young Indian buck would be with his long blond hair hanging from his coup belt. That morning he'd tied his hair behind his neck with a strip of leather and flipped it up under his hat to be cooler as he rode home. Now he was feeling good that it was out of sight and not standing out as a temptation. He wasn't riding into trouble to be relieved of it if he could help it.

Closer whistles and then whoops, like those used to drive cattle, silenced the birds in the branches above him. Settlers with cattle after all, he thought, but he stayed within the edge of the tree stand and relied on being able to see movement beyond it once in a while between the trunks.

"There they are, Thor. They're coming toward the river," he whispered low.

He could make out two men on horseback. They were not moving fast and sat turned in the saddle as if they were watching something behind them.

"Couldn't be cattle, huh, fella? They would be in front of the drovers."

A snap from a whip and then a long high cheer from the men made the hairs stand up on Ingor's arms. That was no cattle-driving cry, and no drover would cheer after snapping a whip. As the two men came fully into view close beyond the trees, Ingor watched in disbelief, but only for the few seconds it took him to assess the situation.

"*Gud i himmel!*" he swore in Norwegian.

Two of the worst examples of humanity that it had ever been his misfortune to know were pulling a buckskin-clad Indian behind their horses. The Indian's hands were tied behind his back with the rope the older man held. The Indian was running bent over and twisted to the side as the rope pulled his wrists forward.

Ingor had suspected that this pair of white men had been low enough to steal animals from his traps, but treating an Indian like this was too low and stupid, even for them. Though he knew only their first names and not the family name, he'd heard they were father and son.

Jimmy, the young man, cried out with another gleeful whoop when his father, Hap, whipped the Indian again. The Indian ducked his head to protect his face. The sudden movement made him lose his balance. He fell and was dragged in the dirt, his arms wrenched up behind him. The men didn't slow up, much less stop when he fell. He bounced along on his hip and his shoulder that was probably dislocated by now.

Ingor clenched his teeth in anger. He couldn't begin to imagine the trouble for the whites in the area if the Indian's relatives discovered what was happening to one of their own. He'd seen enough of the cruelty to know he had no choice but to do something to prevent a war or wide-sweeping revenge that could mean death to him and probably his brother and his family, too.

He checked again to be certain his packhorse was securely tied to the back of his saddle, giving her no choice but to follow at the speed at which Thor ran.

"Get ready to run, big fella," he told Thor. Then, his revolver drawn, he dug his heels into Thor's flanks and galloped toward the three men, shooting Hap's arm as he raised the whip a second time.

The whip fell to the ground. A crack shot because of all his free time to practice, Ingor hadn't missed. He'd learned early on that he had to be accurate to shoot an animal when necessary and not ruin the salability of the fur with bullet holes.

The force of the bullet couldn't have sent the old man to the ground, but he fell anyway. That had to mean the pair was drunk, and Ingor figured they quit thinking and just got nasty when they were drunk. He'd seen them like that once at the Bay trading post in Winnipeg. Once was enough.

"Leave that gun in the holster," Ingor shouted to Jimmy in English. "Reach for it and I shoot you, too."

Jimmy left his revolver on his hip and slid to the ground from his saddle. "Paw." He ran to his father's side and helped him up to his feet. "You shot my Paw. Why the hell'd you go and do something stupid like that?"

Ingor glanced at the Indian. Dressed in a long fringed leather shirt over buckskin leggings, he lay with his face down in the dirt. His long black hair had worked loose from braids and fell across his bloodied face. Ingor saw no movement at all. All that leather to protect him from the coarse grass where they were riding hopefully had saved him from bad abrasions.

"This ain't no business of yours. We were just funning with the redskin," Jimmy whined.

"Fun over, Jimmy," Ingor announced.

"You know my name? Who are you, some sort of Indian lover?"

"Tie him on my packhorse," Ingor ordered, ignoring the questions and riding up next to the Indian.

"You cain't take our injun. Pa, don't let him."

"Do it," Ingor shouted. "And real gentle like," he added in a softer voice. His gun still aimed at the pair, he turned Thor so his packhorse stood beside the Indian.

"Hell, Paw, you gonna let him get away with this? I wanted to play some more."

Hap cradled his shot arm against his chest with his other arm and groaned at the pain. He lifted his hand and saw that it was striped with blood. "Damn it, Jimmy, just do what he says so you can help me stop this here bleeding."

The boy, who Ingor judged was about seventeen, gave him an angry look and stomped toward the Indian. He cut the rope tying his hands behind his back, and managed to lift him over the horse after his father came to help with his good arm. The blood seeping through the buckskins from his wounds left the white men's hands red. They wiped them off on their worn pants that were so dirty already that it appeared to make no difference.

Ingor wished he'd gotten a glimpse of the Indian's face to see if he knew him. He reckoned he would learn who he was soon enough, and prayed that when he could see him, he would not be looking at a dead man. That was all he would need: to be caught by a band of Indians with a dead, tortured Indian tied on his horse.

"Now tie him on with the rope you cut from his wrists," Ingor told Jimmy.

Jimmy did as he was told, securing the body to the packhorse so it wouldn't fall off.

"Now toss the knife," Ingor said flatly.

"What? My knife?" he asked, holding up the potential weapon. "I ain't throwing away a perfectly good skinning knife."

"You throw it in the woods, or I shoot it out of your hand. Then it not good for anything—the knife or your hand." Ingor watched as Jimmy looked to his father for direction. He nodded.

"And give it a good toss," Ingor added. He didn't want Jimmy running to pick it up while the boy was still in throwing distance of his back. After Ingor gave him no choice either, Hap's knife disappeared into the tall grass after Jimmy's.

"Now give me your rifles and revolvers."

"You cain't leave us out here with nothing to protect us from them murdering redskins, or some bear bent on having white meat for supper."

"You find your knives after I'm gone, and I leave your guns at Fort Abercrombie when I get there next. You explain to the major what you do out here and why I take them away. He decide if you get them back."

"Paw, he cain't do that," Jimmy insisted, childishly stamping on the ground with his foot. "How we gonna get them guns back? We cain't tell 'em what we been doing for a little fun."

"Will you shut up, boy?" Hap shouted as he backhanded his son on the side of his head.

"Oooww. Whadja go and do that fer? That hurt." Hap raised his hand to strike him again, but then just cradled his injured arm. Jimmy had already wrapped his arms around his head for protection and stepped out of reach of Hap's hitting arm.

"The guns. Now," Ingor ordered, getting more nervous by the minute. He wanted to move on before the Indian's friends followed the trail to where they were.

Hap handed his revolver to Ingor, handle first, and Jimmy did the same. He got the one rifle they had from his saddle and handed that over, too. Ingor held them braced against his stomach for the time being. He would slip them into his saddlebags the first chance he got.

"My arm's hurt something awful. Get over here, boy," Hap ordered. "Help me tie something around this afore I bleed to death."

"Don't ever let me see you two around here again. You got that? You not get off so easy next time."

Ingor reined Thor toward the east and tightened his grip on the saddle with his thighs. Jimmy hadn't taken more than a step toward his pa when Ingor shot his revolver into the air. The pair's loose horses bolted and ran toward the west. Jimmy whirled around and started after them while Hap shouted after him to help with his arm.

Ingor took advantage of the confusion of the moment and spurred Thor into motion eastward as he holstered his gun. Before the pair disappeared in the grass behind him, he saw Hap running after Jimmy, who had kept after the horses instead of tending his father's arm. They hadn't gone after the knives or watched to see which way Ingor was heading. But he knew it wouldn't take long for them to figure out who he was and where the cabin was. He wouldn't be at all surprised if they came to settle things someday real soon.

Ingor rode hard for a few miles in the open and then cut back into the trees. He slowed his horses and hoped the hard ride hadn't compounded the Indian's injuries. He wanted to do what he could for him and then deliver him to Red Moon in such a way that he could explain that he'd helped him, not hurt him.

How had that drunken pair of idiots gotten a hold of just one Indian in the first place? They sure couldn't have outsmarted his band. Not those two drunks. But if there were others out there looking for this missing one, Ingor could be in big trouble for trying to help.

To free his hands, he stuck the pistols inside his shirtfront. Pulling on the packhorse's reins to move her closer to Thor, he tucked the rifle under the ropes of his bedroll. Before he let go of the rein, he reached down to feel for a pulse in the Indian's neck. It was weak, but he could feel it beating. His neck didn't feel muscular at all. Probably a youngster out on his own for some reason when the drunken pair happened upon him. That could be a lucky break for Ingor if the tribe didn't miss him for a while.

Ingor looked at his sticky fingers and discovered they were bloody. The Indian was bleeding under all that hair, and on his shoulder and hip, too. He would have to stop the bleeding, but not until it was safe for them to stop for a while.

Not wanting to take the chance that Jimmy caught up with their horses, he kept moving in the river to hide his tracks and then turned up to ride along the riverbank. He was heading for a spot he remembered where the high spring waters had undercut the bank. With the lower water level now, the bank would be dry and the spot hidden from above. He felt it was safe enough to stop there because someone riding beyond the trees wouldn't be able to see him or even the horses.

Dismounting there, he put away the pistols in a saddlebag and let the horses drink while he cut the Indian loose. The boy was light, and Ingor had no trouble laying him down on his back on top of his blanket that he'd spread on the riverbank. Searching his head for wounds first, he pushed aside his matted bloody hair and located a gash on the side over his ear. It had been bleeding profusely but had nearly stopped now.

The lump that had formed under the gash was the reason the Indian was still unconscious, Ingor judged. He must have hit a rock as he was dragged across the ground. There was a lot of dirt and blood on his face that his hair stuck to, but Ingor would clean that up later after he'd checked out the rest of his injuries.

Ingor moved to sit on his heels beside the boy's waist and pulled out his hunting knife. He could see blood seeping through tears in the shoulder of his leather tunic. His shirt had to go to get to the wounds to clean them.

In one clean cut, he sliced the leather shirtfront open from the neck to the fringe at the bottom. With it opened that way, he would be able to slide it off without moving the boy much. Later, the boy could have the clean cut sewn together much easier than if Ingor had ripped it open trying to get it off.

That is if there was a "later" for the boy, he thought sadly. He sheathed the blade, took hold of each side of the cut leather and pulled it back to expose his chest.

"*Gud i himmel!*" Ingor whispered hoarsely as he dropped the leather and sat back on his heels and stared.

Chapter 2

Unable to move, Ingor stared down at two perfectly formed breasts with dark tips. And though one was scraped and red, they were the most beautiful breasts he'd ever seen.

He swallowed hard. "I am a dead man if they find us now," he muttered as he rose onto his knees.

Lifting her head on his hand, he turned her face up and pushed back her long tangled hair. This time he studied her face a good deal more carefully. With her hair matted and not in the neat braids she usually wore, he hadn't recognized her before. Now he did. He knew her and he knew he was a dead man if the tribe found them together. He felt chilled despite the summer heat.

He had rescued Still Water, Chief Red Moon's niece.

"How could they do this to one so sweet?"

He knew Still Water had been given her name because she'd never cried as a child. Chief Red Moon had taken Still Water into his own teepee and treated her as his daughter after her parents' deaths from the fever when she was a child.

At that moment, Ingor couldn't imagine being in deeper trouble with the Indians than to have the Chief's kidnapped adopted daughter, who had been beaten to within an inch of her life, on his blanket. He quickly dismissed the thought. Rather than worry about himself, he worried about her. "Still Water. What have they done to you?"

He would do everything in his power to keep her alive. It was the least he could do. After all, it was Still Water who had saved his life the first winter he spent in the Territory. It was the first time he'd ever seen her.

Determined that she would recover, he thought it was important that he know all the pair of drunks had done to her. Everything they might have done. Red Moon's band respected their women and an unmarried woman like Still Water would be an untouched virgin until she married.

Ingor's hand tightened into a fist. "If those two excuses for men touched you, I'll…" A tremor shook him. He'd been about to say that he would kill those men if they had raped her. He stared at her striking high cheekbones and tempting luscious lips. She was beautiful even covered with mud and blood, but he didn't want to think of that now. He had work to do to save her.

Still Water hadn't moved. Moving more quickly now, he removed her shirt completely and worked carefully to wash the dirt and small stones from her scrapes and deeper cuts on her shoulder, arms, and side. Hoping she would stay unconscious and not feel the pain until he finished, he removed her knee-high moccasins and leggings to clean the even deeper gashes on her hip and legs. She had cuts and gashes from head to toe.

Her shoulder, hip, and one ankle were swollen and discolored in addition to the open wounds. While he couldn't feel any broken bones, he tested her shoulder by rotating her arm. He released a sigh of relief when it moved smoothly and he heard no snapping in the joint.

"That good," he said, though knowing she couldn't hear. "It not out of place and it moved good."

After all her wounds were rinsed in the clear flowing water beside them, he turned her and held her head over the river's edge. The flowing water helped him clean her long thick hair. Cradling her head in one hand, he shook his kerchief in the clear water with the other and gently wiped her face clean.

"This feel good?" he asked. "There are not many scratches so you not worry. Most was smeared blood from head. I think cold water help make swelling less." Maybe if he kept talking to her, he thought, she would wake up and respond.

"When I hurt my leg, my brother's wife put snow on it each day to take out swelling."

By then the river had washed most of the blood out of her hair. He finished getting the blood out of the part close around her face by squeezing water over it with his kerchief. The water had rinsed out the soil in the gashes, but he didn't touch them directly so they wouldn't bleed more.

Finally, gently twisting the water from her hair, he tied it at her neck with his wet kerchief and laid the long tresses over the less injured side of her chest.

Next, he wiped as much blood as he could from her tunic and was struggling to get it back on her when she moaned. Worried that she would wake frightened by what he was doing, he froze. His panic receded when she didn't move or speak. He laid her down and pulled the slit leather sides over her breasts the best he could.

"Rest easy, Still Water. *De ikke kan dø. Ingenikke nå,*" he said softly to tell her in Norwegian that she couldn't die. Not now.

Seeing that the weight of her breasts had kept the shirt open, Ingor didn't want to leave it gaping. With the tip of his knife, he punched three little holes on each side of the slit between the soft mounds. He tied the sides together with pieces of leather he'd cut from the bottom fringe. The effect was modest enough—he hoped. Quickly, he pulled on her leggings and laced on her tall moccasins.

Sioux Indian maidens didn't show their bodies to men other than their husbands, but he couldn't have cleaned her wounds any other way. He hoped she would forgive him. Finished with what he knew to do for her, he stayed at her side, looking at her. He always had thought she was beautiful. Now the memory of her pale brown skin and black hair sweeping over him as she cared for him was enough to make him a good deal hotter than the June afternoon warranted. It had been almost more than a man should have to stand to wash her. The dusky cleavage still visible above the ties on her shirt didn't help any either. But he couldn't think that way about her.

He had to get her well and back to her people.

Even now, imagining what had actually happened to her, before he came upon them, haunted him. He hadn't touched her intimately, but he'd seen no blood between her thighs. He wanted to think that meant he'd rescued her in time—before the two men had had their way with her.

Suddenly, Still Water moaned and tossed her head. She had begun shivering. He hadn't thought about the washing and the wet leather making her feel cold. He had to get her warm.

Berating himself for daydreaming instead of taking better care of her, he rose to get his bearings. It was nearly dark. He hadn't realized how much time had passed since he'd stopped. That was stupid. If he didn't know how late it had gotten, he hadn't been aware of his surroundings. With the Indian maiden in his charge, being aware of everything going on around them was now a matter of life or death—his and hers.

They were still too far from his cabin to take shelter there for the night. Riding at a slow pace so Still Water wasn't jostled too much would take more than the daylight hours left in the day. His horse could step into a prairie dog hole and break a leg trying to travel in the dark.

The storm clouds he'd predicted were moving in and the woods darkened. With the two poor excuses for men wandering around looking to do him harm, he didn't dare start a fire to warm her up. It could attract too much attention.

He had nothing more than the blanket she lay on from his bedroll and the saddle blankets. They would have to do. The month of June could still have some frigid nights this far north. He could only hope this wasn't going to be one of them.

Removing the saddles and blankets from the horses, he tied the pair close by on the grassy bank for the night. As the horses began to munch on the grass, he remembered he hadn't eaten since breakfast. But this was not the first time he'd skipped a meal or two. He pulled out a stick of jerky and chewed on it as he went back to Still Water's side. She would probably be awake by morning light and then they would move to his cabin. He would fix her breakfast there to make up for not eating tonight.

Carefully laying the saddle blankets on the ground on top of each other, he lifted Still Water onto them. Her hands felt cold and her heartbeat felt too faint to be good. He had to warm her up fast. The sun had set, leaving him few options.

His rifle and revolver within easy reach and the others in his saddlebag nearby, he pulled off his boots. Lying down beside her, he opened his shirt and rolled her against him. He wrapped the shirt over her and pulled up the blanket up around them both. Rolling onto his back so that she was mostly lying on top of him with her head on his shoulder instead of on the smelly horse blanket, he held her securely in his arms.

He kissed her hair and sighed. Thinking of the injury to her head, he knew she had to wake up soon. And when she did, he hoped that she wouldn't hate him too much for what he'd had to do to help her.

An owl somewhere above him helped him to stay awake and alert most of the night. Thankful, he never heard anything other than the ordinary night sounds that he'd heard so often sleeping outdoors overnight as he checked his trap line.

But when the first light of morning made movement in the woods visible, Still Water lay heavily on top of him as she had the night before—still unconscious. Ingor listened to her pulse and found it was a little stronger, but she still felt cold.

Briefly, he thought about taking her straight to Red Moon's camp so the healers could care for her in a warm teepee. But Ingor had no idea where the band was camped, so the only option he had was to get her to his cabin. There he would build a big fire and wrap her in his furs. When she woke, he would feed her some hot stew to give her strength.

But he had to get her there first.

* * * *

Getting them both up on Thor's back turned out to be difficult. Once the horses were saddled and his bedroll was rolled up and tied on the packhorse along with the tools he'd taken to help Lars build his sod house, Ingor finally managed by walking Thor down river a ways to where the bank was a couple of feet high with a sheer drop to the shallow water.

There with the horse close against the bank, he lifted Still Water into his arms and rested some of her weight in the saddle.

"Steady now, Thor. Steady."

Swinging his own leg over the saddle, he sat on Thor's rump, and after lifting her again, he scooted forward far enough to get his feet in the stirrups. He settled Still Water in the space left and leaned her against him so she wouldn't fall.

"Good, boy." He patted Thor's neck and turned him back to where the packhorse was still tied to a tree. Using one hand, he tied her reins on his saddle, and they turned northeast along the river.

Ingor cradled Still Water in his arms the whole distance to his cabin. "I hate to think I had to carry you tied over the packhorse yesterday," he said in English to Still Water as they rode. "Maybe I not tell you that part when you wake up. I think you be mad enough."

He kept up the one-sided conversation as Thor walked in a smooth gait, but the trip took its toll on her. Her head hung limply over his arm, and she no longer moaned in pain or showed any sign of awakening.

They arrived at his cabin about noon. He untied the packhorse and flipped the tied reins over her neck. Doing the same with Thor's reins, he slid to the ground, Still Water held firmly in his arms.

"Go on," he told the horses. "Go get a drink," he added, knowing they would head straight for the trough beside the stable where there was water collected from the rain plus what he added to it from the river when needed. After being gone so long, he hoped it wasn't empty.

Making Still Water comfortable in his bed was his first priority. He could take off the horses' saddles, brush them down, and put out feed when she was resting comfortably. In the meantime, they wouldn't go far. They knew that staying close to the barn would be rewarded with food.

Pulling open the unlocked door with his foot, he carried her into his one-room log cabin, and held her seated on the foot of the rope-sprung bed. He carefully stripped off her stained clothes and moccasins, and threw back the quilt to lay her down naked with her head on his pillow. He laid her beautiful hair over to one side and replaced the handkerchief that he'd wrapped around it with a leather strip to keep it from pulling as she moved her head.

"I don't like the looks of those gouges on your hip," he said as he checked her wounds. "They're red and nasty looking." He still had hopes that hearing his voice would make her react.

He got the new bottle of whiskey he'd bought at the fort and poured a bit over her angry-looking cuts. He caught the spillage with a washing cloth and used the wet cloth to tie around her elbow where the gashes had begun to bleed again from bending her arm to undress her. He'd learned that from his sister-in-law who insisted it was important to use whiskey to clean wounds. From Still Water's shoulder to her ankle on the side where she had been dragged on the ground, her skin was purple and swollen.

"I think maybe it is good you not awake yet. You feel a lot of pain. But now you rest."

After carefully dabbing each abrasion from her head to her feet, Ingor spread on some of Lissa's salve that had made his leg heal more quickly than he'd expected. But leaving Still Water uncovered long enough to care for her had set her to shivering again. He laid the quilt over her and a few minutes later he had a fire going in the wide fireplace that doubled as his cooking fire. He put on the coffeepot so she could drink something warm when she woke up, and he drank a cup as soon as it was ready. Returning to her side, he stood beside the bed and watched for any movement as he drank it but saw none.

"I go take care of horses now. You just rest. You are safe now, Still Water. I not let anyone hurt you."

With a sigh he headed for the stable, closing the cabin door carefully, making certain the latch caught and the door wouldn't blow open. Unsaddling and grooming the horses took little time. He gave each an extra measure of grain and fresh water in their stalls. He carried a few more pails of water from the river for the trough and then filled the two to take back to the cabin. Still Water looked exactly as she had when he'd left her.

"Maybe the smell of food wake you up." He smiled at the thought and set about to work.

With skill born of living on his own for years, he fried some bacon and mixed up some biscuits that he dropped in a pan to bake in the reflecting oven beside the fire. It probably wouldn't work so well with a new fire instead of glowing coals, but a pan of biscuits, even burned ones, would be good to have on hand.

Hungry as he was, he ate more than half of them as soon as they were done. Breaking each one open, he folded a piece of bacon inside and took a good bite. He washed it down with another cup of coffee.

Once he'd eaten, he sat on the side of the bed. He gently felt Still Water's forehead and then chided himself.

"How can she be feverish, when she's shaking with the cold?" he asked himself out loud. "Don't you worry none, Still Water. The fire go good now, and you be warm in no time." He tucked the blanket up over her shoulders and lifted a few errant strands of her hair from her cheek.

"I be right here, sorting the furs to take to Winnipeg. I must sell them soon or I not have money to buy supplies for next winter. You get a good sleep."

His worry about her deepened when he saw no change that evening after he'd eaten his supper of the leftovers from noon. The bolt locked across the inside of the cabin door, he sat at her side on the plank edge of the bed. Lifting her hand from under the quilt, he could feel it was still cold to his touch. He laid his hand on the side of her face and found it cool.

He frowned, thinking he had to get her warmer. He could pick her up and lay her closer to the fire, but every move would cause more pain and might open her wounds. And too, he couldn't tell if a cracked rib, or other injury that he couldn't see, was getting worse each time he moved her. No, after suffering through the long ride on horseback, moving her was not the answer.

In fact, Ingor didn't see that he had any options left but one. Still Water had to get warm. He'd heard of men who had been injured badly and felt cold just like her. Some had never awakened from their cold sleep and soon died. He couldn't let that happen to Still Water.

So despite the warm summer day outdoors, Ingor put more wood on the fire and walked around behind her to the opposite side of the bed.

"I sorry, Still Water. You might hate me for this, but I know no other way to get you warmed up," he told her as he shed his clothes and hung them over the three stump he used as a chair that sat in the corner of the room. "But you not worry. You safe with me. I never hurt you. You are maiden and Red Moon's niece. You save my life and I only honor you."

Wishing she understood what he said, he lifted the corner of the quilt. "Hell, Chief Red Moon skin me alive if he discovers what I do," he mumbled as he climbed into the bed. "That is, if I not die from wanting her too much," he added.

His persistent arousal had been building since he'd decided to warm her up with his own body heat. Hell, if she was any other woman and awake and willing, he could warm her up in no time.

"No, no," he said propped on one elbow, smiling down at her. "I not do that to you, Still Water. You sleep good because you safe with me. I promise."

He could never live out his fantasies with her because it would ruin her reputation and spoil her in the eyes of her family. Of course, there was always the fact to consider that her uncle, Chief Red Moon, would kill him as slowly as possible, and without a moment's hesitation.

He groaned and tried to think of anything but the soft and lovely body in bed with him. He slid toward her and gathered her into his arms spoon style. Carefully avoiding her bruised hip, he laid his arm over her narrow waist.

"When you wake up, I hope you understand. I think you will—if you not kill me first before I can explain," he added with a little smile.

Unable to sleep in his present condition, he began thinking about how long he had known her. "I still remember the last time I saw you at Red Moon's camp."

Over the past year the Chief had invited Ingor to eat a meal or smoke the peace pipe with him when he went to trade with them. Still Water had moved at the edges of his vision as she served the meal or did whatever Red Moon bid of her. He'd noticed her watching him on more than one occasion. When he glanced directly at her, their gazes would lock for only a moment or two. A maiden, she would always be the one to look away first.

"Do you remember the last time I was in your camp?" he asked without expecting an answer, a grin curling his lips.

Seated at the fire in the chief's teepee, he'd watched her so intently that he'd lost track of what Red Moon was saying to him. Annoyed, the old Chief had twisted in his seat to see what Ingor was looking at. When he discovered it was Still Water, he'd angrily sent her out of the teepee. She'd fled without a word or another glance in his direction. Ingor had stammered an excuse for his inattentiveness, and his conversation with the Chief had continued.

"I didn't see you again until I leave next afternoon. You stand behind the Chief's teepee watching me as I check Thor's saddle. You wore beautiful white leather dress with long fringe. I never saw leather so white. I want to touch it to see if it is soft as your skin."

Their gazes had met over the horse's back, and he'd held hers until once more, she first lowered her head and ducked out of sight.

Now, lying behind her with their bodies curled close together, Ingor let his eyes drift shut. Tired after staying awake most of the night before to keep watch, he was finally falling asleep. Still Water's breathing seemed to get more regular as she relaxed against him. He thought she was shivering less, too.

"You finally warm up. That good," he mumbled. "Now I just need to cool down," he added as he fell asleep with a smile on his face.

His night was fitful and filled with nightmarish dreams. He wasn't dreaming of the last time he saw Still Water in Red Moon's camp. He was dreaming about the first time.

His dream of Still Water stretched back to his first winter in the Dakota Territory. That winter he'd nearly lost his life by being caught away from the cabin in a terrible Dakota Territory blizzard. Any man not as fortunate would have died and frozen as hard as Lot's wife.

He'd never been so cold in his life and unable to keep moving; he was certain he was a dead man.

Chapter 3

The storm that first winter had come upon him without warning. That was his excuse, but he should have known better. All day he'd stayed in the trees along the river, looking for signs of animal dens where he would set his traps. He'd rarely looked at the sky that had been blue when he started out. He'd set his traps, and all the time he'd tried with little success to ignore how cold he was getting as the temperature fell quickly and the wind increased.

He'd felt cold in Norway, but with the mountains north of his village, the bitter cold winds didn't often threaten them with death as it did in Dakota Territory winter. The only real protection he'd found from the killing blast was by the fire in his cabin.

He had already doubled the furs he wore and still his hands and feet hurt from the cold. He'd wrapped his face in fur until all that was visible was a slit he could see through. It hadn't been enough. He was getting dangerously cold, and his cabin was many miles to the east.

Thor, the horse he rode with a travois tied on to carry his harvested furs and traps behind them, was the only horse he owned then. He'd bought his packhorse in the following late spring at the fort. Worried about Thor, Ingor had draped him in furs to stop the wind, too. Snow and ice crusted on their furs, adding to the weight that Thor had to bear as he struggled through ice-crusted snow up to his belly.

At one point Ingor managed to free a frozen fox from the trap and somehow reset it, using his mittened hands after his fingers refused to bend. But he had no strength left after that. He shoved the whole fox under the crisscrossing ropes on the travois.

Even too tired to climb back up into the saddle and desperately wanting a rest, Ingor lay down the center of the travois, on top of his pelts, and ducked his head as he drew his knees up to his chest. Lying on his side, he tucked his hands and feet under the ropes used to hold the pelts, hoping to find some measure of warmth and protection from the freezing wind.

He had wanted to sleep only for a few minutes. Then he would have the strength to ride back to his cabin. As tired as he was, falling asleep was easy. Falling asleep was a blessing often granted people who were freezing to death, he knew. And yet he could not resist.

With no one to order him to stay in his place, Thor began to move to find better shelter from the wind. The jerky movement of his first step was the last thing Ingor felt until a strong light hurt his closed eyes. He blinked them open, intending to see what the light was, but quickly shut them tighter than before. He wanted to bring back the warm darkness where he had found a safe haven from the cold.

Unable to block out the light, he blinked again and saw mounds of furs with dark angry eyes staring down at him and the snow swirling all around them. Was it a circle of coyotes sniffing out their next meal? He couldn't hear them howling, but he wanted desperately to know what they were. He pulled to free his hand from the rope to get his gun, but his arm wouldn't move. His eyes shut again, he couldn't fight the sleep that carried him back to the darkness.

When he woke the next time, he knew he'd died and gone to hell. The whole area around him was filled with smoke and glowed red. He quickly shut his eyes against the gritty burning sensation, and groaned as he tried to move and discovered that he hurt everywhere.

Then hellish tormenting began at once. Some devils poked at his cheekbones and nose and ears, and he gasped at the pain. When they lifted his hand and turned it, he cried out in anguish. His spine arched with the burning agony, but doing that, he pressed more on his legs and his feet hurt even more.

The pain forced him to wake completely. He managed to open his eyes and focused on the harassing devil seated beside him. A knurled crone with dark, age-pleated skin looked down into his face. Long gray braids fell on each side of her head, and a beaded-leather band crossed her forehead. She looked old but surprisingly not fierce.

"You drink," she ordered as she lifted his head.

Maybe, just maybe, he wasn't in hell.

A hand from somewhere else forced a wooden cup between his lips. The warm liquid nearly choked him as it passed over his thick dry tongue and throat. He coughed and ached in all his joints with each spasm. That didn't satisfy her. When he stopped coughing, she nodded her head and the cup was pushed against his teeth again.

"You finish. Drink slow."

This time he concentrated on swallowing the warm liquid a little at a time. He was only beginning to realize how thirsty he had been when the crone nodded her head again. The cup was taken from his lips and the disembodied hand that had held it disappeared from his line of sight. But he didn't have the strength to keep his eyes open anyway. In moments he traveled back into a world of warm darkness where his pain was forgotten.

The next time he became aware of his surroundings, he remembered he'd heard a soft feminine voice chanting. Though he couldn't see her, he could tell she was nearby. He heard no movement, no sound but her velvety aspirate tones. When he blinked his eyes open, her chanting stopped and he'd felt disappointed. She said something, but he didn't understand a word of it.

He tried to speak, but the words died before they were formed. He licked his dry lips with his thick tongue and tried again.

"Where am I?" he managed in a voice so hoarse he hardly recognized it as his own.

Almost silently, she moved to sit on her heels by his shoulder where he could see her. She smiled and her white teeth caught the light from the nearby fire. Her skin was paler than the crone's, though darker than his own even after a summer tan. Her dark hair hung in two braids framing her high cheekbones and slender nose. She looked pleasing but unfamiliar to him. It took him a moment to realize that she was an Indian.

He took in a sharp breath. Why was this one caring for him? Making him stronger before they killed him?

Dressed in leather from head to toe, she seemed to be wearing a short dress over trousers. Fringe cut in the leather ran along the bottom of her tunic and down the side of her trousers. He could see beaded moccasins on her feet that must have taken a long time to make.

He'd seen a few Indians in the towns he'd ridden through as he'd neared the Dakota Territory. Few had been women and not one had been as pleasing to look at as this one.

Smiling, she reached out and laid her long slender fingers over his forehead for a few moments. They felt warm and comforting. His eyes floated shut at her gentle touch only to pop open again when she lifted her hand and spoke. He hadn't understood the guttural sounds, but the smile and the soft touch told him he had nothing to fear from her now.

"Humph. You awake," a much older voice said in broken English.

The crone he'd seen earlier had entered through a buffalo-hide flap that performed as a door to what he now recognized as a teepee. Looking up, he could see the ring of crossed poles and the blue sky beyond. So it was daytime and the storm had passed, but he had no idea how many days had passed since he fell asleep on his travois.

The crone sat on his other side and arranged several small hide bags on her stained doeskin skirt.

Speaking to the young woman in short directives in her native tongue, she took pinches of some the contents of the bags and piled them in her palm. The younger woman brought her a cup of warmed water. She stirred in the mixture of powders and ground leaves and handed it back.

"Drink slow. More later," the crone directed, looking at Ingor.

He lifted his arms to hold the cup and couldn't, but saw his aching hands were bound in strips of wet cloths. The young woman helped him lift his head with one hand and held the cup to his lips with the other so he could drink.

When he'd swallowed the requisite number of sips of the foul tasting liquid, the crone talked to the young woman who mixed the contents of some of the other bags in tepid water in a bowl. He couldn't understand the language that the crone spoke, but he enjoyed watching the lovely young woman as she worked.

Turning to him with that smile he'd found so comforting, she slowly unwrapped his hands. He sucked in his breath to keep from crying out and embarrassing himself. She dipped the strips of cloths in the solution she'd just made and reapplied them to his very painful extremities. It was all he could do to remain silent as she did the same to his feet. He couldn't remember ever being in such pain.

"You hurt here?" the old woman asked as she poked his cheeks.

"Not bad as before," he managed.

"Good. Ugly beard save you." He heard what he thought was a giggle from the young woman, but when he glanced at her, he could see no sign of it.

"Where am I? Who are you? How bad my hands and feet get? They hurt like hell," he said, wanting to know everything at once and hoping they understood him.

The crone spoke to the younger woman in her native tongue, and then looked back at Ingor. "You in the Sioux Chief Red Moon's camp. Your horse bring you here. Her Still Water," she said with a flick of her hand toward his nurse. "Dead brother to Red Moon her father. She say she want care for frozen white man when no one else speaks. So we not take your horse and hides and leave you to die. She can learn much of good medicine." She shrugged. "If she not do good, no one care if you die."

That was very informative, but not what he wanted to hear. He leaned against the pillow of rolled fur under his head as the little strength he'd felt waned. "My horse. Where's my horse? My furs?"

Still Water laid her hand on his shoulder. "Be still, Pale Hair. Horse feel better than you. You cover him good in furs and deep snow protect him from wind. He smart to find cover in thick trees where we find him."

She spoke English and he liked that. Though his own English was far from perfect, he would be able to talk with her. Her soft voice carried no threat, but he hadn't the strength to ask more.

"Good. Thank you, Still Water," he managed, using her name.

The crone rose and handed the small bags one at a time to Still Water, all the while speaking in their native tongue. She was apparently telling her what was inside each one and what to do with them. As the crone prepared to leave, she turned back to Ingor.

"You sleep now. You need something, you say. Still Water here. She bring." Shaking her head, the crone rose to leave.

Yes, Still Water, Ingor thought. What a beautiful name.

Ingor hadn't the strength to keep his eyes open to watch her any longer after the crone left. He heard the leather door of the teepee drop shut and felt the gust of cold wind that opening it had allowed in.

In the months he'd been in Dakota Territory, he had yet to meet an Indian who lived near him. Now he was helpless as a baby, surrounded by them and in their camp. He could yet be a dead man.

He thought of his brother Lars back in Norway who might never learn what happened to him. He and his brother had made an agreement after their mother had died so soon after their father. They worked the farm with their two younger brothers, and when that work was done, they'd hired out as carpenters. They were both saving all they could to go to America. The brothers had all agreed that the two older would leave and the two younger would stay. The farm would not support them all.

When they had saved enough for one passage and a little extra for getting started here, Ingor, the oldest brother, had been the one to leave Norway first. Lars would work another year and save more money. Then he would follow Ingor, who would hopefully have a place for them to live and land to work by the time he arrived. Lars would help to improve what Ingor started—both the house and the land. The two of them should be able to expand to enough land to support two families.

Then the year after that, their Uncle Ole would choose good wives for them both and send the girls over on the first ship out in the spring. They would have money in their dowries to use on their way across the United States as far as the trains would take them. At the end of the line, they would send word to Ingor and Lars, and the men would go pick them up. They would get married in that end-of-the-line town, and then return to Dakota Territory and the homes the men had ready and waiting. At least that was the plan.

Ingor had sent only one letter back to Norway. Before he even arrived at the Dakota Territory, he wrote to Lars that he would build a cabin near the Red River. He described what others had told him of the area in hopes it would help Lars find him. Ingor had done what he said he would, but he could only hope that the letter had made the journey to Norway, and that Lars would come.

But now helpless in an Indian camp, Ingor worried about what Lars would do. It was a big country and unless he got all the way to the Dakota Territory, he would find no one who knew Ingor or where he had gone. The farmer who sold him Thor would never remember his name. He had not even been able to pronounce it. Only some men at the fort would know him. No one else would remember him. Lars would be on his own unless Ingor could get well enough to walk and make it back to the cabin.

The fire crackled. Still Water must have added wood. From the soft rustle of her long deerskin tunic, he knew she had returned to his side. He could stay awake only long enough to feel a veil of comfort come over him just because she was sitting at his side.

When next he woke, the circle of dark eyes was back around him, staring at him. A chill passed over him that would not let him return to the blissfully painless sleep he had known. As the eyes came into focus, he could hardly believe what he saw. The small comfort he felt then was that they were not coyotes.

The chill he'd felt was the wet cloth Still Water passed over his naked chest to wash him. She was kneeling beside him on one side, while four women about her age leaned over to watch eagerly from the opposite side.

He wondered if he was completely naked, but the feeling in his limbs was not back to normal, and he couldn't even tell. He knew that Indian braves thought nothing of being naked. In the summer heat he'd heard of men wearing only loincloths or working completely naked.

But he was not at all comfortable with the thought that all these women were looking at him. The women giggled as they watched his nipples harden into pebbles in the cold.

As they watched, he could be thankful for one thing. The pain in his extremities, plus his embarrassment at being scrutinized, kept his body from reacting to Still Water's gentle touch as it might have on some more private occasion. Yes, for that he was deeply thankful.

Still Water rinsed the cloth in a bowl and spoke sharply to the other women. Instead of moving or doing anything she might have asked, they covered their mouths and giggled more.

"What the hell's so funny?" he croaked.

Still Water would not meet his gaze. She rinsed his chest and patted it dry. "They think much pale hair on chest is funny."

He raised a hand self-consciously to his chest. Touching the warm skin with his fingers caused him to wince. He raised his hand and saw the cloth that had been wrapped around it was gone. He was startled at the condition of his fingers and raised the other to inspect it, too. His fingers were swollen and looked a waxy, dark grayish color.

He tried to raise his head to look at his feet but could not. "My feet," he said. "Are they the same and my hands?"

Still Water washed his arms without answering. Why wouldn't she tell him? Was she afraid to tell him they were worse? He had to know. He knew she had covered them with the same cloths warmed in a basin of water prepared with herbs from the crone. Taking a deep breath and gritting his teeth against the pain, he pulled himself up onto one elbow.

The women watching laughed and chattered excitedly. Still Water addressed them with a short command that Ingor thought must have meant, "Shut up!" The women quieted at once but watched his every move.

He couldn't manage to pull up the fur that covered him from the waist down. He looked up at Still Water. "Show me feet," he ordered. "I must see feet."

His teeth gritted against the pain, Ingor would not take no for an answer. He had to see his feet so he could judge for himself how bad they were. He had to know if he could ever walk again. If he could not, he was a dead man. A man who couldn't get around could not survive in the wilderness.

She met his gaze for a few moments and then with a slight nod, she folded the fur back to his knees and then lifted the cloths from over his feet.

"Damn!" He collapsed back onto the pallet, knowing that he couldn't walk out of this camp now if his life depended on it. He felt so weak that he didn't even think he could crawl out.

His toes on one foot were even darker than his hands while the other was about the same. Even his heels were gray. The worst was that he didn't know if they would heal enough for him to walk again or not. If not, the Indians might just as well kill him.

His nurse re-dipped the cloths before she covered his feet again. The pain he felt deep inside his feet was intense. Once his feet were covered, she folded the fur back across his clean chest. She paused in washing him and was holding his head up and helping him drink a warm but bitter tasting drink when the teepee flap opened.

An Indian man entered and let the flap drop into place behind him. His graying black hair hung over his shoulders and was held off his face with a leather band across his forehead. Several eagle feathers hung from the back of the strip. At his chest he clutched a colorful striped blanket that was wrapped around his shoulders to keep him warm.

The women, who had been watching Still Water minister to Ingor, shrank back as if caught doing something they shouldn't have been doing. They lowered their faces and didn't speak until he spoke sharply to them, and then within seconds they had wrapped themselves in blankets and disappeared from the teepee. Ingor was thankful to lose his audience.

The old Indian sat beyond the fire, facing the door, not far from Ingor's head. He let the blanket fall to the earth behind him and held his hands out to the fire to warm them. He was dressed in a leather tunic and pants with intricate beadwork across the chest and down the side of each leg. A decorative piece of beaded leather hung across his chest. It was covered with beads of several colors.

He spoke more gently to Still Water than he had the other women, and then waited as if for an answer. Ingor finished the drink and Still Water lowered his head to the pallet of furs. Setting down the cup, she folded her hands in her lap.

"My uncle wishes to know the name of Pale Hair whose horse brings him near our camp," she said to Ingor.

Ingor turned his head to meet the old man's gaze. "My name Ingor Oleson," he said. "I very thankful my horse brought me here. I thank you for the care of this kind woman."

Still Water translated what he said, and he couldn't help but wonder how she and the crone knew English when this old man didn't seem to. It wasn't until later in the conversation that he realized that the Indian was commenting on what he said before Still Water had translated. So he understood some English, but Ingor didn't know how much. He only knew he chose not to speak it or to let Ingor in on his secret knowledge.

The man waited patiently as Still Water translated each time one of them spoke, until Ingor had explained that he was a trapper with a cabin near the Red River. Embarrassing Ingor, he had guessed from getting caught in the storm that this was Ingor's first winter in Dakota Territory.

At first pleased at the discovery, Ingor learned the old man was Red Moon, Chief of this band of Sioux Indians. However, Ingor felt a chill as he remembered that the only thing he'd heard at the fort about the Sioux was that they were fierce fighters and hated white people. Not for the first time, the thought occurred to him that they were saving his life only to take it later. It was not a comforting thought.

He was feeling groggy by then, from the drink Still Water had given him, and could barely keep his eyes open. His hands and feet throbbed with each heartbeat. His head lay turned to the side to see the Chief, but he didn't have the strength to lift it anymore.

In a lull in the conversation when he didn't answer, Still Water pushed his hair back from his forehead. He had closed his eyes and hadn't the strength to open them. He must have fallen asleep because when he woke the next day, he could remember nothing more of the Chief's visit after she had stroked his forehead.

Each time Ingor woke over the next few days, he felt stronger. Encouraged, he began to devote himself to two campaigns on which he was certain his life depended. First, he worked to build up his strength again as his hands and feet slowly healed. To accomplish the second, he concentrated on what the Indians said around him in order to learn as much of their language as he could. He often asked Still Water to repeat a word or phrase until he pronounced it close to correctly, or to learn what it meant.

It was several more days before Ingor was confident that he would not lose any fingers or toes, and many more days after that before he could effectively use his hands to feed and care for himself. It took more time before he could walk without pain, but he tried several times each day. He couldn't give up. His brother was depending on him.

In all that time, Still Water had patiently cared for him, performing intimate duties that embarrassed him to no end.

He admired her courage and was thankful that she had convinced her uncle that she could care for the man they called Pale Hair. He'd heard them try, but they could not pronounce Ingor. That made him feel somewhat better about the trouble he had pronouncing the Indian words he was learning.

During the weeks of his recovery, Ingor saw more than once that the braves were angry at the Chief's decision to allow Still Water to care for him. She was a maiden, untouched by a man, and the niece of the Chief who had raised her as a daughter. They knew the intimate relationship she had to have with the white man in order to care for him. The braves came to Red Moon's teepee daily once Ingor was on the mend to talk to their Chief and, Ingor decided, just to see him lying there with Still Water always nearby. The young men stared at him with hatred and a desire to shoot him with many arrows he was certain. Though he could see as the weeks passed, their stares were not without some jealousy, too.

One particular brave, who came often and seemed to have nothing better to do than stay in the teepee and watch whatever Still Water did, was Tall Cloud. Taller than most of the other braves, he was good looking as far as Ingor could assess, but a hardness spoiled his features. He spoke and acted with an air of authority. Ingor didn't know what that authority was based on until he asked Still Water one afternoon after the brave had finally left.

"He think he be Chief one day," she explained.

"How can he be Chief? Is he Red Moon's son?"

She shook her head. "No, Red Moon had two sons, and

they died of the fever at the same time my mother and father die."

"I'm sorry," Ingor said, regretting bringing up the sad memories for her. "Then how could he be Chief? Don't the elders pick chief when Red Moon's time has ended?"

"Tall Cloud says he be Chief because he marry the niece of Red Moon," she said without looking at him.

Ingor nodded, understanding that would give Tall Cloud an edge with the elders. Suddenly, it occurred to him exactly who Red Cloud's niece was.

"He's going to marry you?" he asked, not liking the thought. She was a gentle caring person and deserved someone better than the big gruff bully Tall Cloud.

She shrugged and handed Ingor the herbal tea she had been making for him. "He think he marry me. My uncle say he not ready to decide who I will marry."

She grinned then and Ingor knew she was glad that Red Moon had not promised her to Tall Cloud. Ingor was glad to hear that and took an extra turn around the teepee that afternoon.

* * * *

Toward spring Ingor had decided that he could finally make it back to his cabin on his own. When that decision was made, he got two surprises. One, the tribe would let him leave. They hadn't been curing him only to kill him after all. And two, he was surprised by feeling that he was sorry to leave. Aside from the pain and causing Still Water so much work on his behalf, he'd enjoyed their time together. They'd shared stories of their adventures, always skirting around difficulties between the whites in the Territory and the Indians.

Ingor had never felt so comfortable with a woman before—white or Indian. However, the better he felt, the more his body seemed to enjoy her presence. When she touched him, he began reacting instantly. To avoid embarrassment to him and any hint of threatening her, he did everything for himself as soon as he could and tried not to even touch her. Once he could feed himself, he ate his meals with Chief Red Moon and learned more about his people.

Never again would he believe what he'd heard at the fort about Indian squaws, as the soldiers called them. He'd learned first-hand that the Sioux Indians respected their women and the family protected the maidens until they were married and became their husband's responsibility. Still Water was a maiden to be respected, thanked, and credited with saving his life. He could think of her in no other way.

Before he left the Indian camp, he gifted Red Moon the best of the furs he'd collected plus most of the ones he'd used for covering himself and Thor. Tall Cloud demanded that they take all the furs and leave none for Ingor. He wanted his horse too, but apparently wanted him away from their camp more. Only a horse could take him away fast enough so he allowed that Ingor should keep Thor.

Still Water persuaded the Chief that Ingor needed to keep some to trade for goods for the coming year. Ingor could tell the chief didn't like the idea of his niece speaking up for him, but Ingor was grateful for a few to wear for protection against the cold, which lingered through late spring this far north. He was grateful too that they let him keep his guns and skinning knife. As he rode out of camp that morning with a smile and a wave, he wondered if he would ever see Still Water again.

He found himself wishing that he would.

Chapter 4

During the many months after they saved his life, Ingor had traded with Red Moon's band on several occasions. He could think of no reason why they were so friendly with him except that they knew he was alone and no threat. He had never shown any anger toward them, not even anger at Tall Cloud who stretched his patience to the limit at times.

After trading furs or tools with them, Ingor sat with the men at Red Moon's fire and caught glimpses of Still Water preparing the food they shared. She was always in the shadows and never sat with the men. Their gazes might meet for a few moments, each looking expectantly at the other. However, there was never an appropriate moment to speak to her in camp again with any more than a greeting.

And now…

Now to have her beat up and unconscious in his bed with him taking care of her was unbelievable and dangerous. He couldn't think of the danger to him when he was so worried about her. If she would only wake up. Her cuts and abrasions would soon heal, and he could make arrangements for her to rejoin her band. They would be looking for her. Tall Cloud would be hunting for his woman and would not stop until he found her and killed whoever had taken her. Ingor shuddered a sigh when he thought of what would happen if Tall Cloud found her in his cabin with him.

By the following night, Still Water had not awakened and Ingor was pacing the floor beside the bed. His time during the day had been occupied making more room in the cabin by packing his sorted furs in the rafters of the barn in bundles that he tied securely with rope. He had to get them to the traders in Canada soon before the field mice made meals of them.

All the while he worked, his concern for the unconscious woman in his bed grew. He checked on her often and expanded his pacing from the bed a few steps to the table, to the corner where the furs had been piled, and back again.

Still Water hadn't awakened enough to know where she was or what had happened, but she was reacting to his care. When she moaned and tossed her head, he would hold her up with his arm around her and manage to get her to drink some warm coffee that he dribbled into her mouth. Not responding any more than to swallow, she often choked on the few drops. Then he would see her face etched with the pain she felt. But he wanted to think that was a good sign that she would wake up soon.

Doing everything for her, he'd cared for her as he would a baby. His having to do that didn't bother him. She had cared for him in the same intimate ways. Her not waking up did bother him. He desperately didn't want her to die.

As he wiped her face yet again with a cool damp cloth, he debated going to find someone else to help. First, he thought of taking her to Red Moon. He could make a travois behind the packhorse with a bed of soft furs, and she could lie there for the journey. Maybe Red Moon had a healer in his band who would know what to do to make her wake up.

Or should he take her to Lissa and Lars' place? His sister-in-law would know what to do. Already he had used most of the salve that Lissa had left with him to treat her cuts and scrapes. If he took Still Water there, he could get more. No, he reasoned. That would put them and their new baby in danger if the Indians came nosing around looking for Still Water. It was better that they knew nothing about her.

Hell, Ingor had no idea what would be best. A frustrated sigh escaped his lips as he ran his hands through his hair and then planted his fists on his hips as he watched her. Since he'd gotten her warm the first night by sleeping close to her, she seemed to sleep more easily during the rest of the night. But by morning she'd felt too warm to his touch.

After wiping her heated skin with damp cloths, he kept one over her forehead as his sister-in-law Lissa had done for him the winter before when he'd run a fever. He wiped her lips with a very wet cloth and let drops of water slide into her mouth, which she swallowed.

Without anything but Lissa's salve and whiskey for tending her wounds, there was nothing more he knew to do. He would watch her through one more night, and then if she didn't wake up, he would find help—somewhere. He couldn't just stay here and let her die.

After stepping outside after dark to check on the horses and relieve himself, he returned to the cabin and banked the fire. At least he didn't have to keep the fire going full blast anymore to keep her warm. He'd felt so hot with the fire blazing the day before that he'd gone to the river for a swim to cool off. The cold water had helped bank his desire. But his concern for her and his respect for her helped that too.

As long as he was going to the river, he'd washed some of his clothes including his winter long underwear that he would not be needing again until late fall. Using lye soap, he also got most of Still Water's blood out of the sheet from yesterday and even tried again to get the blood out of her buckskins. The spots lightened some, but the dark stains seemed impossible to remove completely. Until the leather dried and he'd worked it to soften it again, he couldn't put it back on her. Instead, he'd dressed her in one of his flannel shirts and hoped that she wouldn't be too frightened when she woke up and saw it if he wasn't around.

Was there something else he could be doing? The thought that he was failing her after she had saved his life haunted him. He was really out of his ken when it came to taking care of a sick or injured woman. Having had only brothers, he knew little about living with women. He'd often wondered how he would ever manage living in the cabin with a wife. It wasn't idle thinking because his wife-to-be would arrive from Norway next year. Actually, his uncle Ole Oleson was probably already arranging for two women he thought suitable to come to Dakota Territory—one to marry him and the other, his brother Lars.

He shook his head and stripped off his clothes down to his drawers. He had to remember to write a letter to Uncle Ole and tell him that Lars already had a wife. He would have to carry the letter to the fort for the first leg of its journey to Norway. Now that the war that had been raging between the states had ended, there was a better chance that it would be delivered. He could only hope that it would arrive in his little hometown *before* the women were chosen and began their journey to Dakota. The plan was that they would be leaving on the first ship next spring to get all the way to Dakota Territory before the following winter set in.

Ingor sighed and ran his hand through his hair. After checking that the door was bolted, he lifted the quilt and lay down behind Still Water. She moaned softly and rolled against him, her arm leaning against his chest.

"It's only me, Still Water," he said softly. "It's Ingor, friend to Chief Red Moon. Your friend, too. I'll keep you safe. You can rest easy."

She rolled back onto her side facing away from him and slid her backside over until she was nestled against him.

She had moved on her own, he realized. He grinned broadly, happy to see her showing signs of recovery. But when her warm flesh came against his, his grin quickly disappeared.

"Aw, you not want to lie like that, do you?" he asked, feeling his own temperature rise. She said nothing and didn't move away. "Hell, I just think of something else," he vowed.

But all he could think of was her soft skin and beautiful long hair that shone blue-black like a raven's wing. He'd brought some cold river water back with him after washing up, and washed her hair again, the first time with soap. It would not do to have the smell of whiskey or the sight of blood in it to upset her when she woke. The swelling around the gash on her head had gone down a bit which pleased him.

He tried thinking about how to find Red Moon's band and return her to her uncle. They had to be somewhere around where the drunks had been whipping her. But when he thought about her not being in his cabin with him, he was startled by the realization that he would miss her.

"Nay," he told himself sternly. If she were awake and demanding things that all women wanted such as china dishes to eat off of and fancy clothes, then he would not be so disturbed by her leaving. It was only because he was lying with her in his arms that he wanted her to stay.

But would Still Water want those things that he thought white women wanted? Or would she be happier living the simpler way he was accustomed to living? Would she mind going with him and camping under the stars as he checked his trap line during the winter. The two of them would be much warmer bundled up together than he ever had been alone. And he'd feel more content because he wouldn't have to worry about her home alone.

She was used to traveling in all seasons, and might enjoy the treks to Winnipeg each spring to sell his furs. From what he'd seen, the folks in Canada were much more tolerant of the Indians, though not everywhere, he had to admit. And people weren't bashful when it came to showing their hatred of Indians.

He thought she would love having the furs. Certainly she could be a real help in curing the hides before he took them to trade or sell. Yes, he could see that she would fit into his lifestyle a lot better than a Norwegian bride would. He had worried more than a little bit that his bride from back home might not like what she found when she finally got here. If she wanted all those fancy things that he thought all white women wanted, what was he going to do then? He didn't have any of them and he didn't have the money to buy them even if there was a store nearby that carried them.

Still Water stirred and took his hand in hers, holding it between her breasts over her heart.

As pleased as he was that she was moving under her own power, Ingor still gritted his teeth. It was going to be another long night, and he could count on needing another cold dip in the river come morning.

That is, if she didn't wake, while he was asleep close behind her, and slit his throat.

* * * *

As the night air cooled with the fire banked, Still Water tucked in tighter against the heat beside her. Her vivid dreams credited the cocoon of warmth to an attractive brave, who wrapped his long strong arms around her and held her close to protect her. Their bodies knit together perfectly, and before long their lips met in tentative kisses that soon became searing. His tongue sought entrance to her mouth, and though surprised, she welcomed the new sensation.

His warm fingers opened her shirt, baring her breasts. He caressed the soft mound and teased the tip until it was a high firm peak. He toyed with the hard tip with his tongue and kissed her again. His thigh slid between hers as their bare legs entwined intimately.

She arched her body to expose her neck as he trailed kisses down the slope of her jaw to between her breasts. Her heart raced as she ran her fingers into his long hair. He pressed against her thigh, making her moan as hot waves of new sensations swept over her. Never had she felt this special before. Surely this brave's touch was pure magic.

She raised her arms to caress his shoulders, but a sudden intense pain radiated from one of her shoulders. She cried out with the pain that startled her awake.

Her dream evaporated as she opened her eyes and discovered a nearly naked white man beside her. He was the one who had been kissing her breast.

"Still Water?" he asked in a hoarse voice.

In the dim light all she could see was long pale hair covering his face. Who was he? How dare he touch her so intimately?

And then in an instant she remembered all that had happened, and she screamed. Two men had kidnapped her as she gathered herbs with other women. One had held his hand over her mouth to keep her silent and then they had carried her away. It had taken both of them to hold her in her struggle to be free. The one time she managed to break free, they caught her and hit the side of her head with their fists. When she woke, she was tied behind their horse. They made her stand and run to keep up. Hoping her people would hear her, she wailed high and long. The men only jerked the rope, knocking her down.

"You shut up, squaw, or you be even more sorry."

Not willing to give in, she wailed again as soon as she was back on her feet. The older man snapped his whip at her, but she dodged it. That only made him angrier. He raised his whip to strike her again when the younger one yelled at him.

"Stop it, Paw. We don't want to kill her before we have our fun with her, now do we?"

The older one hesitated and then curled up the whip. But he kept it in his hand, ready to strike again.

At that point she vowed that she would not give them the satisfaction of thinking she was afraid. And she would kill them, or herself, before she would submit her body to theirs. Now, one of them had her nearly naked in bed with him. She would keep her vow and kill him, or die trying.

With lightening speed she grabbed his hand from her breast and bit it until she tasted blood. The man cried out and looked at her as he jerked back his hand. She used the moment to free her legs from under his and sat up, pushing back the quilt. Her shoulder hurt so much she felt nauseated from the pain.

Shouting something, he knelt behind her and grabbed her wrists, holding them together over her breasts. He would not let her flee. And she would not let him see how much he humiliated her.

"Still Water," the man shouted. "Take it easy. I'm not going to hurt you. You safe with me. It's Ingor. You remember me. I'm not the man who stole you from your people. I could never do that. You safe now. You safe now."

Her head pounded with a deep ache at each of her rapid heartbeats. The room spun around her. Her shoulder and hip throbbed painfully, but she looked back over her shoulder at his face. It slipped in and out of focus. She tried to concentrate on what he was saying to keep from passing out.

"I your friend, Still Water. Ingor, the trapper. I not hurt you. Please, lie down and try not to move. You open wounds again."

His gentle but firm voice slowly penetrated the fog in her head, but the meaning of his strange words floated away. She knew that with his superior strength holding her in place she couldn't escape. Not now anyway. But there would be other chances.

She ceased her struggling and let him help her lie down. She peered at him again through a veil of her hair now tangled over her face. His blue-eyed gaze was steady as he watched her. His shoulder-length blond hair hung forward on each side of his head. She had seen him before.

"It's me, Ingor. Friend to Red Moon. Friend to all in his

family. Friend to you, Still Water. Let me help you."

Even in the little firelight, she could make out his yellow hair. Yes, she knew this man. She had thought he was an honorable man. "You?" She swallowed hard past her disappointment in seeing him. "You did this terrible thing to me?"

"*Gud i himmel*! No," he breathed as he closed his eyes and his face filled with pain. "I could never hurt you." He lifted the light quilt to cover her. "I do my best to help you since I took you from those bad men."

"You take me from those two?"

"Yes. You safe here."

He rose from the bed and stood with his back to her as he pulled on his pants. He looked around, seeking his shirt, and they both realized that she was wearing it. Still Water felt the warmth rise into her cheeks as she quickly buttoned the shirt. He crossed to a peg on the log wall and pulled on another shirt that had been hanging there.

"When I get you away from those bastards, I clean you up the best I can."

He looked down at his feet and she knew he was remembering bathing her naked body.

"Oh, and I put salve on scrapes," he said, looking back at her. "My brother's wife gave me some extra. It's good. It saved my life. You remember my bad leg."

"Ah, that not important now." He dismissed his own problems with a wave of his hand. "Your wounds all heal good." He kept his eyes diverted now by watching the fire.

Rolling onto her side slowly in pain, she watched him

cross to the fireplace and stir the embers. When flames reappeared, he added a few small logs. As he put the coffeepot on the iron tripod over the fire, she tried to push herself up on her elbows. Pain shot through her one arm and shoulder. She gasped and fell back down to the straw mattress, cradling her bad arm with the good.

"Hey, easy there. You got too beat up to sit up. Just lie still and rest. I get you something to eat and you feel better then."

Her head still pounded. She raised her good arm and discovered the lump on the side above her ear.

He had been watching her. "I think that lump is the reason you've slept for two days and three nights."

"I was gone from my people for that long?"

He nodded.

"What will Red Moon think?" Tears suddenly burned at the back of her eyes. "He will think I am dead."

She could stand the pain she felt in her body, but she didn't want to cause any pain for the uncle she loved like the father he had been to her.

He finished measuring the coffee grounds into the pot and set it over the flames. Returning to the bedside, he sat on the wood edge of the frame that supported the ropes on which the straw-filled pallet lay. He pulled the quilt up farther to cover her shoulders.

"You not be sad. As soon as you can move good with no pain, I take you to Red Moon."

She frowned. "He go to Canada where our people can be

safe. He may be hard to find."

"We find him; I promise you."

She looked up at his smiling face and felt a little more reassured. He always had been kind to her.

He looked away again. "I...I sorry I was the one to find you, Still Water," he said softly. He looked at her then, concern written all over his face. "But that was better than leaving you in hands of those two devils. I...I real sorry for what I must do to take care of you here."

Unbidden tears stung in her eyes again and this time a few spilled down her cheeks. He wanted nothing to do with her, but the responsibility had been forced on him because he could not leave her with her kidnappers. But now she could see that he was another white man who wanted her people out of the way, far away from where they wanted to live.

After all the times she'd seen him and heard him in her uncle's teepee, she had thought he was different. But maybe she had just wanted him to be different. If she were ever in trouble, she would have chosen him to be the one to help her. She thought he would do his best. His trades with Red Moon had been honest and fair. He was always respectful of her uncle and of her. And she liked his long blond hair and blue eyes in such contrast to her own dark coloring.

While she had felt a thrill when she woke and felt his body close to hers, he was sorry he'd had to get involved. She did not think she could complain though. He had taken good care of her from what she could see.

She had learned about the ways of men. Once she understood he was not lying close to her to try to rape her, she could feel that for a few moments at least, he had desired her. But he was probably dreaming of a white woman when they awoke in each other's arms. Her lips thinned as she felt anger at her foolish hope that this man could care for her. She should be content that he would return her to Red Moon.

"You must hurt something awful. You rest and I make us some breakfast."

He turned to prepare the food and she looked around the rustic cabin. It was neat and orderly for a man who had no woman to look after him and do for him. There were pegs driven into the logs all around the room on which he'd hung his clothes, outerwear and gear. He had a rope stretched between two of the pegs and she saw her tunic and leggings hanging there. Had he tried to clean them? One side was nearly in shreds. No wonder she ached so much.

She remembered the two men kidnapping her, but she remembered nothing of what happened after she fell while running behind their horse. She pushed back the hairs from her face and investigated the bump on her head more completely. She felt relieved that she could move both her arms and tried her legs. While she didn't think there were any broken bones, he had been correct. Her scrapes and bumped head would hurt for some time. She couldn't guess how long it would be before she could raise her injured arm or ride a horse and use the muscles in the painful shoulder.

With the quilt protecting her modesty, she systematically checked out her wounds. While she no longer feared Ingor or felt the immediate need to escape, she needed to be aware of how she was physically and how soon she would have the strength to leave. He would not want her to stay a minute longer than she had to so that he could be relieved of the burden of looking after her. Her leaving might also save his life. They both knew what would happen if her uncle, or worse, Tall Cloud, found them together here.

Chapter 5

Ingor watched Still Water out of the corner of his eye, and knew she was trying to discover just how badly she had been injured. Only she could tell for sure if there was something wrong inside, something like a broken rib, but from the way she was moving, he didn't think there was. Nothing had stopped her from fighting against him when they woke.

She winced when her hand ran over her bruises, but she could turn her body just fine. She poked her foot out from the side of the quilt and turned her foot. Her ankle was swollen and dark, but she was able to move it. He felt relief that there didn't seem to be anything broken. If those two men came to exact vengeance, she would have a better chance to escape harm.

He cut up and boiled some venison jerky, and poured her a cup of the broth. "Let me put this blanket roll behind you so you can sit up a little and lean on it," he said, reaching for his blanket roll that had been hanging from one of the pegs.

She muttered something that he didn't understand, but

allowed him to lift her shoulders and slip the roll behind her. She exhaled a ragged breath as she leaned against it, and he knew that even with his help, sitting up had caused her a great deal of pain.

And having a man care for her in the situation where she was not married to him could only be adding to her pain. He wished his bride-to-be were here already from Norway. Then she could care for Still Water to save her the embarrassment of having him do what she couldn't do for herself.

His brow knitted as he acknowledged that the idea of his bride here in the cabin now didn't sit as well with him as he'd first thought it would. *He* wanted to be the one to take care of Still Water, not anyone else. And would his Norwegian bride even want to help an Indian? If she came out here thinking bad of Indians the way some of the folks he'd learned about at the fort thought, then she wouldn't even want her in the cabin. She might get the vapors at the idea of her sitting in their bed. He shook his head at the thought.

Once Still Water was comfortable, Ingor held the cup until she wrapped her fingers around it and took a sip. She looked squarely at him and thanked him in her native tongue. That was a phrase he knew from his time with her tribe.

Actually he knew quite a lot of her native tongue. He kicked himself mentally for not using it when she first woke up. She might have understood him sooner and not been so afraid. She pulled the cup back to her lips and drank again.

"Take it easy on this. You not eat in days, and you want

to start out slow." He spoke in English, glad she understood him.

She nodded. "This good," she said.

He grinned and her face created a beautiful smile. "Now I know you hungry if you think this man's plain broth good."

Her cheeks revealed a little tinge of pink and her dark eyes sparkled. He couldn't get over that she was much prettier than he had realized from seeing her at Red Moon's camp. Taking care of her for a while would be no chore at all. In fact, he would downright enjoy having her as company.

"Hungry is good. I glad you awake now. You cold and shivering at first, but yesterday, you too warm. I see big lump on head, but I very worried when you not wake up."

When he was certain that she could handle the cup on her own, he let her take it. He rose and sat at the table where he ate some biscuits and bacon left from the night before. She said nothing, but he could hear the catches in her breathing that signaled her pain as she bent to drink from the cup. She didn't look at him, and he missed seeing her smile when it wasn't there.

"I know you want to know," he began and then hesitated. "Ah, after I take you away from those bastards, we camp by the river for the night. You not wake up and I cannot do much more than clean you up some." He drank the end of his coffee and not anxious to get back to his tale, he got up and refilled his cup. He waited until he was settled at the table again to continue.

"We too far west to come here to my cabin by nightfall. I

not know how bad you are hurt."

She remained silent, but he could feel her dark gaze on him. What was she thinking?

"You understand?"

She nodded and then her face became pinched with pain.

He pushed his empty plate away and looked around the cabin. His saw her tunic and other clothes on the line stretched beyond the bed. "I try to wash out blood," he said with a shrug, pointing to them. "I must cut them off you, so it take some mending to make them fit to wear again."

She looked down at his shirt that she wore and raised her gaze to meet his with her unspoken question.

"I wash that shirt and some winter things at the same time. You wear it until we get something else for you."

"I sew my clothes. They be fine," she assured him.

He swung in his chair to face her but didn't rise from it. "I think maybe you should to wear my shirt under your tunic. You see many tears to sew up. To get it off, I must cut up front. I sure hated to, but...." He raised his hands in a helpless gesture and then dropped them to his thighs. "Sorry."

She raised her hand to between her breasts and knew that she was thinking about his looking at her naked body. The pink returned to her tanned cheeks, and she lowered her eyes.

"Ah, hell. There's nothing else I can do, Still Water. I feel bad with you unmarried, but no one around besides me."

She tried to smile, but he could see her lower lip quivering. "No, I thank you," she managed softly. "You save my life.

I am better here with you. Not want to be with those men who take me away. I rather be with you." She looked up shyly and then quickly looked back at the quilt.

He ran his hand through his long hair and wished he'd tied it back. It was getting hot in the cabin with the fire built up to cook and to keep Still Water comfortable.

"I did what I could. Those men…ah, they not do nothing to you, did they? I mean, I know they hurt you bad dragging you. Ah…nothing like between a man and a woman…"

She frowned, silently questioning what he meant.

He took a deep breath. "Hell, they not force themselves on you, did they?" he said in a rush. He didn't understand why, but it was important to him to find out that she hadn't been violated. He didn't want her hurt in that way.

She shook her head and looked away. Then she looked back suddenly as if she had thought of something new. "They not…not do anything unless after I hit head when I fell." Looking away, she added in a weaker voice, "If they did after that, I not know it."

Ingor released the breath he'd been holding. "Hell, no. Not do it then." He crossed to sit on the bed beside her. "I saw you when you fell, and Thor raced to get you. They not touch you after that. I swear not then."

He didn't go on to say he'd had to tie her to his pack-horse. That might be humiliating for her. She heaved a sigh, and Ingor knew she was as relieved as he'd been.

"Thank you," she whispered. "You do so much for me."

Their gazes locked and held this time. He wanted to go

on looking into those obsidian depths. He raised his hand to touch the softness of her cheek when he caught himself. He slapped his hand against his thigh and looked away.

"No need to thank me after all you did for me, but I… I wonder how those men take you from your people?"

"I was washing herbs and berries at a stream to get mud off from rain splashing," she said quietly. "The two men point their guns at me and put dirty cloth in my mouth. The old one makes the young one put me over the old one's lap on his horse, and we ride away from camp. The other women not see us go because they not come to the river for water then."

She paused and took a deep breath, wincing at the pain in her side. "The old man touch me in ways I not like. I get loose twice by sliding free and falling to ground. Only they catch me and hit me so hard my head spins inside. But I didn't want his hands on me. He should not touch me that way. My uncle would kill him slowly if he knew. I fought with him and scratched his face."

Tears welled in her eyes and she squeezed them shut to force them out. "When we farther from the river, they tied a rope on my hands behind my back and the other end to the saddle. They make me run behind." She turned her head until their gazes met again. "If you not rescue me when you did, I be dragged until I dead." She looked away. "Or until I am so hurt I cannot fight what they want to do."

This time Ingor didn't hesitate. He brushed a few errant tears from her cheek and cupped her jaw in his palm. "You not have to worry about them now. They all gone. You safe here with me. I make sure of that."

"Thank you," she repeated in a hoarse voice.

Their gazes held for a few moments, but when Ingor began to think of ways she could thank him that he was certain that they would both enjoy, he knew it was time to get away from her side.

"Well, I must get to chopping wood. I gone from home for two months helping my brother build a sod house west of here. You not worry. I stay close to cabin. You try and sleep some more. You need to build up your strength, but if you need me, you call."

She smiled weakly and laid her hand on the back of his where it rested on his thigh. "Thank you."

"You not need to keep saying that. I happy to help."

He looked down at the slender but strong tan fingers. They could prepare a meal, bead a moccasin, and skin and cut up a rabbit or a buffalo, all with equal ease. Her hand was more beautiful than any white one that he'd seen, even those with longer, neatly trimmed nails.

He turned his hand under hers and lifted hers in it. He squeezed it gently and laid it on the blanket. He rose and lifted the bedroll from behind her so she could relax on the pillow. "Sleep now," he murmured. "I keep good watch outside."

Her eyes floated shut with a small smile on her lips. He took a deep breath and headed outside to the woodpile. A few hours of hard work followed by a cold dip in the river was just what he needed.

* * * *

Over the next week the woodpile grew faster than a pile of dirt outside a new prairie dog tunnel. Ingor took time out to hunt a couple rabbits for a pot of rabbit stew that he kept slow cooking over the fire for a few days. The thickened liquid was good over the dry biscuits he'd baked. Still Water seemed to tolerate the change in the menu to solid food. In fact it seemed to give her some strength back, but she was still so weak that he was wary of letting her get out of bed except when absolutely necessary.

Everyday he returned to the ax, hoping to wear off the way he felt each time he helped her sit up to eat or to rise for the short trip to the end of the bed to use the chamber pot. He hated that she was embarrassed each time she needed it, but she was still too weak to even stand on her own. She would hang on to the corner of the bed frame as he turned his back. He was happy to give her what small amount of privacy he could, but he sure worried that she would pass out and hit her head again if he didn't help her go back and forth.

When she was done, he would sweep her up into his arms and lay her down gently. By then she was always so exhausted that she could only smile her thanks before she slipped off to sleep again.

He swung the ax into the cut end of another log and then stretched his aching back. The humid air pasted his shirt to his skin, making him decide to take that dip in the river now to cool off. After checking to see that Still Water was still asleep, he grabbed his rifle and walked through the stand of trees to the river.

Checking the snares he had set near a rabbit hole that morning, he quickly dispatched the two he found trapped. He would skin them and then fry them for supper after he cooled off, he decided as he undressed and walked into the water.

He floated for a while in the cool water, and then reluctantly walked up the back where he pulled his pants and boots back on. Skinning the rabbits there where other wildlife would find and eat the remains, he was startled when he heard a horse blow close by. Pretending not to hear, he reached toward his shirt as if to put it on. Diving for his rifle instead, he rolled sideways on the riverbank and came up to his feet, aiming the rifle toward the sound.

A lone Indian brave sat erect and proud on a sorrel horse, watching him from the opposite side of the river. Ingor could see no firearms, but he wore a knife at his waist. A bow and quiver of arrows hung over his bare back. Ingor knew that if he wanted to, the brave could throw the knife into his heart before he could jump for cover.

Wearing only a breechcloth and moccasins, the Indian rested his hands on his bare thighs within easy reach of his knife. The front section of the sides of his long, straight black hair were braided and tied with a leather strap. The rest flowed down his back over his shoulders.

Ingor relaxed his stance and lowered the butt of his rifle toward the ground. "Tall Cloud, my friend," he called, hoping it was the truth. "You try to frighten a man when he takes a bath after a morning of hard work?"

"Many days you cut much wood for snow when no snow fall in summer. Now you clean two rabbits for one man."

Ingor felt his heart racing, but he nodded calmly. "Little for a trapper to do in summer, and I thought I would lay in some wood before I head north to sell my furs." He strolled back to where his rinsed out shirt was spread on a bush to dry. It was still wet, and he made no attempt to pick it up to put it on.

"Instead of watching me cut all that wood, you could have offered to help." He grinned, now hoping Tall Cloud couldn't see how nervous he felt.

The brave had been watching his cabin for days. Was he watching for Still Water? He had to have been. There was no other reason for him to be this far east. In any case Ingor had been right not to let Still Water step out the door, or even to dry her clothes outside. The brave would not be sitting on his horse on the opposite side of the river if he had any inkling that Still Water lay in his bed as they spoke.

"What brings you this far east?" Ingor asked as if he didn't know.

"I look for my woman who disappeared."

Ingor felt his blood run cold. "Your woman? I didn't know you had taken a wife. Who do you honor to call your woman?"

Tall Cloud shifted slightly on the horse's back. "She not my wife yet, but I have spoken to Red Moon, and he promised Still Water to me. She would be mine now if she had not been stolen from me."

Ingor released the breath he'd been holding and nodded. "Still Water. I remember her kindness for me from Red Cloud's teepee."

He didn't think it would hurt to remind Tall Cloud that he and Red Moon were friends, and it might help. If the brave discovered Still Water holed up in his cabin, he would skin Ingor alive, literally, inch by inch. "I see her last month when Red Moon honors me and invites me to sit at his fire. Now she disappeared?"

"She was stolen away. I find her trail and marks of two horses. Other horses come, but they all split up and disappear in the wind."

Ingor couldn't help but wish Tall Cloud had caught up with the two miscreants. On second thought, they might have sent Tall Cloud right to his cabin.

"This spring for two moons, I go west of here to help my brother and his family build a sod house." Ingor shook his head. "Since then, no strangers pass here," Ingor responded to cloud the notion it might have been him. "When Still Water disappear?"

"Already too many days have passed since I see her," he said as he shifted again and reached to reset the reins in his left hand, leaving his right free to throw the knife. He raised his gaze to hold Ingor's. "When I find the men who took her, I will kill them very slowly, and they will suffer much more than Still Water suffered in their hands."

Despite the width of the flowing water between them, Ingor felt the brave's hatred and anger. He nodded. "I hope no harm has come to your woman."

Tall Cloud stared at him. Ingor concentrated on not moving a muscle. He could give the brave no reason to cross the water and discover what was making him nervous. Suddenly, he thought of the rabbits lying at his feet.

"You would honor me if you would take one of my rabbits, Tall Cloud. A man hunting for his lost woman not have time to hunt for food."

After another nerve-wracking moment, Tall Cloud nodded. Without another word, Tall Cloud rode into the water toward Ingor, who walked to the water's edge. He handed the skinned rabbit to the brave who tucked it in the blanket roll he carried tied behind him.

"Good hunting," Ingor added in what he hoped was a strong voice.

Tall Cloud nodded and reined his horse around and disappeared into the tree stand on the other side of the river. Ingor sat down hard on a nearby log and gulped in breaths of air. He pulled the large handkerchief from his pants' pocket and wiped his sweating brow. If the brave had noticed how much he was sweating, he hoped he would think it was due to the summer heat.

Suddenly realizing that Tall Cloud might be watching, he went through the motions of checking his boot for a stone to show that his sitting had a purpose other than because fear had turned his legs to mush, and they had failed to support him.

Rising, he grabbed his damp shirt and the second rabbit, and strolled back to the cabin. He hung up his shirt on a bush by the door to finish drying. Stalling going inside, he checked on the animals in the barn before picking up some firewood and heading into the cabin to make lunch. The last thing he wanted do was give Tall Cloud the impression that he was anxious to get inside.

But he was. And he was even more anxious when he walked in the door and looked at the bed.

The bed was empty.

Ingor tossed his armful of firewood in the general direction of the pile beside the fireplace. He looked in every corner and saw nothing out of place. The sheet that had been over Still Water had been pushed back, but not yanked away as it would have been if Tall Cloud had found her and taken her away. Had she left the cabin without his knowing it? *Gud*, it was a wonder Tall Cloud hadn't seen her through the trees.

He heard her moan before he saw her. Running around the foot of the bed, he found her lying on the floor beyond it.

"Still Water," he said, rushing to kneel at her side.

She moaned as he lifted her into his arms and rose, holding her against his chest. Circling the bed, he gently laid her on the straw pallet.

"What happen to you? Why you on the floor?"

The shirt that she wore lay open low enough to expose one breast. He drew in a sharp breath as he slid her feet under the sheet. He jerked the covering up over her, tamping down the desire that had slammed into him like a giant ocean wave pounding against the sheer cliff sides of the fjords in his homeland.

She moaned again and raised her hand to her head. Her eyelids fluttered and then slowly opened. "Head hurts much."

He sat beside her and took her hand in one of his. With his other hand, he gently lifted her hair from her forehead where her hand had been. A narrow new red welt was swelling.

"What happened? How do you hit your head again?"

"I need chamber pot. After I'm done, I try to get back in bed and all goes black."

"Maybe you hit your head on the bed frame. Now you have new lump and new headache."

He rose and crossed to the basin of water on the small table on the kitchen side of the cabin. He rinsed out a clean square of cloth. She smiled when he laid the damp cloth on her forehead.

"That feel good."

"Good. You rest while I fix us something to eat."

Her head tipped toward him, she watched as he cut up the rabbit and dipped it in some flour before frying it in bacon grease. He lifted the floorboards that hid his root cellar and reached for a couple wild onions he still had. He noted that the small dug out area under the floor was nearly empty. Caring for Sweet Water had taken all his attention and he hadn't even checked to see that the escape route from there to the woodpile behind the cabin was still open. He had dug it out just big enough for him to crawl through in case he had trouble with the Indians. At the outside end, all he had to do was push away the stacked wood and he could run away through the trees.

All the while he was cooking, he knew he should tell Still Water that Tall Cloud had come looking for her, if for no other reason than to prepare her for when he found her.

Ingor could imagine what Tall Cloud would do to him, but what would he do to Still Water when he'd figured out she had stayed in the cabin with him willingly as she healed?

He could tell Tall Cloud that he had promised to take her to Red Moon when she was well enough to travel, but would Tall Cloud have expected her to sneak away earlier and find her way home even as beaten and bruised as she was? Would she suffer terrible consequences for having stayed longer to regain her strength?

Later, by supper's end, the fried rabbit and onions were gone, but Ingor still hadn't told her. He left the cabin to empty the chamber pot and caught site of movement in the trees. The sun was slow to disappear in the west during the long summer days. With no darkness until very late, the Indian would have no trouble watching what he was doing. And he would either think it very odd that he used a chamber pot instead of just going outside, or hopefully he would think he was just emptying a bowl of water.

But if Tall Cloud was watching him, the only way to know what he was thinking was to see if Ingor lived through the night.

Chapter 6

As he slept on the floor on a pile of furs that night, Ingor stayed awake as much as he could, half-expecting Tall Cloud to try to come through the door at any moment. The next day he never saw Tall Cloud, but he could still feel his presence.

It was then that he decided to tell Still Water that Tall Cloud had come looking for her. He was not entirely certain why he waited until it was too late to turn her over easily to Tall Cloud. He just knew that giving her up was not something he wanted to do.

"I... You should know that your people were here looking for you," he began after supper that night. He heard her gasp. Her onyx eyes were wide with fear. He set down the empty bowl that had held the stew he'd made for her and sat on the side of the bed. "Tall Cloud."

She pushed with her palms against the bed and shrank down farther into the roll of blankets against which she leaned. She looked at the door and back at Ingor. "He is here?"

Ingor shook his head. "Two days ago we talk by the river. He…he say that you his woman. He say that Chief Red Moon promise you to him."

"No, no, it cannot be." She looked down at her hands as she twisted the quilt in her fingers. "All women in camp want to be his woman, yet he speaks for me—the only woman who does not want to be wife to him."

"You don't?" Ingor asked, not quite sure why he was comforted by hearing that. "He is fine strong brave and would care for you well. Give you many sons."

"No, I cannot be wife to him. I know this and say this for many years since I became a woman. Years ago when he first asked for me, I said no."

"That long time to have a woman say no. And yet he keep trying?"

She leaned her head back and Ingor could see that she was not looking at the rafters of his cabin; she was looking back into the past.

"After my coming-of-age ceremony, I was proud to be a woman. I look forward to being a proud brave's wife. I want to bear him many sons. So I look at the braves and watch them when they did not know it. I want to pick the one who would be best for me. One who could win my heart."

She smiled. "Whenever the young women are around, the braves like to show off. It is fun to watch. Each one tries to look better and stronger than the others."

"What do they do?" Ingor asked. He moved closer and sat on the tree-trunk chair beside the bed.

"If the women are picking berries in the woods, they will try to shoot a rabbit with their bow and arrow to show how good they are. Or if we are spreading out the buffalo skins to stretch and dry, they would make a race with their horses. Some would even stand on their horses' backs and ride by."

The smile disappeared from Ingor's face. There was no way he could do that. A little annoyed, he asked, "Was that not fun to watch?"

"Most of the time, yes."

"And did Tall Cloud win contests?"

"Most of the time, yes," she repeated. "But winning most of the contests was not enough for Tall Cloud."

"I not understand."

She took a deep breath as if preparing to get out whatever she had to say that would be difficult.

"There is much laughing and fun at first. But then one time the boy who shot the rabbit can't find it because Tall Cloud has taken it and pulled out the arrow. Then he puts in his own arrow, and he claims he shot the first rabbit. The other boy's arrow cannot be found, but I see this. I know that Tall Cloud broke the other boy's arrow and hid it in a hole in an old tree."

"Did you tell him you knew?"

"The other boy insisted he had hit the rabbit and when I started to say that he had, Tall Cloud took my arm and with a smile on his face, he squeezed it hard. I know this is threat that if I say what I know, he will get even with me later. He frightened me and so I said nothing. It is only a game and was soon over. But for days Tall Cloud brags to everyone that he is the best shot."

Ingor rubbed his palms on his thighs. "Uh… Does his winning most of time impress you?"

"He not impress me. Even when he wins, I wonder what he did to cheat. No, he frightens me, and I know that each time he does something bad to make sure he wins. One race he threw dry dirt in the eye of the winning horse. The racing horse cannot see and stops so Tall Cloud wins."

"Others must have seen that."

"Two riders very close and suddenly one stops. There is much dust and who can say how it happened. But I know from the way he smiles and looks at me." She shuddered at the memory. "Even his smile is a threat."

"I understand now why you not want him for husband."

"So often he asks Red Moon for Still Water for wife, but because I refuse him, Red Moon tells him he must wait until I am ready."

Ingor saw tears welling in her eyes. "What is it? What's wrong? Do you have big pain somewhere?"

"Yes," she said, blinking rapidly. "I have big pain here." She placed her hand over her heart. "This spring he asked Red Moon again. Only this time Tall Cloud said he would not wait. I have seen eighteen summers. He said he would take me as his wife by the end of this summer—if I want him or not."

"But Red Moon not marry you to Tall Cloud if that not what you want."

She shook her head. "I try to tell my uncle when he speaks to me of this, but he will not understand. It was different for the old ones. The women married the one their father picked for them and did not argue or refuse. But I cannot marry one I fear. Red Moon says I should be proud to be Tall Cloud's woman. I must try again to tell him I can't, but with no new thing to say…"

Ingor took a deep breath and felt a strange measure of relief that she would always deny Tall Cloud's request, but worried that she couldn't deny him much longer.

"Now he is looking for me—with Red Moon's blessings, I am sure. But if he brings me back, Red Moon will have two choices of what to do with me."

"Be Tall Cloud's wife or not," Ingor concluded.

She shook her head slowly. "No."

"I not understand."

"My uncle can insist I marry Tall Cloud for saving me."

"Or?"

She spoke softly and didn't look up at him. "Because I was taken by white men, he can set me aside and say I am no better than a dog. Even Tall Cloud would not want me then. I would be forced to work like a slave and never have a family of my own."

Ingor couldn't believe what he was hearing. It wasn't her fault that the bastards stole her by the river. How could they treat her so badly?

She looked up and frowned. "How did Tall Cloud come to look for me here by your cabin?"

"Well, I not know, except not many white men around to check on. Tall Cloud seemed to be alone. He stayed around here for a few days to watch this cabin, but he gone now. He say he trails two horses from the place you were stolen. Then he find place where I take you from those men. Maybe he trails my two horses from there to the woods, but not this far. I walk horses in water for long way to hide where we go."

"Tall Cloud is a good tracker." She looked up at him. "Maybe he could trail your horses all the way to your cabin."

"No, he say he lost the trail in woods, but he come on to cabin because he knows I am here. No other trapper live near here."

"But he did not come in to get me. Does he not know I am here?"

"No, Still Water. I…I not tell him you are here."

"No?" she breathed. Her wide-eyed gaze locked on his.

"He wants to find you and take you back, but I think you too sick to travel. I not tell him you here. Now maybe he go back and try to trail other two horses some more. I not know how much track left after rain yesterday."

"If only a few marks, Tall Cloud will find them. He is the best tracker. But if he does not find me, I think he will be back." She struggled to sit up. "I cannot stay here."

She reached over to hold his hand tightly between both of hers. He was shocked at seeing so much concern on her face.

"You are not safe with me here."

"But I keep you safe."

She shook her head while holding his gaze. "If I cough while you outside, he knows I am here. I do not want you hurt, and Tall Cloud would kill you in front of me just to have revenge on me for refusing him. I could not bear to see you hurt."

"You let me worry about keeping you safe. Tall Cloud will spend three, maybe four days, trailing other two horses. That trail all he has to go on. But I shoot in the air and scatter those horses good. They go west and those two drunks must take whole day to find them. Then they must hole up until the old one's gunshot wound heals. So they hard to find. And Tall Cloud also must watch out for army patrols."

"Army tell Chief Red Moon he must go live where army wants," she said, her voice catching. "Red Moon say he move whole camp to Canada and not obey army." Her lower lip trembled. "Red Moon's people ready to move north when I taken. They must have moved without me by now. What will I do? I will be left behind all alone."

Suddenly overwhelmed, Still Water hid her face in her hands. Ingor couldn't bear to have her feel so unhappy and lost on top of all the pain she suffered from the beating she endured. He moved the few inches to sit on the edge of the bed. Once there he gathered her into his arms and held her gently against his chest. She didn't give in to sobbing like he thought she would, but he felt the dampness of a few tears on his shirt. She was a courageous woman, no doubt about it. He admired that and was proud of her.

"All you need do is stay here in cabin. You get well and

strong again. You stay out of sight and safe until you can travel. Then I must get my furs to the traders in Canada. On the way I take you to Red Moon."

"But..."

"No, you no worry. Let me worry about Tall Cloud and about getting you back to your people."

Her hands were between them, resting on his chest. She clutched his shirt and straightened enough to look up at him. Ingor kept his arms around her. "No, you can't take me back. There is more."

"More? What you mean?"

"Everyone knows Tall Cloud wanted me as his woman. He brags that he will have me. But now they all think I have been taken from my people by white men. If they see you with me, they will think it is you who took me. They will think I have been with a man who is not my husband. Because of that Red Moon not take me back. And Tall Cloud will want his revenge. If he cannot find the two men who steal me, then he will take his revenge on us when we find my uncle. He is good at revenge."

"They can't do that. You were stolen from them. You not do one thing wrong. I tell Red Moon you are safe with me and that I honor you."

She moved her fingers hesitantly on his hard chest and looked up to meet his gaze. "You can tell him, but since I am here with you..."

"But we not do anything wrong. I promise. I tell him."

Shaking her head, she whispered, "But I have."

Ingor's anger flared. Had those two vermin raped her, and she tried to hide it from him? "Those two. Did they..."

She laid her fingers over his lips to silence them. "No, not them. Here in this cabin—you and me."

"Here? But we do nothing wrong." He looked at her mouth and remembered the delicious kisses. "I know I sleep naked with you, but I only make you warm."

"We were naked together?"

Ingor cursed himself as he remembered that she had been unconscious and hadn't known that before. He had the bottoms of his long johns on when she woke up and saw him in bed with her. He shrugged.

"I not know what else to do. You lie close and I wrap my arms and legs around you. Then you get warm." She got warm just like he was getting warm now remembering the feeling of her soft skin pressing against his.

She stared at him, her lips slightly parted. He could see she was breathing faster now. Well, she had a right to be upset, he thought.

"You are beautiful woman, Still Water. I am a man and I...I want you for long time now, since I see you in Red Moon's teepee. But I swear to you, I only touch you when I must clean your wounds and keep you warm—until we wake up together."

She smiled, calling his attention to her lips once again. "I understand, but I did not know we were naked together."

"Oh, don't remind me," he groaned. He closed his eyes and tipped his head up, trying to forget the image.

"It is not you. It is me."

He jerked his head down and met her gaze. "You, but you not..." He stopped when he saw her knowing smile.

"Yes, it is me. In my heart I have wished for you—for long time now."

Ingor swallowed hard as the meaning of what she said shook him. He looked down at her full lips, delicious as a deep red wine, and this time he couldn't look away. At that moment he thought he would die if he couldn't taste them. He slowly lowered his head until his lips barely touched hers. He felt the heat as their breaths mingled. Turning his head slightly, he rubbed against her lips again with a feather-light touch.

The shock he felt at the arousing contact jolted him to the core. He looked into her eyes, and though hooded with heavy lids, they mirrored the desire he felt. He closed the little distance between them to kiss her again, straining his self-control to the very limit to keep from taking her on the spot.

Instead, he pressed his lips against hers, turning and nipping softly. She uttered a low sound of pleasure, and he knew he had to stop. He couldn't do this to her. He would ruin her completely in the eyes of her people.

Moving away at that moment ranked right up there as one of the hardest things he'd ever done. Nonetheless, he smiled and slowly took his arms from around her. Rising, he glanced back and saw the questioning frown on her face. She hadn't wanted him to stop either and that made it even harder for him to walk out of the cabin, but he did.

The moon lit his way as he walked to the nearest tree to lean against it and cool down. The first thing he saw was the reflection of the moonlight on the blade of the knife pointed at his stomach. Looking up, he met Tall Cloud's hard stare.

Ingor struggled to take a deep breath. Fear had closed his throat, but now it was fear for himself and for Still Water if this brave found her.

"I...I have no more rabbit to offer my friend, Tall Cloud," Ingor managed.

He frantically looked around for a reason to be outside so late. He saw the water pail and pointed at it. "I was just going for some water."

"No," Tall Cloud announced, kicking the pail aside. "Go," he added, swinging the point of the knife toward the cabin door.

Ingor's chest pounded with his rapid heartbeats. "Go? Ya, I go to the river for water."

"In cabin. Go."

Ingor started to object when Tall Cloud pressed the tip of the knife to his neck. "Now."

Why hadn't he taken his rifle? Ingor's mind raced to find another action to take other than going into the cabin, but feeling a liquid run down from his neck that had to be his own blood, he knew he could not. If Tall Cloud killed him now, he would have no chance at all to protect Still Water.

He stepped back from the blade and slowly turned to the door. Tall Cloud reached passed him and pulled open the door. The light from the fire illuminated them both where they stood just outside it.

"This," Tall Cloud grunted, shaking his fist with something in it in Ingor's face. "I find this by river."

He opened his fist and Ingor saw a piece of leather with fringe cut along one side. Stalling for time, he took the leather and looked more closely. "It is wet and muddy. It could be by river for a long time."

"Still Water make fringe like this. If she is here, I kill you so slowly you will wish a hundred times that you are dead."

He shoved Ingor into the small cabin. Falling onto the bed, he quickly stood and backed away past the fire. A quick glance told him the bed was empty. Had she hidden on the floor beyond the bed where she had passed out a few days earlier?

It took seconds for Tall Cloud to walk beyond the bed to check the floor and even to look under it. They both could see no one hiding under the small table or behind the cut logs he used as chairs.

Thinking maybe she was a witch and could disappear, Ingor looked at Tall Cloud. "She is not here. And I promise you that if I find her, I will return her to her uncle. She would be safe with me for I owe her my life that she saved in the big storm two winters ago. You know this is true."

Tall Cloud stared at him for several moments and then stormed out of the cabin, leaving the door open. Ingor stood panting as he listened to the sounds of a horse's hooves disappear into the night.

The grating of wood rubbing against wood brought him

out of his stupor. Turning toward the small work area he had to prepare food on, he saw the floor planks rise slowly. Releasing the breath he had been holding, he slammed the cabin door and pulled down the iron rod to lock the door before he crossed back to the root cellar. Dropping the opened trapdoor on the floor beyond the hole, he knelt to help Still Water up from the hole under the floor. Lifting her into his arms, he carried her to the bed and gently set her down. She remained curled up, her leather clothes that she had pulled from the rope where they had dried, crushed against her with both arms wrapped around them.

"How did you…" he started to ask, but then he remembered. He had gotten onions out to fry with the rabbit. She had seen that the space had been big enough for him to step into to reach the vegetables. It had been the one and only way she could have saved their lives, and she had done exactly that.

He sat beside her and held her against his chest for several minutes until their hearts beat more normally. Then he took her clothes and put them on the chair and lifted the blanket up to cover her as she lay down.

"He gone now," he assured her. He wanted so badly for it to be true.

Not until the next morning did Ingor finally feel confident the brave had moved on to look elsewhere. But he might be back. Ingor knew it was time to pack up his furs and head north. He could only give Still Water a day or two more to build up her strength.

* * * *

"Company halt!"

Ingor had heard the patrol approach. Working in the shade of a tree in his denim trousers with no shirt on, he'd been sharpening one of his traps with a file.

At the first sound of horses in the distance, he'd determined who they were. Hurrying into the cabin before they were close enough to see what he was doing, he made certain Still Water knew the Army was passing.

"You must stay inside and not make any sounds."

"What if they come inside?"

Ingor looked around the cabin. The only door was behind him and there were no windows. "I make sure they not come in, but if I can't stop them, you know what to do."

He grabbed a can of oil as his excuse for going inside in case the Army had spyglasses and were watching him. He shut the cabin door securely and returned to the tree under which he'd been sharpening the trap.

He'd finished the sharpening and had soaked a rag with oil to rub over the black metal by the time the Army pulled up several yards beyond where he sat. Ingor put down the rag and got to his feet. Not wanting them any closer to his cabin, he walked out to them.

"Stay in your saddles, men. We won't be stopped long," Sergeant Decker shouted as he slid off his saddle and approached Ingor.

"You're a ways off the trail," Ingor said with a smile to greet the officer as they shook hands.

"Came by here just to see you. Wanted to warn you so's you could warn the other trappers in these parts."

"Warn us? About what?"

"We got orders to move the rest of them Indians out of the area this summer. This prairie is open to homesteaders now, and we don't want no trouble from them."

"My own brother comes here now," Ingor said with a proud grin. "He settled two day's ride west of here. I helped him build a good sturdy sod house."

"Then you know how important it is to get them Indians out of here as fast as possible, and with as little trouble as possible."

"I never have trouble from the Indians so far," Ingor responded. "The only time white man get into trouble is when he take something that belongs to the Indian."

The soldier spit some of his tobacco on the ground. "Next thing you'll be saying is that this here territory belongs to them and we have no rights to it 'cause they were here first." The Sergeant laughed at his own joke, as did the other men close enough to hear it.

Ingor shrugged. "Well, they live here all their life. I live here and they do me no harm."

"You sound like the Indian-lover that two men back at the fort was complaining about."

Ingor shook his head. "Nobody complain about me. I help my brother build his soddy, and now I must get traps ready and get my furs to Canada. Summer is short out here."

"Ain't that the truth? Hell, them two at the fort was so

drunk all the time they probably made it all up anyway." He looked behind Ingor at the cabin. "But the way you live all alone out here, you're practically like one of them Indians. Don't know how you stand it alone. It's no wonder you ain't got a wife. She'd go plum crazy out here all alone."

Ingor grinned. "I live only way a man can if he want to stay alive in this land."

"Yeah, well, the pair we met up with said some big white guy traveling with an Indian squaw stole their horses and their guns. He even stole their knives and shot one of 'em. They caught up with their horses, but they was at the fort to do some trading for guns since theirs were gone. You wouldn't have any idea who the horse thief might'a been, would you?"

Ingor snorted. "Wait a minute. You tell me one white man and one Indian squaw rob two white men who have guns and knives? Hell, I not believe such a thing," Ingor said through a laugh. "They must be drunk. That can't be true."

"You're probably right, but I thought you might have seen a stranger."

Ingor shook his head. "No stranger, but I keep my eye on my horses," Ingor said with a casual wave toward the two horses that stood in a small fenced coral next to the stables where they were eating grass. "Thanks for warning. If horse thief in territory, I want to know about him."

"If those two men have their say in the matter, the pair that robbed them won't be around long. They're waiting 'til the old man could shoot again, and then they were going out to find 'em. I expect they left the fort soon after we did."

The Sergeant took off his hat and wiped his sweating brow on his stained uniform shirtsleeve. "Too hot in the summer and way too cold in the winter. I don't know how you boys stay alive all alone out here. Hell, it ain't noon yet and the temperature is too hot to leave the shade of the tree you was working under."

Ingor glanced up at the endless blue sky. "Ain't getting no relief from the heat today."

Leaning down for his rag, he wiped his sweaty palms on it only to get the oil on him that he'd poured for the trap. Even so he thought that the two of them talking about the weather had to mean that the Sergeant didn't truly suspect him. And for certain, the Sergeant knew nothing of Still Water or that she was taken from her people by force. He would have mentioned it, but from what he'd said, he wouldn't have cared about her. On top of being nervous, that thought made Ingor angry, and he wanted the Army to leave his land. Now.

"Putting off leaving not make it easier," Ingor said with a shrug.

"You're right. Just thought you'd like to know we're on our way to move Red Moon to live in government custody."

Ingor shook his head. "I not think he like that much."

"I don't give a damn what that old redskin wants," the officer said in a raised voice. "My orders are to clear his band out of this area to make it safe for the homesteaders coming in, and I intend to do just that." Ingor nodded but said nothing more. "You know where they're camping now?" he asked as an after thought.

Ingor knew when the Sergeant shook his head that he had just given Ingor the real reason he'd stopped. He didn't know where Red Moon was and he was hoping Ingor would. Why else would they ride a day and a half north of the fort just to see him before they swung west? He shook his head.

"I not see his band since I work my trapline last winter. I not see them when I come from my brother's place. They could be far out west at the Missouri River now. Probably are in this heat. They not want to take chance of water drying up like in rivers around here."

"Damn, that far? Well, we ain't stopping 'til we find 'em and round 'em up." He circled his horse and mounted. He ordered his men to straighten their column and prepare to pull out. Gathering his reins in his gloved hand, the Sergeant looked down at Ingor. "I'd hate to think that you might know where they are and not tell me."

"I promise you, Sergeant, Chief Red Moon is partial to the land well west and south of here. I not see him coming from my brother's place. You watch for my brother Lars and his family two days straight west of here. It good you see they doing okay. I help them long time and now I have little time to get traps ready and get my furs north."

"You ain't done that yet?"

"Hell, no. Laid up last winter. My leg been hurting something fierce since I get back here," Ingor lied. He pulled up his pant leg and showed the Sergeant his scars from the trap clamping on it last winter. "Some days the broken bone aches so bad I not walk."

"I heard you got caught in one of your own traps," the sergeant said with a laugh at Ingor's expense.

"I think I was smarter than that," Ingor said with a grin to join in the joke.

Sergeant Decker laughed harder. He stared at Ingor for a good while longer before reining his horse around and leading the company to the southwest. "You take it easy," he called over his shoulder.

The column disappeared from his view riding two men abreast into the prairie grass that was tall enough to hide their feet in the stirrups. The grasses swayed in the variable wind and closed in after the last horse like a wave rolling over the wake of a boat on a fjord.

"Keep going southwest," Ingor muttered to himself when he knew they could not hear him. "That should give Red Cloud plenty of time to move north ahead of you."

He added the trap he'd been oiling to the others that were ready to use and hanging in the barn, and washed up at the horse trough. He hurried back to the cabin only when he was certain the Army unit hadn't doubled back.

Time had just run out and he was worried. He had to talk to Still Water. He couldn't wait any longer. They were not safe in the cabin. They had to get far away from Tall Cloud, from the two men who stole her, and now from the Army, too. The sergeant wouldn't hesitate relocating her apart from her family. Then they would have a good chance of never seeing each other again. In his heart he didn't want that to happen.

Inside the cabin, he found her slicing strips from the salt pork to cook for their lunch. The trapdoor was open and his loaded revolver lay on the table beside where she was working.

Chapter 7

Ingor looked at Still Water with a proud smile and then at the gun again. Stepping closer, he picked it up and put it back in the holster hanging from a peg on the wall beside the door. "You won't need this."

"I won't let them take me," she said levelly as she went right on with her work.

Ingor froze with his hands over the strap on the peg. He looked at the revolver. He saw it all clearly then and understood how desperate she felt. Still Water had taken the revolver to use on herself if the Sergeant had come to the cabin to take her for relocation.

Would she rather die than go with Tall Cloud, too, if he came back and found her? He dropped his arms to his side and turned slowly to face her.

The bruising was gone from her cheek now. He still noticed her wince once in a while from a pain in her hip and ankle, but the swelling was down and the discoloration nearly gone. She was well enough to travel, and yet they had not left to find Red Moon.

When she had looked up and smiled as he'd come in, he couldn't help but think how comforting it would be to come home to a woman who would smile at him like that everyday. He ran into few people in the territory and even fewer of them smiled. Most were grizzled old trappers who had nothing to smile about.

"Ah, the patrol, could you hear what we said?" he began, wondering if she'd heard the bad news.

She shook her head. "I not hear without opening door and I could not do that." She went back to cutting another slice.

"I not think it safe for us here anymore," he burst out, walking over to stand on the opposite side of the table.

She slowly lowered the slab of meat to lie on the warm surface and set the long-bladed knife beside it. Clutching the side of the table with her greasy fingers as if she needed its support, she said, "You want me to leave today." It was not a question. She was stating what she saw as the inevitable.

"No!" he said harshly, hitting the table with the palm of his hand. When he saw her shrink back in fear, he immediately tempered his voice. "No, that's not what I mean at all, Still Water."

She watched him warily as he circled the table and took a square of cloth to begin to wipe the grease from her hands. "What I mean is that *we* need to leave. Both of us. Army looks for Red Moon and Tall Cloud looks for you. Now those two drunken bastards who took you look for me to get even.

The Army stop here because I know most of what goes on around here."

Pausing with her hands still in his, he looked into the fry pan where she had been laying the slices of fatty pork. "I'm not sure I can keep you safe here anymore. I think we are better off out there."

She looked into his face, trusting but questioning. "Where? Where we go?"

He drew in a deep breath. "Look, I must go to Winnipeg with pelts to sell them and trade for goods. I not get there yet this year."

She pulled her hand from his. "I will not stop you. Do you leave today? I go away now then."

"No, no," he said, reaching to capture her shoulders, holding her gently but firmly so he wouldn't hurt her. "You not understand. What I try to say is that I take you to find Red Moon on the way to Winnipeg. I explain to Red Moon what happened to you. And I make him understand you still the maiden you are before all this. Then he must take you back into his teepee. And you will be safe going north to Canada with them. The Army can't go into Canada."

"But the Army go looking already. They find him first—before Canada."

He shook his head. "Not if they head southwest and look for him where I sent them. I think of where I found you. You said Red Moon moving farther north from there so I send army south. I think we have a few days before the sergeant figure that out."

"And what of Tall Cloud? What if he finds me first? He will kill you." She dropped her gaze. "Or make you wish you are dead. He will kill us both."

Ingor dropped his hands from her shoulders. "All we can do is watch out for him. The *last* thing I want is for him to be the one who finds you."

Their gazes met and he thought her eyes looked shinier than usual from tears gathering there. After only a moment she nodded. "When we go?"

"It too late in the day now. We start before first light in morning. Fix food tonight that we eat on the trail without fire. It plenty warm out at night so we not miss fire except for cooking. We not let anyone see or smell where we are after we leave."

She nodded, and he started to turn away when she stopped him with a hand on his arm. "Thank you," she whispered. "I do not know any other man who would help me and protect me like you do, Ingor."

He felt his control slipping and fought his desire for her that filled him suddenly. But as he turned to meet her gaze, he saw the mirror image of his desire in her face. Something inside him, that had managed until then to hold him back from touching her, snapped.

Suddenly, Still Water was in his arms and Ingor was kissing her, caressing her. They couldn't get close enough together.

He had been working outside with no shirt on. She pulled at the buttons on his shirt that she wore to open it. He pushed it off over her shoulders and let it fall to the dirt floor. Then soft breasts pressed against his hard chest. His palms swept over her back, wanting to touch all of her at once, yet restraining himself so his touch wasn't hurting her.

He kissed her bruised shoulder, and she raised her arms to cradle his head and bring his lips back to hers.

The rest of his clothes seemed to melt away, and they kissed even more frantically. Their bodies would not be denied and they fell onto the bed together.

And then he was doing all the loving things he'd wanted to do for weeks, and more. Her breasts were soft and just the right size to fill his hands. He delighted in making the dusky tips stand up firm. She moaned softly and he had to kiss her again.

For this joyous time she was his and his alone to have and take pleasure together.

Only she wasn't his.

She was a Sioux maiden to be honored, not ravaged.

He raised up, leaning on his elbows that were braced on either side of her shoulders.

"*Gud i himmel*! What have I done?" He stared at her wide eyes with little memory of having gotten into bed with her. "*Gud*, I am sorry. I should not do this. I am so sorry."

Her eyes widened in shock at his words. Or was it hurt he saw there before she looked away? Her loose hair fell over her face and he left it to mask her expression.

"Damn!" He swung off the bed and pulled on his trousers over his painfully rigid sex. He heard the rustle of the dried grasses in the pallet, and knew that Still Water was dressing herself, too.

Ingor's shoulders bowed under the burden of guilt. He'd come so close to dishonoring her. He had taken a huge chance to rescue her from the very same fate at the hands of two other men. How could he have been so insensitive? He cared for her too much to ruin her in the eyes of her family.

But when she'd slipped into his arms, he'd lost all of his power to reason. He only knew that he wanted her. It didn't matter that she was an Indian. It didn't matter that she wasn't blond like most Norwegian women. He wanted her. He might even need her.

"Still Water, I..." he began, his back still to her to give her privacy to dress and time to recover.

He wanted to tell her that stopping had been the hardest thing he'd ever done, and the very last thing he wanted to do. But instead, he said, "I'll get the horses ready to leave in the morning. You get food ready."

He stepped closer to the door to put more distance between them. If he got close to her again, he wouldn't be able to stop next time. "Pack whatever you want to take—what you think we need."

She didn't respond, and he hadn't expected her to. She'd been helping her family pack to move with each season all her life. Now, he was certain, she could do it by rote.

He grabbed a shirt from a peg and stepped into his boots without looking at her. He couldn't stand to see the pain he'd caused reflected in her eyes.

As he strode to the stable, he berated himself time and time again. Still Water was not one of the loose women he'd seen in town saloons as he rode west. She was an Indian maiden, the virginal niece of the Chief. And he had no right to touch her, no matter how much he wanted her, or how much he was coming to care for her.

He grabbed a sack and filled it with grain to feed the horses on their journey. After tying it carefully, he grabbed another and did the same. He would return Still Water to Red Moon as he'd promised. Then he wouldn't blame the Chief one bit if he didn't waste a minute before literally skinning Ingor alive for the way he'd treated his niece. Ingor could think of no greater insult to give Red Moon who had given him only aid and friendship when he was new to this territory.

Tying the sacks together so they would ride over the back of a saddle, he flipped them over the half door of the barn and turned back to the horses to check their hooves.

As he cleaned them, he couldn't stop thinking about her.

* * * *

Now, after nursing Still Water back to health as she had patiently cared first for him two winters before, they prepared to go find Red Moon's camp. Ingor made two bedrolls from his blankets and the quilt from his bed, and tied one on the back of each saddle. He packed the cloth bags containing their food with the sacks of horse feed on both horses to distribute the weight. He kept a few pelts separate from the others to gift Red Moon. Much as he might like to carry Still Water on his lap, she would ride the packhorse so they could make better time. But that, he realized, meant there was not enough room to carry the furs he had to sell.

He'd thought of trailing a travois loaded with his furs, but that would slow them down. Instead, he had to change his plans. He would return Still Water to Red Moon, and then if they didn't kill him, he would return to his cabin for the remaining furs and take them to Winnipeg to sell. If he didn't get held up by an early snow storm, that second trip would bring him back to the cabin in the fall when he should be setting out his trapline to begin the harvest of furs all over again. In the meantime, he thought the furs were safe tied in rolled bundles and hidden in the roof rafters of the stable. He could only hope that four-legged critters didn't find them and decide they would make a soft nest.

Ever mindful of the danger into which they would be riding, Ingor insisted Still Water wear his plaid shirt over her repaired dress to hide it. He also asked her to cover her shiny ebony hair with an old hat of his. At least from a distance, no one could tell she was an Indian or a woman.

She hid the tails of her braids under the shirt and without his asking, even cut the fringe from her leggings and tall shoes. Not having spent any time in the sun as she healed hidden in his cabin, her skin tone was no darker than his was after working outside without a shirt each day and getting tanned in the sun.

He tied on the last bag of food she handed him, and he noticed that her hand trembled as he took it from her. He looked up at her face, but she would not meet his gaze. He figured she was too angry with him for his treatment of her.

When the horses were ready, he returned to the cabin. She had spread out the embers in the fire so it would safely extinguish itself, and cleaned up the cabin so that everything was back into place for his return.

As he closed the door behind them, she waited patiently to follow him to the horses tied by the barn. Crossing to her, he gently grasped her shoulders. She looked at his chest and didn't raise her face to his. He lifted her chin with a bent finger, and their gazes finally met.

There was so much he wanted to say about how much he'd enjoyed the weeks together. About how lonely he would be in his empty cabin without her. But how could he say he'd enjoyed the time when she'd been in so much pain and lonely away from her people.

"Are you ready to go?" he finally managed. She nodded.

The sky was just beginning to show light in the early dawn. He looked at her closely and wondered if they would ever meet again. Though he had vowed never to touch her again, his will was too weak. He lowered his head to savor her lush lips once more. She uttered a soft sound that was nearly his undoing. He wanted to take her in his arms and...

No, no, he could not. But he smiled and dropped his hands to his side. She quickly turned away.

"Then let's leave," he said, his voice breaking.

Glancing at the sky, he noticed high dark clouds gathering to the southwest. Good. A storm would help slow up the

Army and give him a better chance of finding Red Moon first. After giving her a hand up on the packhorse, he mounted Thor and led the way into the woods.

The cottonwood trees along the river covered their trail with white puffy seeds that imitated the snow cover due in a few months. They stopped only briefly to eat a biscuit and a piece of cold bacon for nooning. By late afternoon they had left the river and turned northwest. The storm hit them out in the open prairie a few hours before sunset.

Ingor would have kept on riding if it hadn't been for the wind that blew the cold rain sideways and drenched them completely in minutes. He pointed to a scrubby forested rise in the distance and called out, "We can find shelter there."

He was not certain she had heard him, but she nodded and dug her heels into the packhorse's flanks and followed at his quick pace. Circling to the downwind side of the rise, they rode up into the trees.

Tying the horses so the thunder and lightning of the storm would not cause them to bolt and run, they worked together to gather tree branches. He cut ones he could reach from the trees with his ax, and she dragged them to their campsite. Leaning them against a fallen tree whose thick branches had brought it to rest a few feet from the ground, they fashioned a shelter of sorts. By pushing away the wet leaves from the soil under it, they had relatively dry ground to lay their bedrolls on.

"I wish we could chance a fire to warm us up," Ingor said as they worked.

"We may be only half day from Red Moon. The storm will end tonight and we get dry tomorrow."

A half day. Only a half day more to see her pretty face, to enjoy her company and quiet comments, to feel her close by. Leaving her with Red Moon would be like leaving a part of himself.

He fed the horses some grain and loosened their cinches. The saddles and blankets were soaked but would keep the hard rain from their backs for the night in case it turned to hail.

With the animals taken care of the best he could under the circumstances, he grabbed a saddlebag of food and a canteen before he ducked under the branches and sat down beside Still Water. Pulling his blanket up to wrap around them both for warmth, he opened the bag so they could eat supper.

The biscuits were soggy but filling as they huddled close together and ate in silence. The wind howled in the trees above them, and the rain brought down leaves along with the torrents of water around them. Ingor couldn't claim they were dry, but they were better off than they would have been if they had stopped out in the open.

There was nothing more to be done after they ate. With a stray hope that the lightning would not bring down a tree near them, they fell asleep, snuggled close to keep each other warm, Still Water in his arms with her back to him.

The silence as much as the early sunlight woke them the next morning. Cold and therefore aching as usual since nearly freezing to death two winters before, Ingor rose and walked stiffly to ready the horses. Still Water handed him two strips of deer jerky. He popped the end one into his mouth to chew on for breakfast, and the other into his pocket for later.

In no time at all, the bedrolls were shaken out and tied in rolls on the tightened saddles. Riding out of the forested area into the open allowed the sun to warm and dry them out. Each time they stopped, Still Water retied the blankets to expose a new damp section to be dried. By the time Ingor wanted to stop for nooning, their clothes were dry and they felt much more comfortable.

A long low rise stretched out ahead of them in the endless prairie. He stopped Thor and she rode up to his side. He had been about to say they would ride to the top where they could see what was ahead, and then eat. He didn't get a chance to speak. Still Water grasped his lower arm and squeezed it hard.

"Whoa," she said firmly to hold their horses where they were. "Do not move at all, and it will be easier on us," she said in a steady voice. "Do not even look at your guns."

Chapter 8

When Still Water had released his arm and sat with her hands resting on the pommel of her saddle, Ingor followed her example. On the rise ahead that had been empty moments before was a line of a dozen or so horses that had come into view. Riding in the wide line toward them, he saw that each horse carried a Sioux warrior. Many had a spear in their hands and all carried a bow and arrows angled over their backs. He knew without being able to see them that each would have a knife and many would have tomahawks tied on their belts. They might even carry rifles.

This is it, Ingor thought. He expected to hear the whine of an arrow flying through the air that would kill him at any second now. He could only pray that Still Water didn't suffer a worse fate.

"Whatever they do to me, I want you to know I not regret one minute of time I spend with you," he said softly as he turned to look at her.

She met his gaze and he thought he saw a bit of a smile. "I

will tell my uncle we are even now. I save your life and now you have saved mine."

He had no time to say that his feelings for her were beyond being thankful for her nursing. The braves on their galloping horses surrounded them. At the lead was Tall Cloud, who stopped and faced them, their horses a few feet apart. He looked at Ingor with such hatred that he almost felt the stare as a physical blow. But then he looked at Still Water. The disgust Ingor saw in his face then was enough to make his blood boil. He straightened and would have said or done something to protect Still Water, but she spoke before he could.

While she had nursed him back to health, she had taught him enough of her language to know she told Tall Cloud that she was safely returned to her uncle's care by this white man, who was friend to Red Moon and his people. She thanked Tall Cloud for coming to insure their safety for the last few miles to the camp.

Tall Cloud uttered a few words too loud and fast for Ingor to translate, but the nasty way he'd said them highlighted the contempt in which he held Still Water. Then he turned and directed his men to surround them with a swing of his spear.

Ingor had wanted to greet him, call him *dakhotah*, the Sioux word for friend. But it was just as well that he didn't have the chance. Anyone who looked at Still Water, with the lack of respect as Tall Cloud had, was not his friend. What other choice was left other than to be his enemy? Ingor tightened his grip on the reins to keep from doing something he knew would be stupid.

Tall Cloud reined his horse around and in angry silence led the way to Red Moon's camp where they seemed ready to move on. There were no teepees for shelter. The leather walls were tied on packhorses or on travois with the rest of their possessions for the families' ride north.

Tall Cloud led the way to the west of the group where Red Moon sat on a blanket in prayerful contemplation. The old man rose as they approached. When he recognized Still Water, a smile filled his face.

"My prayers have been answered, my daughter," he said in his native tongue. He opened his arms and Still Water slid off the packhorse and ran into his embrace. He gave a hand signal to Tall Cloud that Ingor didn't know, but it must have meant that he should go away and leave them.

Tall Cloud grunted his disapproval and stormed away with the other braves. Ingor breathed a deep sigh of relief and his pulse raced a little less. Knowing what might have happened, he was happy to have the Chief accept her back into the fold. Not until that moment did Ingor have any hope that he would live to see the sun set.

Still Water began at once to tell her uncle the whole story of how Ingor had saved her life. As the Indians ended their period of rest and began the trek north again, he urged her to walk beside him. Ingor could translate most of what she said as she told him everything that had happened to her after she disappeared.

Red Moon stopped then and insisted Ingor ride behind them with the packhorse's reins tied to Thor's saddle. Ingor knew that Red Moon wanted to talk without Ingor being able to hear them. He could do nothing but go along with his request.

"Please do as he asks," she said when he hesitated at first. He'd wanted to listen to be certain she would be safe and accepted back into the band. He wished he could add his support to her not becoming Tall Cloud's wife, but he knew his comments would hold no weight.

With a glance at Red Moon, he mounted Thor and kept a discreet distance behind them. He could hear some of what they said, but not enough. His muscles tensed, as he stayed ready for whatever would happen.

As they walked, Red Moon listened to all Still Water said about the two white men who had stolen her away and how Ingor had risked his life to rescue her. He asked questions, too. He learned all the details about being in the cabin alone with Ingor and how he had cared for her.

"It was just as I had cared for him," she explained. "He only thought of saving my life because I had saved his."

The expression on the Chief's wrinkled face never changed, and Still Water could not tell what he thought of the whole situation. At the end of her story, he asked the question that was the hardest for her to answer. As with all his earlier questions, she never thought of lying to him to make the answer easier.

"You look very fit. Why have you not returned to your people before now?" he asked.

She lowered her head and felt an embarrassed warmth

rise across her neck and cheeks. She had been healed enough to return to them at least two weeks earlier and yet she had not. He had been right to ask.

"I couldn't return before the Pale Hair could bring me, Uncle. I am riding on his horse to find you. Two winters ago I saved his life, and this summer he paid his debt to me and to our people by saving mine."

She paused and took a deep breath to fortify herself. "But in payment for saving my life, I gave him more. Though he never dishonored me, I also have given him my heart, Uncle."

Red Moon stopped walking and jerked his head up to look into her face. He asked her another hard question. She shook her head and met his gaze squarely to let him know she spoke only the truth.

"No, Uncle. I have given him my heart freely, but he took nothing from me. He does not even know that he owns my heart. I am the maiden I was when I went to gather herbs the day I was stolen. I swear it to you on the love that I hold for you," she replied, her heart racing.

He stared at her for several more seconds, and then nodded sharply before he continued at his slow pace. He was silent for a long time, but she walked beside him without speaking.

Still Water knew Ingor was getting impatient. He was shifting in his saddle and she could hear his loud sighs of frustration, but she did not dare look back at him.

Ingor was at the end of his patience. "Still Water," he quietly called.

She looked back then to see him watching her and smiled at him. But then she raised two fingers over her lips as if to silence him. He looked at her a moment longer and then nodded. If she needed more time to do her explaining to Red Moon, then he would give it to her. He straightened in the saddle and said no more while he waited. If he was allowed to leave in one piece, he wanted to be certain she would be accepted by her uncle.

A few more minutes passed in silence before Red Moon paused his walking. He raised his arm holding the staff that he had been leaning on as an aid to his old legs. The people around him stopped and several of the braves, who had appeared with Tall Cloud to usher them into camp, rode over to circle the group.

Ingor was startled when Red Moon began half-talking and half-chanting to his people in a loud but tremulous voice. Ingor couldn't tell what he was chanting and didn't understand what was happening or going to happen.

Two of the Indian warriors rode over next to Ingor. Using hand gestures in addition to their harsh native words, they ordered him to dismount and stand beside Still Water. Worried by what might happen to Still Water, he was happy to oblige. He raised his leg over Thor's neck and slid to the ground, his hands high and away from the gun that he always wore on his hip.

The smile she gave him when he came to her and put his hand on her back at her waist made him want to think that nothing had gone wrong. But something was going on and he wished he knew what. When he looked up and saw that Tall Cloud had dismounted and joined the group with a hateful glare, he felt uneasy again. He flexed his fingers and prepared to draw his weapon. If Tall Cloud hurt Still Water, he would kill him even though he knew he would die doing it.

Tall Cloud shouted at Red Moon, interrupting his chanting. Red Moon spoke a few angry words. He pointed to Still Water and Tall Cloud responded just as angrily. They were talking too fast for Ingor to understand all their words. But even if he had missed the words, he knew what Tall Cloud meant when he pointed to Still Water and then spat on the ground before he mounted his horse and galloped away.

Ingor looked down to see tears filling Still Water's eyes. He wanted to even the score with Tall Cloud and make him apologize. But that would have to wait for another day. He tightened his arm around her.

"Are you all right?" he asked quietly.

She sniffled and smiled up at him and then directed her attention back to Red Moon.

Ingor wanted to ask what was going on, but Red Moon had gone back to his chanting, and he didn't want to interrupt. Ingor tried to guess at what he was saying when the old man took Still Water's hand and placed it in Ingor's. He turned to his people gathered around them. Here, Ingor understood that he was calling for a blessing on them for their travels. He asked the Great Spirit to hold them safe from war and hunger.

Red Moon finished and looked at Still Water. She looked

up at Ingor and said, "I will care for him as he has cared for me."

The old man looked at Ingor as if expecting him to say something. He looked to Still Water for a clue as to what was going on.

"My uncle asks if you will continue to care for me as you have this summer," she said softly, laying her hand on his chest.

"You know I would care for you whenever and wherever you needed me," he promised, looking into her dark gaze and covering her hand with his.

Red Moon nodded. "Then it is done," he said, speaking this time in English. He laid his hand on top of Still Water's and Ingor's. "Thank you, friend," he said to Ingor in English. "I hope the Great Spirit gives me days great in number so these tired eyes may see you both again."

"Thank you for your blessing, Uncle," she said. "And may the Great Spirit keep The People safe and see you to your journey's end."

Red Moon nodded to her and then to Ingor before he lowered his hand and turned away. Two of the braves helped Red Moon up onto the back of a horse. Bent over with the weight of his people on his back, he held onto a handful of the horse's mane. As his horse walked north, the others followed.

Still Water pulled Ingor back when he started to turn toward their horses. "Wait," she said.

He didn't understand. Hadn't Red Moon just thanked him for helping Still Water? He couldn't be leaving Still Water behind, not when he had just showed her such affection. Didn't he believe that she was worthy of staying with them? She couldn't be cast out. Ingor felt his anger grow as the band moved away.

"Wait," he called as he tried to move again to stop them, to get them to take her with them.

Still Water reached for his arm and held him firmly where they stood. "May I watch them go for just a minute longer," she asked then, her voice breaking with emotion. "I may never see them again."

Ingor turned to face her. "How can they do this to you? How can they go off and leave you?"

"Leave me?" she asked, looking up at him with a frown. "No, it is not my people who leave me. It is I who chooses to stay here—with you."

Ingor was stunned at her reply, and he would admit to anyone who asked that he still didn't understand all that was happening. He thought the old man was thanking the Great Spirit that his adopted daughter had been returned to him, and then he blessed her. So why did he ride off, leaving her standing there?

Looking around, Ingor realized that standing in the open as they were doing was not a good idea. He had to get them to cover and then there would be time to get Still Water to tell him all of what had just happened.

"Come on. Standing out here, we look like two ducks on a pond waiting to get shot."

With his hands on her small waist, he lifted her onto the

packhorse. He mounted Thor and they headed east, the best direction, he judged, to miss running into the sergeant and his patrol.

If Red Moon didn't want Still Water with him, then Ingor would do his damndest to keep her safe until he figured out something better. He had no idea exactly where the Army patrol was by then. But in their quest to see that Red Cloud's people were moved, he suspected they weren't far. He could only hope that he and Still Water could avoid them.

After they had gone a few miles, he was still angry that Red Moon had ridden off and left Still Water despite her making excuses for him.

By the time they stopped by a small stream that still offered enough water this late in the summer for the horses to drink, he was concerned that Still Water hadn't said much since leaving her uncle. He knew she had to feel bad about it and that made him even angrier. He didn't want her to be hurt.

"We haven't come all that far," he told her after dismounting for a break while the horses drank the water. "We could still catch up to Red Moon."

Their gazes met, both brows knit with concern for the other.

"You want me to leave?"

"I want you to be happy."

She stared at him a moment longer and then nodded. "Then we go on together—you and me. Being with you makes me happy and I make sure you not sorry you take me with you."

They rode east and then south until late afternoon. They had stopped only briefly at noon to eat the end of the bacon and the last two flapjacks Still Water had cooked for the journey and wrapped in a cloth.

Still Water hadn't spoken during the ride and neither had he. Their voices could carry far over the flat prairie, and they didn't want to announce their movements to anyone nearby. But that wasn't the only reason. Ingor was still trying to figure out what had happened and what they would do now.

At the end of the day, they had stopped and were standing just a few feet apart. Nothing was standing in the way of a little quiet conversation. He kept hoping she would explain, but finally he had to ask.

"Tell me what go on back there with Red Moon. I hate the way Tall Cloud look at you. I want to hit him when he spit at you. I thought Red Moon believe you when you explained what happened."

She nodded. "Yes, he could tell I was speaking the truth."

"Then why did he go off without you?" he asked, his impatience growing.

Still Water began to retie the food bag and check to see that nothing was left on the ground. She tied the bag on her saddle, not having explained yet.

Ingor couldn't stand it another minute. He walked up behind her and laid his hand on her shoulder to turn her so she would face him. "Tell me. I not speak your language enough to understand much of what they say, and I not understand any words that Red Moon sings."

She nodded slowly and looked up. Their gazes locked. "My uncle thanked you and the Great Spirit for returning me to them as I was when I left."

Ingor released the breath he'd been holding. "Then he believed that I not hurt you or…or do anything that would…would change you."

She smiled and laid her palms on his chest. He felt their warmth through his shirt. "He believed that I am the maiden that left the camp two months ago."

"Then what went wrong? Why didn't he take you with him?"

"My uncle wished to give you the greatest gift he could for saving my life and returning me to him."

"I not want any gift from him," he insisted. He moved his hands up and down on her shoulders a few inches but not letting go. "I take care of you because I want to. Besides, they going to need everyone to survive the winter in Canada."

She nodded. "Yes, this is why he gave you the gift that he did. It was all the more valuable."

Ingor frowned. He hated that he didn't understand yet. "What gift?"

She could no longer meet his gaze. She looked down at her hands spread on his chest, and took a deep breath. His heart was pounding and he wondered if she could feel it.

"My uncle gave you the gift of me—as your wife."

Ingor gasped and squeezed her shoulders in shock. "What?"

She looked up, and for a second or two, he saw fear in

her eyes. He hated seeing it there and pulled her against him more gently. He circled her with his arms and kissed her hair.

"Oh, Still Water. As my wife?"

She nodded, her head moving against his chest. "It was not the full Sioux ceremony. We had no time to prepare. We had no time to make our vows to each other. He had precious little time to give us his blessing, but he made us man and wife. In the eyes of my people now, I am your woman. That is why Tall Cloud was so angry at us both."

She lifted her head and looked at him. "But I know that white people will not believe we are man and wife."

"Why not? No preacher is within hundred miles of here. I hear folks make their own vows by themselves, and then they married with no preacher at all. Besides, it not matter to me what other people think. If your people have blessed our marriage, that good enough for me."

"Then you don't mind that he gives me to you as your wife?"

Ingor smiled. "I think we do very good together. I like having you with me."

She smiled too, but it was not as joyous a smile as he wished to see on his wife's face. "I will also understand if the time comes when you do not want it to be so. Then I will leave."

Suddenly, Ingor couldn't help but think of the two Norwegian brides-to-be who were coming to Dakota Territory to marry him and Lars. But all he had to tell them now was that both the Oleson brothers were already married.

"That time never come. I not want you to leave me, Still Water." He cradled her jaw in his palm. "Not ever," he said, meaning every word.

He almost added that Red Moon had accomplished what he hadn't had the nerve to do himself. He had done his duty and returned Still Water to her people, but it was the last thing he'd wanted to do. All along, he'd wanted her to stay with him and now she could.

She was the kind of wife a man like him needed. He had no fancy clothes or dishes or ways of doing things. He lived off the land and worked hard to stay alive. He would work hard to provide for her and he knew she would do her share too. Yes, he thought, she was a better wife than ten Norwegian women.

Smiling at the thought, he lowered his head to kiss her. He felt her melt against him and knew the kiss easily and quickly could develop into much, much more. But it wasn't safe here and so he ended the kiss reluctantly.

He ran his thumb across her lower lip that was slightly swollen from his kisses. "We must leave now and ride to dark. I not want Army to find us."

They mounted their horses and continued southeast at a steady pace, riding side by side. Ingor had begun to think of a place to stop for the night when Still Water raised her arm and pointed to the horizon. A cloud of dust rose in a long line, the leading edge coming toward them.

"It's the Army and if scouts out ahead, they might know we here already." He reached to hold her arm. "You ride straight east to those trees. They not far. Wait for me there. If something happens to me, ride around the Army and head southwest until you find James River. Take that south and find my brother Lars. Tell him that you my wife, and he'll take care of you. I promise." He curled his hand around her neck and leaned over to kiss her hard.

"No, no, I not leave you," she insisted.

"Yes, you must. Our wedding will make no difference to the Army. Now, duck down and ride for those trees. Let the tall grass hide you and pray they don't see your dust."

She held his gaze. "I go to trees, but I wait for you there. I won't leave without you."

He kissed her again and watched as she bent low in the saddle and dug her heels into the horse's flanks. Ingor directed Thor on a course that would take him directly to meet the Army patrol as she disappeared into the trees. He hoped they would think any dust they saw was his, coming from the east. He waved and the sergeant left the column to ride to meet him.

"You're a long way from home," the sergeant called.

Ingor shrugged. "The territory is open for homesteading now. I thought I look around before I head to Winnipeg with the furs."

"Funny you would pick now to do it, just when we're out in this god-forsaken prairie looking for Red Moon."

"Well, I sure not go looking around in the winter," Ingor replied with a laugh, trying to deflect the suspicion he'd heard in the sergeant's comment. "This is last chance I get this year.

But I not see anything I like better than back in the wide valley of the Red."

"You ain't seen nothing of a white man traveling with an Indian who mighta stole them fellas' horses and weapons, did ya?"

"No, Sergeant. As matter a fact, I not see anyone at all."

"That a fact?" the Sergeant asked, studying him. "Say, how come you ain't got your packhorse with you?"

Ingor tamped down a moment of panic and did his best with a lie. "I let brother use horse to pull plow. He want to work more land to plant next spring."

The sergeant seemed to relax in his saddle. "We passed by his place. He had a bunch of horses in a corral. Why'd he need another one of yours?"

"If I leave her home alone, she have no one to feed her. Lars take good care of her," he explained, the lie getting easier, but his heart racing faster.

"It wouldn't go good for you if I discovered you had warned Red Moon that we were coming to find him."

"Sergeant, wherever Red Moon is, he know where you are for some time now. He not need me to warn him."

"I suppose you're right." He took off his uniform hat and wiped his forehead and the band of his hat with his kerchief before tugging it firmly back in place.

"But I see no sign of him." Ingor waved an arm casually out toward the northeast where he wanted the Sergeant to think he'd just been.

The sergeant straightened his back and turned his head to

stretch his sore neck muscles. While they had been talking, the column of men had passed them heading north. "I'd best get caught up to my men. I think we're on the right trail. We'll find him this time if he don't beat us to Canada."

Ingor laid his reins across his left hand and turned the horse to face east. "I keep an eye out for those horse thieves, Sergeant. I not want to lose mine."

The officer nodded. "You do that," he said and spurred his horse into a gallop north.

Ingor rode at a steady but calm canter for as long as he thought the Army could see him. The minute they were out of sight, he leaned forward and let Thor loose into a gallop back toward the trees. He wanted to find his wife and make sure she was safe.

Chapter 9

Ingor found Still Water waiting dangerously close by the edge of the trees where she had stayed to watch the encounter. At least happy she had remained in the saddle and ready to ride if necessary, he didn't have the heart to scold her for not going farther into the trees. Cradling her jaws with his hands, he leaned over and kissed her hard.

"Come on. We've got to get out of here. I not think Sergeant smart enough to double back and check on me, but I not want to be here if he does."

Staying in the cover of the trees as long as they could, they set out east again and rode until well past sunset. When the sky was barely light enough to see by, they made camp without a fire on the bank of a river that still ran clear so late in the year.

Ingor could not dismiss the fact that this was the first time they were making camp as man and wife.

* * * *

Still Water was accustomed to moving about in camp in

the pitch black of a moonless night. Granted, more often than not, she'd had campfires dotting the landscape that she didn't have tonight.

When they'd first arrived at camp, she noticed a deep curve in the lazy river where the grass grew right up to the edge of the water. That was perfect fresh feed for their horses. After their cold supper, she walked to the river by the grass while Ingor laid out the bedrolls.

She took off Ingor's hat and the shirt, which she wore over her leather clothes, as well as her protective high moccasins. Her tunic and leggings followed. She unbraided her hair as she stepped into the river. The mud on the bottom oozed between her toes, but the cool water felt refreshing.

The water was never more than waist deep, but by kneeling, she was able to wash her hair and her body of the dust and sweat from their journey. Taking handfuls of sandy mud from the bottom, she rubbed her skin clean. She was happy to find that her wounds no longer hurt at all when she rubbed over them. Her shoulder sometimes gave her trouble when she lifted or pulled something heavy, but that was the only time it hurt.

After rinsing off thoroughly, she walked up the gradual bank of grass. She wrung as much water as she could from her long hair and picked up the pile of clothes to return naked to their camp a few yards into the trees.

A sliver of a moon had risen while she bathed, and dappled pale light shone through the trees on the campsite. Ingor had laid out the blankets side by side near the saddles. The hobbled horses were grazing nearby.

Hearing her coming, he had pulled his gun from his holster, but the moment he saw her, he dropped it back in. Meeting her gaze, he unbuckled the holster from his hips and lowered it to the ground beside the rifle within arm's reach of his blanket. He held his hand out to her but said nothing. He only smiled as his gaze swept over her body.

Encouraged though feeling shy, she stepped to the end of the bedrolls and laid her clothes on the corner of the quilt. Turning back to him, she raised her hand to lay it in his. He pulled her close and for a moment they stood holding hands and gazing into each other's eyes.

Still Water smiled. "With the stars filling the sky above us and Mother Earth as our only witnesses, I give myself to you, my husband, for as long as you want me. This life you saved belongs to you now. I will do my best to honor you, to help you, and to care for you all my days," she vowed in a soft voice.

He returned her smile. "I accept your great gift and I treasure it. This life of mine that you saved when others thought me dead now belongs to you. You can count on me to protect you, and know this: I will never desert you," he vowed to her.

He raised his hand to rub the backs of his knuckles over her soft cheek. Like striking a sulfur match, his touch ignited flaming heat that sped throughout her body. Turning her head, she kissed his bent fingers and the flame within her flared up higher. Gathering her into his arms, he kissed her.

"Your clothes feel rough against my skin," she said with a smile when their lips had parted. She dared to unbutton his shirt and tug it loose. Slipping her arms around him inside the shirt, she pressed her aching breasts against his bare chest. "That feels much better."

"Your hair's wet and you're shivering. Do you want to put your clothes back on?"

She shook her head. "Not yet."

Forever. That's how long Still Water felt she could stand there in his arms. Luxuriating in the feel of his fingers stroking her head and then combing through her hair, she felt completely contented. Not from the summer air, a heat of a different kind flowed through her to keep her warm. Being close felt so right, but it was not enough.

"You kiss me again?" she asked, looking up at him.

"Anytime you want me to."

His lips felt warm and soft as they met hers at an angle. Slightly parted, their lips rocked and turned like two lovers getting comfortable in a soft pine-needle bed in the forest.

Too soon he lightened the pressure and barely brushed her lips with his before he outlined their contours with the tip of his tongue. Finding that the most comfortable spot on that imaginary pine-needle bed was in the center and entwined together, their lips met again as their tongues dipped, tasted, and tantalized.

Just when she wanted more from him, much more, he retreated from his gentle invasion. She whimpered as he feathered her swollen lips with light kisses. Then his lips were gone and hers felt cold. He stepped back only a small step, but the heat within her dissipated, and she was left feeling bereft.

"Make me your wife," she said in aspirate tones, holding his arms so he could move no further away.

"You sure, Still Water? There no going back once I do."

Her smile broadened. "I never more sure of anything. I've waited all my life for you, for tonight."

"Then we've waited long enough, my wife, haven't we?"

With her whispered "yes", they waited no longer. There under the wide canopy of stars, fantasies and dreams held by two caring people for months, maybe since they first met, became reality.

When he discovered the barrier that proved her to be the maiden he knew she was, he stopped. "Are you sure, Still Water? I not want you unhappy with me later."

She saw his set jaw, felt his taught muscles and knew what stopping had cost him. She answered his query with her lips covering his so there could be no more words, only feelings. There would be no more stopping on this special night with him. Only total sharing, holding nothing back.

In trying to give more than they received, each achieved even more. Still Water knew she was thankful to him that she was able to wait for this night with him. He led her to an ecstasy she could never have imagined or experienced with anyone other than this man whom she had come to love.

Ingor could not hold back from making love with Still Water again at the first light of day. Wishing they could spend the day this way together, he walked with her to the river where they quickly washed up, comfortable with their nakedness. Within a few minutes of efficient activity, they were on their horses heading for his cabin.

They rode in silence so as not to be heard, and for hours, Ingor thought about the startling depth of his desire for his new Indian wife. He knew that one night with her would never satisfy his need for her. Even as he rode, his body reacted to his vivid thoughts of taking her that night in his comfortable bed.

He thought Red Moon was a wise man and had done the right thing in marrying them. When Still Water had said she would rather be with him than go with the tribe, maybe the old Chief had seen that Ingor wanted her as his wife, too.

But it wouldn't be easy for them. Other than his brother and a few Canadian trappers he knew, and one of them had an Indian wife, he didn't know a white man who didn't hate or at least fear Indians.

What would the men at the fort think when they learned his wife was a Sioux?

Gud i himmel! What would his brother Lars and his wife Lissa think?

* * * *

Riding near the river in the trees, they approached the cabin around noon. Thor sidestepped nervously. Ingor trusted the horse's sense and signaled with a raised hand for Still Water to stop. Backing Thor to stand next to the packhorse she rode, he leaned closer.

"Something wrong. You stay here with horses. I go on ahead on foot to get a look at the cabin."

"Be careful," she mouthed.

He smiled and kissed her quick while he had the chance. Silently dismounting, he handed her Thor's reins and pointed toward the river. She nodded and turned the horses in that direction, but not before Ingor lifted his rifle from his saddle.

"Now you don't want to go down that way when Paw's waiting for you at the cabin," Jimmy said from a hidden position behind Ingor.

Ingor spun around, but held his fire when he saw Jimmy step from behind a tree with a gun trained on Still Water.

"Now since you gone to so much gol-darned effort to rescue her, seems to me you don't want her shot, do you?" He grinned broadly, exposing his darkened teeth.

Ingor lowered his rifle slowly. "You right about that. I not want her shot."

"Then drop them guns. I'll just see how you like them tossed into the high grass where trying to find them is like looking for a spoon of sugar dropped on a snow bank."

Ingor lifted the revolver from the holster with his free hand. Instead of tossing them toward the high grass, he quickly tossed both firearms beyond the base of a gnarled oak tree closer to the river. He'd set many traps near that tree to mark their location, and if he could get free of these degenerates, he could find them easily.

"Damn it, I said to toss them in the grass," Jimmy wailed.

"We in woods. I not strong enough to throw that far."

"Well, hell, just get going." He waved his pistol toward the cabin.

Ingor moved to mount Thor, but Jimmy stopped him.

"Oh, no you don't. You get them reins from her and lead both them horses back to the cabin."

Buying time until he could get the upper hand, Ingor did as he was told. He had Still Water to think about now. He couldn't let anything happen to her. He would keep her safe or he would die trying, and as long as the simpleton had the gun pointed at them, he might.

"Hey, Paw, lookee here what I found in them woods," Jimmy called out when the cabin was in sight.

"Boy, where the hell you been? I want my supper," Hap shouted back, but when he stepped outside and saw the trio coming toward him, he laughed. "Boy, when you go fishing, you bring home some big fish."

"I didn't get no fish, but I found them. They was riding back here just as pretty as you please."

Jimmy waved the gun he held toward the cabin. "Get on inside wheres I can tie you up. We'll be a lot safer that way."

Ingor helped Still Water down from her horse and tried to stand between her and the gun trained on them. "Who take care of the horses?"

"We should take care of 'em. They'll bring good money," Hap decided. "You go with him to put up the horses, and I'll take her inside. She can start fixing our supper."

"She stays with me," Ingor insisted, putting out his arm to keep her behind him.

"The hell she does. And if you want her left alone, you just get the horses to the barn."

Nodding his assurance to Still Water, Ingor led the horses to the barn. He pulled off their saddles, wiped them down with handfuls of straw, and fed and watered them in record time. Jimmy had to run to keep up with him as he returned to the cabin and swung the door open wide.

Hap was seated with his feet up on the table, a jug of whiskey in his hand. "That was fast," the older man said.

"Don't drink it all, paw," Jimmy complained as he grabbed the jug and took a long pull on it.

Ingor moved to stand between them and Still Water and watched them for a few moments to assess their situation. The two of them were dressed in the same dirty denim trousers and plaid shirts that they had been wearing when he rescued Still Water from them. From the way they smelled, he would have to guess that they'd worn the same clothes day and night since acquiring them who knows how long ago.

Each of them had a scruffy beard. Ingor expected that. He grew a beard himself to protect his skin from the freezing wind in the winter and the sun in the summer. The men each wore their hat in the cabin and, Ingor realized, he had left his in the barn where he'd hung it on a peg before caring for the horses.

Turning his head only slightly, he glanced at Still Water. She was filling a large frying pan with strips of bacon. Spoon bread made from coarse-ground wheat sat in a bowl ready to fry in the bacon fat when the strips of meat were done cooking. The were lucky that the promise of food had made Hap keep his hands off her.

Looking around the cabin, Ingor discovered that the intruders had trashed the place. The straw mattress was split open and the food cache under the wooden trapdoor in the kitchen area was open and empty as far as he could see from where he stood. But he saw no daylight down there so he hoped the tunnel had not been discovered. They might need to use it yet.

"I see you make yourselves at home," he said, wondering what else they had found.

His furs were still layered and tied into bundles in the barn, ready to take to Winnipeg. He had seen them still tucked in the rafters when he put up the horses. Though they might suffer some mouse damage, he'd thought the dry summer air blowing through the barn would be better for them than the stagnant air in the windowless cabin while he was gone. The furs and the small bag of coins he had stashed in the bottom of the barrel of beans were the only things of value that he would need from the cabin when he and Still Water escaped.

"We feel right at home," Hap said. "This is a mighty nice cabin you got here. Not like them dirty sod huts. We're going to enjoy living here."

"Yeah," Jimmy agreed. "Say, where'd you get all these straight logs. I went through them woods to go fishing and I never seen a straight tree out there. They's all crooked from the wind."

"Ya, I get trees for walls in Minnesota. A farmer there help me cut them and bring them back in his wagon. Many tall pines grow east of here."

"Say, I never thought of doing that," Jimmy replied.

"That takes money, you stupid boy," Hap told his son. Turning back to Ingor, he said, "Nice cabin, but other than the whiskey, we ain't found nothing worth having. If you can pay a farmer for them logs, you must have some cash money. Where is it?"

Hap had his revolver leveled at him. His hand was shaking so much that Ingor prayed he wouldn't squeeze the trigger by accident. He smiled. At hearing they'd found nothing of value, he almost laughed with relief. That had to mean they hadn't found his precious stash of coins. "I trade furs for food, not money. What I need money for? No store around here."

"Damn," Hap swore. "Gimme that jug, boy. I need another drink."

Ingor turned to Still Water, who was stirring the coarse-ground bread mixture. He heard and smelled the bacon sizzling on the fire. Hap and Jimmy fought over who got the next swig from the jug. They were so set on getting their next swallow that they had forgotten their plan to tie him up, and he wasn't going to remind them.

Suddenly, Ingor got an idea that just might work to get them free of those two. He turned more and stood with his back to the men, who must have figured that without guns, he was no danger to them.

"Let me help you," he offered to Still Water. "I'll get the

beans." With his back to the other men, he winked at her and hoped that was enough to let her know he had a plan. She nodded and said nothing, which was perfect. He took a bowl from the box behind her.

Keeping his body between the wooden bean barrel and the men, he dug into the bottom and pulled out a little sack. While putting some beans in the bowl with his free hand, he folded over the top of the little bag to keep the coins from jingling, and stuffed it into his pocket. He set the bowl by where Still Water was working and put the top back on the barrel. Seeing the dishcloth, he pulled it off the counter and stuffed it into his pocket with the tail sticking out, to make a more obvious reason for the bulge from the sack of coins. It was all the money he'd saved since getting to America and he wasn't going to hand it over easily.

"But beans not get soft by the time rest of supper is ready, will they?" he asked. Still Water shook her head but remained silent.

He turned and looked around the cabin one more time to mentally say goodbye to all he owned. If his plan worked, the cabin would burn to the ground before he could stop it. If his plan didn't work, he'd be dead.

"Anybody knows beans take all day to cook," Jimmy slurred with a laugh and a burp.

Hap took advantage of the diversion and swiped the jug from his son. Jimmy pulled out the tree-stump chair from the table next to his father to sit down, and then promptly tripped over the wide base. It took some effort for him to get up and sit down.

When he had, he yelled, "When's supper? I'm hungry."

"Have some more of this then," Hap said, pushing the jug toward him, "And shut up your yelling."

Standing before the fire, Still Water lifted the cooked bacon from the pan of sizzling fat and laid them on a tin plate which she set on the plank counter in the kitchen area. When she was going to return to put the wheat cakes on to cook, Ingor grasped her arm. Checking that the men weren't watching, he motioned her toward the door with a nod of his head.

Taking her place near the fire as she slowly stepped toward the door, he reached for the folded towel she'd used as a pad to protect her hands and lifted the pan of bubbling fat from the fire. Thinking of nothing but saving their lives, he tipped it and let some fat slosh over the side into the fire. Instantly, the pan of fat burst into flames. Angrier than he had ever been, he yelled as if burned and turned. In one fluid motion he sprayed the burning fat over the table and the two bastards seated at it.

Yelping in pain as he batted at the flames, Jimmy jumped up and pulled his gun. Ingor let the pan fly, hitting his arm. The gun went off, hitting Hap next to him, who slumped to the floor, engulfed in flames. Yelling for his pa to get up, Jimmy batted at the fire that the burning grease had started again on his own arm. Crying out in pain, he had only succeeded in hurting his hands.

The mattress straw strewn on the floor from their search

of the cabin provided more fuel for the fire. The bed frame caught fire too and then the cabin log wall. Far enough from the fire to be safe for a few moments longer, Still Water pulled the spare saddlebags from the peg on the wall and stuffed them with food staples and the cooked bacon. Having food once they escaped would be as important as escaping the fire.

"Get out of here," Ingor yelled.

Desperate now for fresh air to breathe, he grabbed one of the bags she'd filled and pushed her to the door. The strap of the other bag over her arm, she opened the door, unwittingly letting a burst of oxygen into the cabin. The flames leapt high to the wooden roof with a sudden roar. She screamed and covered her face with her hands.

"Get out. Get the horses," Ingor ordered, guiding her shoulders out the door. She turned back and grabbed the second bag from him.

"You're not going anywhere," Jimmy yelled as he lunged to stop them. "You killed my pa, you dirty snake."

Ingor blocked his body with the door and saw Still Water run toward the barn. Maddened by the flames burning his arm, Jimmy threw open the door to the wall with a growl and renewed energy. He grabbed the frying pan Ingor had thrown at him. Backing away, Ingor raised his arm in self-defense when Jimmy swung it and hit his shoulder as he tried to escape out the door.

Ingor yelped as the blow slammed him against the doorway. Stunned by the pain, Ingor paused too long. Jimmy jumped at him and pressed his hands against his neck, trying to kill him. Ingor raised his knee with all his might, but dizzy from Jimmy's hands cutting off his air, he was losing strength fast. He could hear the roar and feel the heat from the intense fire as his cabin burned around them.

Working frantically, Still Water bridled the horses and just slung the saddles on their backs before she led them from the barn to tie them to a tree well away from the fire. She intended to return for the furs and sacks of feed when she saw Jimmy trying to kill her husband in the doorway. Determined to save him, she ran to the door and picked up a thick log from the firewood pile outside the cabin. Brandishing it in both hands, she hit Jimmy as hard as she could on the back of his head. Despite the roar of the fire, she heard the sickening crunch when it hit. Jimmy fell on top of Ingor, a dead weight.

Ingor didn't move to get out from under him.

"Ingor! Come," she called, coughing, choking on the smoke now pouring out through the top half of the doorway.

Ingor still didn't move.

Chapter 10

Still Water knew she had to get him out of there before the roof fell in on him where he lay. Pushing with her feet, she rolled Jimmy off him into the cabin, but Ingor showed no signs of moving.

"Ingor, get up," she shouted to no avail.

Wanting to think only that Ingor was still alive, it was up to her to get him to safety. Putting an arm under each of Ingor's, she pulled with all her might. She managed only a few inches when her injured shoulder shot pain all down her arm and across her chest. Frightened for their lives, she knew she had no choice. She could think of no other way to get him out, and she couldn't stop trying. She pulled his unconscious body again and again, gaining a precious foot or two with each pull. Her overworked back muscles seared with pain on each attempt.

Even several feet outside the cabin, she could feel the heat of the fire hotter than any bad sunburn. But she wouldn't leave him. Coughing from the smoke, she pulled him back all the way to a safe distance where she'd left the horses. She laid a hand on his chest and felt it rise and fall. So relieved that he was still alive at that point, she ran back to the barn to save what else she could.

The ceiling planks had burned through in the cabin and the sod roof had begun to fall into the room with a showy spectacle of sparks and flames. It wasn't long before the log walls collapsed, some falling in and some out.

Working frantically to save the equipment in case the barn caught fire, she ran in and out carrying everything that she could find. Her lungs hurt with each rapid breath from the exertion and she coughed more often. Her tears washed her stinging eyes as she dragged each of the sacks of grain Ingor had readied for their trip. She set them beside the horses and made another trip for their blankets. Ingor hadn't bothered to untie their bedrolls or the remaining food from the saddles, and she was glad, knowing they would need them to survive the coming cold weathers.

The cabin was fully engulfed in flames by this time. The last wall fell inward as the supporting logs failed. Thousands of huge sparks blew outward. Knowing the barn could be next, her strength seemed to increase with her level of panic. Had it not, the heavy saddles would have been her undoing.

Still Water knew she no longer had to fear that Jimmy or Hap would come out after them, but the grass in front of the cabin had caught fire where a few logs and the myriad of sparks had landed.

She had to move Ingor to a safer place. Kneeling on the

ground beside Ingor's shoulder, she pushed his hair back from his face. An angry red welt crossed his neck, and she wondered if his windpipe had been crushed. Despite the crackling of the thick cabin logs burning behind her, she could hear that his breathing was quick and raspy.

"Ingor, can you hear me? You must wake up. I can't lift you up onto Thor. Please wake up and help me before the fire moves farther."

Ingor showed no signs of having heard her. The horses pranced sideways and neighed nervously. Saddling them took twice the normal time because they were so skittish this close to the fire. She finished saddling them and prayed to the Great Spirit that she would think of a way to lift Ingor into the saddle by the time she was done tying on their goods.

She glanced at Ingor and saw no movement other than his shallow breathing. Undoing the knot holding his coiled rope to the saddle, she returned to where he lay. If she had to, she would tie the rope under his armpits and drag him away. Bruises on his backside would be better than burns.

A glance back at the fire told her that the fire in the worn and spotty grass in front of the cabin had burned out. That was not the case on the sides of the cabin where the grass grew higher and thicker, closer to the cabin. Fires had already started there.

She knelt again at Ingor's side before tying on the rope. "Please, Ingor, I love you too much not to get you to safety. Please, Pale One, I love you. Wake up and help me get you on Thor."

"You love me?" Ingor croaked, blinking his eyes open and looking up at her.

Startled that he actually woke up, she laughed with relief and kissed him hard. "Oh, my husband, you woke up. We must get you on the horse and get away."

"Tell me once more first," he insisted.

"I love you," she said with a smile, and then she changed her voice to order, "Now get up."

Ingor shook his head and immediately regretted it because of the pain that gripped his neck. He raised his hand to cover it protectively and swallowed hard.

"I love you, too," he said, barely able to speak.

She stopped tugging at his arm. "You do?"

He smiled and swallowed again. "Yes, I do and I promise to work harder to keep you safe from now on."

"Oh, Ingor," she said. "You did protect me. You saved us both."

He lifted his arms to hold her shoulders and pulled her down to kiss her. The crashing roar as the fireplace chimney fell in startled them both back to reality.

"The furs. We have to save the furs before the barn catches fire."

Ingor had just managed to get to his feet when they heard shouting and the pounding of horses' hooves on the dry packed earth. They looked up to see Lars and his wife Lissa's brother, Wally, racing up on horseback.

"What happened?" Wally shouted as they tied the horses to a tree so the fire wouldn't make them run.

"Long story, but must save furs. Bundles in rafters of barn," he told them in his hoarse voice. Ingor started toward the barn, but Lars grabbed his arm.

"I'll get them. You stay here. The barn is good distance from the cabin. Maybe we can save it, too," Lars shouted.

Thor rose on his hind feet and pawed the air.

"Wally, you help them get horses farther from the flames. We got to calm horses."

At once Lars ran to retrieve the furs. He pulled the travois Ingor used on his trapline with its leather bed out the barn door and mounded the bundles on it. Then he picked up the poles and ran with them to the others. They had moved the horses and goods farther from the fire. Then they all set about to try to save the barn. Grabbing the pails, they ran to the river to fill them. Returning to the barn, they wet down the side of the barn facing the cabin, and the grass and weeds on the ground between them.

Nearly exhausted already, Still Water only made one trip. After that she remained at the river, standing knee deep in the water. The men brought the pails to her, and while they leaned their hands on their knees and fought for a few deep breaths of fresh air, she filled the pails and handed them back. They ran back to wet the barn and the ground all over again.

"I think we've won," Ingor told Still Water much later when the flames over the cabin no longer sailed to the treetops. He gave her a hand up to the muddy back of the river and hugged her. "The cabin fire too low to spread now, but not possible without your help. You saved my life again."

Together they all carried the last pails of water back to the cabin site. These they used to water the horses before the firefighters plopped down on the grass beside them. They all had blistered hands and smoke-blackened faces streaked with sweat. Ingor coughed and fought to get his breath.

"Thank you, brother," Ingor said when he could speak, but his voice was still hoarse. "I don't know why you and Wally come here today, but you save barn."

"We saw the smoke and rode ahead," Wally explained.

"Lissa comes with the baby in the wagon," Lars explained. "We have some grain we cut and I think she want to see other people."

"Yeah, there's nobody around us out there," Wally put in with a laugh. "But that's not the real reason. The Army scared her good. They talked about Indians out to get the whites and..." Wally stopped in mid-sentence and looked at the Indian woman, who had been helping so much, leaning against the tree. "Pardon me, ma'am," he said to Still Water before turning back to Ingor and adding in a loud whisper, "Who's she?"

Ingor laughed at Wally's attempt to be polite and inquisitive at the same time. "I tell you," he said, sitting up and reaching to hold her hand. "This beautiful woman is my wife. Her name is Still Water, and she is the niece of Chief Red Moon of the Sioux."

Both newcomers stared open-mouthed at Still Water. Ingor watched her blush, though the soot on her cheeks hid much of the color. He gave her hand a little squeeze. "She is the one who saved my life the first winter in Dakota Territory. I told you about her."

"But she's your wife?" Wally asked with a grin.

They had no chance to talk more because they heard a wagon creaking through the grass toward the cabin. Lars jumped up to help Lissa when she arrived, while the others rose more slowly.

"Lars," Lissa cried. "What happened? Are you all right?"

He lifted her, with the baby in her arms, down from the wagon. With his arm around her, he ushered her over to the others while Wally tied the horses in the shade of a tree well away from the smoke and flames still rising from the burning embers.

"Oh, no. It *was* your cabin that made all that smoke. What happened?" Lissa walked over to Ingor who had gotten to his feet. "I'm so sorry. Are you hurt?" she asked him.

Everyone held out their blistered hands from hefting the pails of water and Wally, Lissa and Lars laughed. "Just like after the wood shop fire," Wally explained to Ingor and Still Water.

"Here goes another good petticoat for bandages," Lissa complained. "First, I'll need some clean water to clean your hands with."

"I get it," Still Water offered softly.

"Wait." Ingor put his arm around his wife to stop her. "Lissa, this is Still Water."

Lissa smiled broadly. "The woman who saved your life

two winters ago. We have much to thank you for. I'm pleased to meet you."

"See? She remembers," Ingor said with a nudge in Lars' ribs.

"Yes, I remember her pretty name and I'm glad to have a chance to thank her, too," Lissa said with a broad smile. "And this is Eric, our son."

Still Water nodded with a shy smile. "I get water now."

"Not yet," Ingor insisted, catching her again when she tried to walk away. "What Lissa not know yet is that Still Water is my wife."

Lissa looked at Ingor with wide eyes. "Your wife?" she asked. "When was the wedding? How did we miss it?"

"It long story, but we married just before coming here."

"Well, congratulations. You were just at our homestead this spring and you said nothing about her all the time you were there helping us."

"He's a fast worker," Wally put in with a laugh.

"We all go to the river and clean up. We tell you then," Ingor offered.

"I'll get the food we brought, too," Lissa offered. "We haven't eaten since breakfast, and we can eat down there by the river away from the smoke."

"We not eat either. We broke our fast with only deer jerky this morning," Ingor said. "I am hungry."

"We do have a little food to offer that we rescued from the fire," Still Water added.

Ingor met Still Water's gaze. He was certain that they

both were thinking of the coarse-ground wheat bread that she had been ready to fry when he started the fire. He took her hand in his. When she winced, he looked at the palm of her hand and found blisters on every finger and across her palm.

"We get your hands cleaned and bandaged," he said, taking care of his bride. "Get cleaned up before food."

****

The meal they shared was a break from the realization that Ingor and Still Water had just lost their home. Ingor told his brother and his family all about Still Water being stolen from her tribe up to the brief Sioux wedding ceremony as Red Moon and his people were leaving for Canada.

"The Army was looking for them when they stopped by our soddy. They not like seeing us out there all alone, but when I tell them I am brother of Ingor, they say maybe Sioux leave us alone since they leave you alone," Lars explained.

"I not bother them and they not bother me. I make honest trades and we get along," Ingor replied. "But now I wed to Sioux. Everyone can leave us alone, I think."

"Do you really think they will?" Lissa asked softly.

"What you mean?" Ingor asked.

"Well, the Sioux recognize that you are married, but do you think that the Army will? From what we heard at the fort last Christmas, they don't hold marriage of a white man to an Indian woman as being a legal marriage."

"How you say that? Why not?" Ingor asked hotly.

Still Water laid her hand on his arm while Lars, protective of his wife, put his hand over Lissa's.

"Lissa is right, brother. Instead of snapping at her like turtle, you should listen to her."

"I'm sorry I yell." Repentant, Ingor's shoulders slumped.

"I understand," Lissa replied. With a smile she added, "I wish the circumstances were happier, but we all welcome you into the family, Still Water."

"Thank you," Still Water replied.

"I am happy you welcome my wife into family. That make me proud," Ingor said.

"You consider yourself man and wife. We can do no less," Lars said solemnly. He grinned suddenly and slapped his brother on the back. "I not believe you finally married, big brother." They all laughed at that.

"I wish the Army stay out of my life. We just want to be left alone," Ingor added, laying his hand over his wife's where it still rested on his arm.

"If the Army doesn't catch up to Red Moon's band before they cross into Canada, what else can they do? They have no jurisdiction in Canada," Lissa said.

"They not catch Red Moon. They hide in Canada where they are safe from the Army," Still Water said confidently.

"But the Army is pushing out any other Indians they find—Sioux or anyone," Wally put in. "No one's safe."

Still Water gasped. "No one?"

"What's wrong?" Ingor asked.

"What about this Sioux?" she asked, her finger pointing at her own chest. "Can they take me away from you?"

"*Gud i himmel*, do you think they could?" Ingor asked

Lars and Lissa. "Is that what you try to tell me?"

No one replied because no one knew for certain, but they all feared it was true.

* * * *

The combined food was soon eaten, and the men returned to the cabin site where the fire was still burning in the thick logs that had made up the walls of the cabin. Several rows of stones of the chimney over the fireplace still stood, rising from the flames like a blackened tower.

Lissa sat under a tree nursing Eric with Still Water at her side, keeping her company. Half-heartedly, the men poked at the burning logs, knowing the fire would not die down for some time. They managed to pull away some logs that had fallen away from the cabin when the roof collapsed. Several had not burned much. They doused them with water just to be certain they weren't burning, and hoped to be able to use them again.

"If you can't use them with the burned side turned out, you can always use them for firewood," Wally said brightly as he and Lars pulled the unburned end of one farther from the fire before they poured water on it too.

"Careful you don't get burned again," Lissa called.

"We not get burned," Lars assured her.

"We had enough of that in Philadelphia," Wally said. "Now that was a fire that was hot and quick with all the milled wood in there. But none of those pieces were as thick as these logs."

"These could burn for days," Ingor said sadly. "All that work to bring them here from Minnesota wasted."

"I wondered where you get them," Lars put in.

Ingor told him about his trek to find logs. "When I come, I not have plow to cut sod for the house." He shrugged. "And I think sod house not be nice as yours, so I get logs like in Norway. But now I see sod house would be good and easier. Log house is much hard work."

"I never thought I'd be living in a sod house either," Lissa said. "But it's been cool this summer, and I expect it will be warm this winter. It's very good."

"And it won't burn to the ground," Wally commented.

With no more logs to pull out for possible reuse, the men stood watching the flames they had stirred up.

"We have to wait until logs not hot to search for anything worth saving," Lars said, stating the obvious.

"I can see the cooking pots still in the fireplace. They should be good, wouldn't they?" Wally asked.

"Good and hot right now," Ingor judged. "We see if they crack in big fire. Then no good."

Lissa was done feeding the baby and Wally wandered over to ask Still Water about Red Moon's band. As he listened, he sat cross-legged and whittled on a wooden toy as he always did in his spare time.

Seeing Wally join the women, Ingor nudged Lars' sleeve and jerked his head toward the river. Then he called casually, "We go clean up. We be right back."

Ingor led the way without saying more. He wanted to get farther away from the others so they couldn't hear what he had to tell his brother.

Chapter 11

Ingor led him to the river east of the cabin. Two horses were tied to trees near the water's edge. He untied them and led them to drink. Tying them again where they could reach the grass, he walked on with Lars following.

He headed right for the big tree where he had thrown his pistol and rifle. Very glad that Jimmie was not very smart, he found them quickly. In short order, he had cleaned the dirt from them and checked that they were loaded. He dropped the pistol into the holster on his hip and carried the rifle parallel to the ground.

When they got back to the horses, Ingor untied their reins and took them with him back toward the cabin.

"You have more horses out here in trees?"

Ingor nodded. "I do now."

They reached the spot in the river behind the cabin that he always used to clean up. He tied the horses again and he and Lars walked toward the water.

"What is it? What's wrong?" Lars asked in Norwegian as

they bent over to wash the soot off their hands before enjoying a cool drink themselves.

Replying in his native tongue also, Ingor said, "You haven't insisted I tell you how the fire got started and why there are two extra horses tied back here."

Lars shrugged. "I knew you had a good reason to wait to tell me."

Ingor smiled and sat on a fallen tree trunk. He picked at the wet strips of cloth Lissa had wrapped over his blisters, and then the story came tumbling out. First, he told Lars about the two men who had died in the cabin. Then he went back to the beginning of the story and told him about rescuing Still Water from them.

"You took a big chance. They could have shot you."

Ingor nodded. "That's when I discovered that I would do anything for her."

Lars grinned at his big brother's admission.

"I wanted to kill them that day when they took her. Today I killed one to protect Still Water, and she hit the other one over the head while he was trying to kill me. I don't know if she killed him or the fire did." He rubbed his throat that was still sore and inflamed.

"Sounds like the pair got exactly what they deserved," Lars concluded. "I don't think there will be anything left to bury after fire dies."

"No?" Ingor asked.

Lars shook his head.

Ingor nodded. "Good. Then we don't have to tell Lissa

and Wally about them being in there. I'll tell Still Water that it is our secret. We will never speak of them again—as if we never saw them here."

"I think that's a good idea."

The brothers sat a couple of minutes in companionable silence.

"I never thought I would kill a man," Ingor said. "I would not want to again." At the same time, he knew it would do whatever he had to in order to protect himself and his wife.

The songs of the birds and the merry splash of the river churning over a few rocks near shore illustrated the beauty that coexisted with the brutality that they had witnessed.

"I came to Dakota Territory to settle down and make good life for us and the wives Uncle Ole send from home," Ingor said.

"Now Dakota Territory is home, but we have chosen our own wives, not the ones from Uncle Ole. I like this way better," Lars said.

"I was going to write a letter to Uncle Ole and tell him not to send the women," Ingor noted guiltily. "Already the letter might not be in time to stop them."

Lars laughed. "Can you imagine what would happen if they knocked on our doors one day and announced to our wives who they were?"

The brothers laughed at the thought. After a short silence, Ingor offered, "That would not be funny. We should not laugh. Maybe we should think of what to do with them if they come."

Lars nodded. "But I send a letter. Lissa wants to visit others at the fort. They will send it on."

They chatted a little longer in Norwegian before they strolled back to the others and switched to English.

"We bring wheat and oats from our harvest. They grow quickly in the rich soil here."

"We do something with this load of grain now," Ingor announced as the men approached the wagon that Lissa had driven in. "It dark before we know it. Moon is too small to see much by."

Not having any place to store all the wheat and oats that Lars had brought, Ingor emptied the sacks of oats into the wooden feed bin he'd built in the barn. He'd made the log walls thick and fit them together tightly to keep the field mice out. He liked that Thor and the packhorse would be fed this winter with good oats. They burned up a lot of feed just keeping warm. He laid only a couple sacks with wheat for he and Still Water to use until he could get his cabin rebuilt. Not having a mill nearby, they would have to stone grind it as they needed it.

"We take the rest of the wheat back home and keep it for you," Lars offered. "Wally build nice thick wood boxes for Lissa for grain. He can build more. You come get it when you want it."

"I don't know when we get cabin built again," Ingor said.

"Then you will wait for the fire to go out and built again here?" Lars asked.

Ingor looked around the area and then at Still Water. "It

good here. I have fine trapline. Cabin close to river for fresh water and even when it swell in the spring, it not get wet up this high." Still Water nodded. "But before we build, we take the ashes out and bury them in the woods."

Lars nodded his understanding that Ingor wanted to remove the burned bodies along with the charcoal first.

"In the meantime, you could sleep out of the rain in the barn," Lissa suggested. "The weather is still good for your horses to be outside in the corral for now."

Ingor didn't want to dwell on all the horses he had to deal with. "That all we can do," Ingor said to Still Water, figuring she would be disappointed at living in a barn, even for just a while. If she was, she didn't show it and that lightened the burden of responsibility he felt. Hopefully she thought the new barn was better than a teepee with a hole in the middle of the roof. "I glad I build big barn."

"We will be dry and warm in the barn and that good," Still Water agreed, smiling up at him.

The three men spent the little time that remained of the afternoon cleaning out the end stall in the barn. They scraped the dirt floor until it was clean of the animal litter, and then they scraped some more to expose a fresh layer of soil that the horses hadn't soiled.

Lissa showed Still Water how to wet the swept surface with a pail of water, and then wait until it dried into a hard-packed smooth floor. With the Dakota wind blowing through the barn, it dried quickly.

They hung what belongings they didn't need to take to

Winipeg over the door to the stall until Ingor could get pegs up. His drill had been in the cabin, so he didn't know how he would manage that without it.

"I lost many tools," he said to Lars. "Even the ones you carry all the way from Philadelphia for me. And the nails."

"Well, the handles on the tools probably gone, but if the heat of the fire not ruin the temper, the heads of the tools still work," Lars said.

"I can help whittle some new handles for you," Wally offered. "I can get 'em real smooth."

For the first time that day, Ingor grinned, feeling that everything would work out for the better. "Ya, maybe they still work. I had them rolled in oilcloth so they not rust, and stored in food box that I dig under the kitchen floor. I saw them there earlier today—before we get out of fire."

"With the fire above them, they might be just fine," Lars said. "But I know one thing. I not going back to Philadelphia to buy more."

They all laughed at that and it felt good.

"You never did say what started the fire," Wally put in.

"Bacon grease," Ingor said, perhaps a little too quickly. "It burned and got splashed on the bed." He shrugged, very thankful when no one asked any more questions.

* * * *

As the sun was setting below colorful stripes in the western sky, Lars and Lissa were the first to go wash up at river before they turned in for the night. While the others watched the sleeping baby, Lissa un-bandaged his hands and washed them. Lars winced when the torn blisters on his hands hit the water.

Lissa held his hands in hers. "I remember the first time I bandaged your hands. You were such a wonderful help during the fire at father's workshop."

"And you looked so beautiful with smears of soot on your face."

"I must have looked funny," she replied with a little laugh.

"No, you look beautiful," he insisted as he leaned down and kissed her thoroughly.

After a few minutes in each other's arms, she rinsed the strips of cotton cloth and carefully wrapped them back around his hands.

"I wish I had some of my salve here with us. As soon as we get home, I'll put some on our hands."

"Lissa?" Lars asked softly.

She looked up with a questioning frown.

"You are happy as my wife and the mother of my son, aren't you?"

She smiled and wrapped her arms around his waist. "I'm very happy, and I wish the same happiness for your brother."

"Me too. So you not mind having Still Water as your sister."

She shook her head. "Why should I? I've always wanted a sister and I think she'll make a fine one."

"And you not mind that she is Indian? Your friends in Philadelphia not like that. They not even talk to her."

"My love, I am a lifetime away from the friends I had back east. Out here we have learned to make our own rules to live by." She smiled. "Do you remember that Indian woman, the one who was with child? She came into our camp late one night on the trail from Philadelphia."

"How could I forget? I thought they would scalp us all, but that didn't stop you from fixing them food and helping her."

"And they didn't hurt us at all. They ate the food we offered and she birthed her baby right there."

"And they stole more food when they left," Lars put in.

"Yes, but they were hungry and needed our help. I was glad they stopped at our camp. She taught me most of what I knew about having babies. And though I was frightened of them the whole time, I think they were scared of us, too."

"I think she wanted your help birthing the baby. I do nothing but sit with the rifle on my lap."

Lissa smiled. "She could have done it by herself, I think." Lars nodded. "What I'm saying is that Still Water's tan skin doesn't change the fact that she is a caring and loving person. And if Ingor can love her, which he obviously does, we can, too."

"Thank you."

Lars kissed her and would have liked to stay by the river for a much longer time, but Wally called to them to come watch the baby so he could clean up.

* * * *

With little food left between them for supper, Wally

saved the meal by catching two rabbits on his way to the river for water for everyone to drink. Proud of his catch, he didn't mind cleaning them and sitting by the burning timbers turning a long green branch he'd speared them on. It wasn't much meat for so many people, but once it was cooked, they each got a hot piece to enjoy along with some biscuits and jam that Lissa had brought for Ingor. This gave Still Water a welcome rest from all the lifting and running she had done to keep Ingor alive and save their goods for the trip north.

With the cabin fire to see by as they prepared to turn in for the night, Lars and Lissa spread blankets on the remaining grain contained in the wagon. They would sleep with the baby between them and the star-filled sky above them. Wally spread out his bedroll under a tree near the wagon.

Ingor and Still Water bedded down the other side of the barn near the woods. Newly married, he wanted some privacy from the others.

"They not think it strange for us to be way over here?" Still Water asked softly.

Ingor tugged her into his arms. "Wally maybe, but not Lars and Lissa," he said with a smile. "They understand."

Until late into the night when, sated and exhausted, they finally fell asleep, they were both very glad to be away from the others.

* * * *

"Are you awake?" Still Water whispered when the quarter moon was high in the sky. She lay spoon style with her back tucked against Ingor, their legs bent together.

"I am now," he murmured.

"I must speak with you, Ingor. I see trouble ahead for you."

"Trouble for me?" he asked in a more alert voice.

"Yes. I think from what your brother says today, that there can only be trouble for you—a white man who has an Indian wife."

He squeezed her closer. "You let me worry about any trouble. I take care of it."

"If the Army comes and takes me, there is nothing you can do."

"I not let them take you. I think of something," he promised firmly.

She thought about that and realized he'd almost fallen back asleep.

"It is all my fault. I bring this trouble to you when you were just trying to help me. I'm sorry, husband."

"You're sorry you married me?"

She shook her head and rolled onto her back close against him. "Never. But I am a burden to you. My uncle married us without even asking you what you wanted to do. He just gave me to you."

"Your uncle is wise man. He see that I want you."

Still Water treasured his admission that he had wanted her.

"You are good to me, husband. I love you, but not just for saving my life or taking me back to my people. I love you for long time."

He smiled and kissed her. She laid her hand on the side of his face. His beard tickled her palm. She wished the light from the fire and moon was brighter. She wanted to memorize each feature so she could remember his face all her days.

"Because of this big love I have for you, Pale One, I can show you an escape you when you need it from the burden my uncle gives you."

He leaned his head on his palm supported by his bent elbow and met her gaze. "What you say?"

"You are a good man. We have saved each other's life and in Indian way, we are even now. There is no shame in leaving me. I can find my uncle…"

He didn't let her go on. "Leave you? Who say anything about leaving you? When we make our vows together, I promise you that I not leave you. Do you remember?"

She nodded. "Yes," she whispered.

"Well, then you not even think of you *or* me leaving." He kissed her hard. "You leave and I find you and bring you back."

"But I am offering you your freedom. Other whites will not think you bad for leaving an Indian wife."

"Still Water, I not care about what others say. Out here a man can do pretty much what he wants. If anyone not like me to have Indian wife, they can move on and not come back."

"But the Army. They not think we married."

He sighed. "Yes, and I admit that is problem. But I not look for an easy way out of our marriage. I love you, Still Water, and that gives me only one choice. I have to figure a way to get the Army to agree that we are married."

"How can we do that?"

"Well, I see only one way. We have to get white preacher or Justice of the Peace to marry us again."

"But where is one?"

He chuckled. "Well, we could find some in Minnesota, but I not sure they like the idea of marrying us. No, I see we must go to Canada. Red Moon is taking his people to Canada to be free of the United States Army's orders to relocate, and we must go to Canada to marry and be free of them, too."

"There is this preacher or Justice of the Peace to marry us there?"

"It's a big country. We ought to be able to find one in Winipeg on this trip with the furs. He give us paper that says we married. Then the Army will have to agree that we really man and wife. They not take you away from me."

Still Water sighed. Did she dare hope that such a thing was possible?

"Now let's get some sleep," Ingor urged. "We can't work on the cabin until fire's completely out and we bring in more logs. While we wait, we go to Canada to sell the furs and to find a man who will marry us. Maybe we take the dead men's horses to sell in Canada too. We not want them here where someone may recognize them. We leave in the morning."

She lifted her head and kissed him. "Yes, my husband."

Chapter 12

The following morning, Ingor watched expectantly with Still Water at his side as Lars and Lissa looked at each other before she answered.

"You want me to what?" Lissa asked Lars as the first light grayed the black in the sky.

"I'm just asking if you will trade clothes with Still Water, or loan her the other dress you have with you. They're leaving for Canada to get married right and proper, and to sell his furs. He wants a white woman's dress for her so she won't attract more attention as an Indian. You have another dress in the wagon."

Lissa looked down at the faded pink calico dress she wore. "This is hardly a wedding dress, and the other one's no better. They're work dresses that are stained with baby spit-up. Oh, and I have a trunk of such pretty ones at home that I'll never wear out here. I'd be happy to give you one of those. They would be much better for a wedding."

"No, we not want anything fancy, just plain dress," Ingor

insisted. His demeanor softened considerably then and he toyed with his hat. "I not want people to notice us." He dropped his gaze to his hat in his hand. "And… And I think Indian in fancy dress not look like…like good woman to other white people," he told them.

"Oh," Lissa said. Her cheeks colored, showing she understood that a fancy dress would be more likely worn by a loose woman.

"She can wear your other one, can't she? You can even keep the apron. She not want to wear apron to get married," Lars explained.

"No, I suppose not," Lissa said.

"You call this planning a wedding?" Wally asked, trying not to laugh and failing after overhearing most of the conversation.

"You think this is funny, do you?" Lissa snapped.

Wally's laughter won out. "You could trade and wear her leggings and tunic. You wore my pants most of the time on the trail to Dakota once it got cold. Seems to me you can hardly object to wearing them now," he argued.

Lissa looked daggers at him, but her gaze softened as she looked back at Still Water, who had not said a word. She just stood patiently but self-consciously beside Ingor. "Do you think it will fit you?"

"I think so, but if you not want me…" she offered softly.

"No, Still Water. Don't think that for a minute. I just didn't understand at first why you wanted it. But I'm all for you and Ingor getting married in the white man's way, and I'd be happy to give you a dress to keep you safer at his side. I'll get the other one and you can choose. We can change in the barn."

After Lissa detoured to the wagon, the two women disappeared into the barn and several minutes later came out with Lissa's spare dress on Still Water. It was calico like the one on Lissa, with long sleeves and a high collar. Little buttons fastened the top to a bit below the waist, handy for nursing the baby.

Despite Lars' comments about Lissa keeping the apron, her apron had been tied over the dress. Still Water also wore her bonnet with a bow tied under her chin, hiding all her hair from view.

"She want to wear the apron to a wedding, Lissa?" Lars asked, not giving up on his notions of a wedding dress.

"The dress is too large for her," Lissa explained. "She needs it to make it look like it's truly her dress."

Wally was grinning and Lissa asked sharply, "What's so funny now?"

"Without the bonnet for the ride back to the homestead, you're going to get your face sun-colored. Then you'll look like an Indian."

Lissa swatted his arm and pulled Wally's hat off his head and put it on her own head. "Now I won't," she said smugly.

Ingor had not moved from where he'd been standing and staring at Still Water. When everyone's gaze fell on him, he said softly, "I've never seen you in a bonnet like that. You not look like yourself. Your own uncle not know you at a distance."

"That's what we're trying to do, isn't it? Make her look like someone different?" Lissa asked. "Show him your hair, too."

With shy reluctance, Still Water untied the bonnet and lifted it off her head. Lissa took her shoulders and turned her so her back was to the men.

"See? Her hair is pulled back, braided into just one braid that I wrapped around and around in a bun low on the back of her head. The bonnet should keep it in place, but I wish I had more pins to make it more secure," Lissa said. "It might come down, but she'll be all right as long as she keeps the bonnet on. The hair should fall into the bonnet and stay there."

"But can she fix it that way, or are you going with them as her maid?" Wally asked.

"She can certainly manage one braid and twisting it into a bun," Lissa insisted. "I showed her how."

"I can't get over how you've changed," Ingor said, still staring at her. She smiled shyly.

"Say, how is she going to ride in a saddle in a dress?" Wally asked. "You rode here in a wagon and that skirt's not very wide."

Still Water held the sides of the skirt out and frowned. "I not think of that."

"A proper lady in Philadelphia would ride sidesaddle if she wasn't riding in a wagon," Lissa told them.

A couple of grunts from the others told her what they thought of that idea. There wasn't a sidesaddle within all of Dakota Territory as far as they knew.

"I have leather tops on my moccasins covering my leg to my knee. I can lift up the skirt high enough to sit on the saddle." She started to lift her skirt to her knees to show them when Ingor reached for her arm to stop her.

"Only around me," Ingor insisted. "I not have any other man gawking at your legs."

She frowned. "But we not always know when other people will meet us on the road. And what I do in Winnipeg or when we see farms and outposts?"

Ingor held his hands out to his side and shrugged. He slapped them down against his thighs and thought a few moments. "I know. You ride with me. We put all bags and furs on the packhorse and Thor can carry the two of us." His grin told the others that he would enjoy traveling that way, too.

"After hours of riding, your legs will feel like you walk through a sticker bush," Still Water insisted. "You cannot ride with me on your lap for that long."

"I not mind, but we start out with you in saddle on packhorse. It will be several days before we see other people. When we see town or farm ahead, you ride on Thor with me."

Still Water nodded and turned to Lissa. "Thank you for all your help."

"It's fun having a sister to share clothes with," Lissa replied. "And I'm very glad we got to meet you while we were here." She took Still Water's hands and squeezed them affectionately. "You'll have to get Ingor to bring you out to our home. We'd love to have you stay with us."

And then it was time for them to leave. Ingor shook Lars' and Wally's hands. "Thanks for your help."

They looked at the cabin fire that had burned low though some of the logs still glowed. The smoke rose in several places before it was taken by the wind.

"We start to build new cabin when we get back," Ingor said. "The fire should be cold by then."

"We bring wheat back and help," Lars promised. Ingor smiled and hugged his brother, slapping him on his back.

And then it was time to leave. Ingor lifted Still Water onto the packhorse's saddle. She twisted one leg over his neck and sat astride. He helped tuck in her skirt and apron around her legs above her high shoes to keep them from getting chaffed on the saddle. He checked the stack of furs that was tied behind her.

"The Indian way of wearing leather pants and the long shirt that falls to the knees when you dismount makes more sense for riding and it look nice on a woman," he said. "Dress is no good for riding."

"Thank you," Still Water said softly to Lissa. "I will take good care of your things."

"Consider them all yours. I brought out more than I'll ever need."

"Oh, but…"

"And when you get back, maybe you'll show me how to make a pair of leather leggings for myself for riding. And if you want to, you can take your pick from the rest of the dresses that I don't wear," Lissa offered.

"That is if she not use them all for curtains or tablecloths before then," Wally joked. "We got flowers everywhere from cloth that used to be skirts on dresses."

"You think you see your uncle Red Moon and the others in Canada," Lars asked.

Still Water only shook her head until Ingor said, "Canada is a big, big country. Her uncle smart. He hide where no one can find him."

"When will you be back? Winter comes on fast," Lissa said with a frown.

"Hell, with the crazy weather up here, it could snow tomorrow," Wally announced.

"Wallace, mind your language. There's a young child present," Lissa scolded.

"Young child? You mean Eric? He's just a baby and can't understand what I said."

"Just mind your sister," Lars ordered.

Ingor laughed at the domestic scene and climbed into Thor's saddle. "I can't say when we be back."

He looked at the burning cabin's burning embers, and then at the barn. "We have much work here before winter come. That barn mighty cold then, even with animals in it. We not have a fire in there with all that straw. Besides, fire would scare the horses."

"We come help you," Lars insisted. "And we take care of the other two horses until you get back. Wally can wash them down and when they get fed good, no one know them anymore."

Ingor understood that Lars was confident that no one would recognize them as the two miscreant's horses. He looked sheepish and thanked them. He had forgotten about the other horses belonging to the pair who died in the fire.

"They sure need grooming. I hope you didn't pay much for them," Wally remarked, not knowing how Ingor had acquired them.

"They cost more than I ever think," Ingor said, shaking his head.

"We put them in with ours and teach to pull plow," Lars said with a laugh.

"And if you return too late to finish the cabin this fall, you can come and stay with us," Lissa offered.

"Right. We stayed with you last winter. Now it's your turn to stay with us," Wally reasoned.

"It would be fun to have the company. It's very lonely on the prairie. The winters are very long," Lissa said less brightly.

"Thank you," was all that Ingor said.

He smiled as he reined Thor around to stand next to Still Water on the packhorse. After another round of goodbyes, the two rode off, going east along the woods. They would give the horses time to limber up after standing for days before they broke into a canter.

"Stay safe," Lars called.

Ingor looked back one more time and saw Lars standing with his arm around Lissa. They both waved when they saw him turn in the saddle. He waved, too, and smiled broadly.

All the while he felt envious of Lars' happy family situation. Someday, he would have it for himself—he and Still Water.

His family wouldn't have any fancy Eastern ways. Still Water would never have the fancy dresses he had seen in Lissa's truck. He glanced over at her and smiled. She was twisting her head and tugging at the neck of the dress.

When she realized he was watching her, she said, "This dress not feel soft like leather. It itches me."

"Sorry you have to wear it, but it might save our lives."

She nodded and Ingor's heart swelled, knowing that he had found the perfect wife to live with and raise a family his way, the way of a trapper living off the land the best he could.

He and Still Water were going to Canada so they would be safe. He just hoped they would be able to arrange things so they could come home to Dakota again. But right then, he didn't know if it would ever be safe for the two of them to go back.

* * * *

Still Water followed behind Ingor as they rode along the narrow trappers' path going north beside the western bank of the north-flowing Red River. Sticking to the worn path made their journey easy for the first two days. They timed their meals to coincide with the rest periods they gave the horses so there were fewer stops. They did not meet another person, so they had made good time and didn't have to worry about anyone seeing Still Water.

On the third evening, they stopped where a river flowed into the Red from the west.

"This not far from the border," Ingor told her. "There is a mound of dirt with rocks over it to mark where we cross into Canada. That is less than one mile ahead."

"They must have rain northwest of here. It makes river too wide and deep to cross here."

"We follow it upstream," Ingor decided. "We find a place there."

They rode west until they found a shallower area where they could safely cross without getting all wet. They had to keep the furs dry if they were going to be worth anything at all, and as cool as it was this late in the day, they didn't want to get wet either.

"The packhorse doesn't like getting bath," Still Water said as her mount sidestepped and neighed nervously when they began to cross. "She fight me all the way."

"She never take much to the water. I gentle with her to get her to change her ways. Not easy. She still only like water to drink," he added with a smile.

Ingor reached down and took a rein to keep the packhorse close at Thor's side where she couldn't rear up and be a danger to either one of them. He knew Still Water was an excellent rider, but he was taking no chances.

"Get up there," he told Thor with the added inducement of his heels in his side.

Steady and dependable Thor headed straight across, delivering them both safely to the other side. Ingor handed over her rein and they rode up the riverbank.

"There few trees on north side," Ingor said, standing in

his saddle to spot a place to camp for the night.

"There are a few by that bend farther to the west," Still Water offered after looking that way.

"That is better than no trees. At least we have shelter."

"But don't you think we should ride on past the rocky mound into Canada? What if someone find me here?" Still Water asked.

"I not let anything happen to you. And bend in the river means we have fresh fish for supper," he said with a grin.

"That would be good," she said, rubbing her stomach that was empty.

She suddenly looked down at what she was wearing and remembered she wasn't traveling with her usual bag of goods tied to her belt that included fishing items. "I have no bag with hook or line here, but they are in pack roll."

"I have mine," he said, turning Thor west. "I take fishing hooks and line to Lars' homestead, so they still in my saddle-bag. I never take them out at the cabin."

"Good you not have time to unpack." She laughed with delight, looking forward to a meal of something other than roasted wheat cakes and venison jerky. The flour she'd managed to pack in the fire was almost gone anyway. She would even welcome some pemmican, ground buffalo meat mixed with fat and berries, a staple of her tribe. As they rode, she studied the plants near the river and found more possibilities for their supper.

Ingor fed the horses a measure of oats by pouring it in his hat and holding it for each one to eat. Knocking the horse slobber from the brim by hitting it over his thigh, he held it in the river to rinse it out before set it back on his head. Once they were fed and watered, he tied the horses for the night where they could graze. He set the saddles nearer the fire she had made and spread out the horse blankets to dry the sweat.

She let him know she was going to walk along the river to gather a few things for dinner and find a good fishing hole. When she came back to camp, he looked up and couldn't help but laugh.

She had pulled her skirt forward between her legs and tucked under the tie belt of the apron. That made a pants-like covering out of it, leaving her legs uncovered from her knees down. Her bonnet had become a basket in which she carried the greens, roots and berries that she had gathered. Her hair that she had twisted into a bun that morning, the way Lissa had shown her, had fallen free down her back in a single braid that was loose at the end.

"I look funny?" she asked, feeling a good deal more upset than inquisitive about his laughter.

"Oh, no, Still Water, you look beautiful. But you must only do that with your dress and hair when no one else is around. Only me."

Holding her bonnet basket in one hand, she fisted the other and planted it on her hip. "And who else do you see here?"

He laughed even harder and then started coughing. "Oh, stop. My throat still hurts when I laugh."

She lost her angry stance immediately and hurried to

stand in front of him. She opened the collar of his shirt to check on his neck. The redness had faded but not completely.

"It still hurts?"

Taking hold of her shoulders, he kissed her gently. "It gets better each day, but my voice still sounds funny, don't you think?"

"It is deeper than before, but it sounds good."

"So you like man with deep voice?" He kissed her cheek and then the side of her neck. He pulled her earlobe into his mouth and sucked on it.

"I like you with a deep voice or any voice."

"Why not show me how much you like me?"

She smiled and turned her head toward him so he stopped nuzzling her neck. "If I show you now, you will not have fish for supper."

"The fish," he exclaimed. "I forget all about them. See what you do to me?"

"Wait until after dark. I will do many other things to you."

"I hold you to that promise," he said with a grin.

Ingor found the fishing hook and line he'd packed wrapped around a short stick. He started toward the bend in the river when Still Water stopped him.

"Wait. The fish will like these," she said, pulling two good-sized worms from her bonnet where she had carried them with the roots and leaves she had gathered. He took them with thanks and added a kiss for good measure.

While he fished, she mixed up thick wheat cakes and

sprinkled cut-up wild onions she had found on most of them. The last two she mixed in the few dark berries that the birds had missed and she'd found still hanging from the prickly branches.

They were roasting wrapped around the end of sticks stuck in the ground circling the fire when Ingor returned with two large catfish. Using his hunting knife, he gutted them and cut the tough skin in strips that he pulled off to expose the flesh. Still Water rubbed each one with some wild onion. Having no fry pan, she threaded the filets on green sticks and set them over the heat of the fire where they could roast without burning.

Ingor glanced up at the sky. "It might rain tonight. Let's do what we can to make some shelter."

While the food cooked, they gathered small branches to lay over a fallen tree to make a lean-to shelter as they had before. Only a few were from evergreens as they were sparse in that area, but they seemed to work as a roof when it started to rain toward dawn. As the temperature dropped, and the couple quickly came up with several ways to get warmer than they had been.

Unable to get back to sleep then, they ate the wheat cakes with berries in them that Still Water had cooked the night before and saved for breaking their fast. But when they were ready to leave, it was still raining, and it was cold.

"I put on my leggings under my dress, but I wish I could wear my leather tunic around me now to keep warm and dry," Still Water said.

"No one should see you in that for now, but I got something even better."

Ingor reached for a fur bundle and pulled out two large tanned deer hides from the bottom of the stack. He cut a T-shaped hole in the center and each one and pulled them down onto their shoulders. He took the long narrow sections from the deer's legs and tied them together on each side so the hide wouldn't blow in the wind.

"These keep us dry and much warmer."

"You are very clever like Indian, husband," she said, tying on her bonnet and hoping it would remain stiff-brimmed and keep the rain out of her face.

Smiling, he helped her onto her horse. After tucking in her skirt around her leather leggings, he mounted Thor.

"Look. This bonnet keeps the rain out of my face, but the water still drips down my neck," she said with a laugh as they rode northeast to the Red River where they would turn north again.

"The border's not far now. We will see more people around, so we must keep a sharp eye out."

As they rode north past the rock-covered mound marking the border, they breathed a little easier. They were safe—from the United States Army anyway.

Ingor and Still Water rode north all day without seeing anyone. But then they had left the more traveled path beside the Red River soon after entering Canada in favor of riding where they would be out of sight of any other travelers. Ingor didn't want anyone to come upon them without warning with

Still Water's dress hiked up to her knees. Besides exposing her Indian moccasins and leggings, he didn't want her thought of in the terms that anyone would think seeing a woman's skirts that high.

By late that afternoon the rain had stopped and they took off their leather covers when the sun came out and the temperature rose. They would need them again with the evening chill.

"The rain slowed us up. Think you can ride 'til closer to dark to make up time?" Ingor asked.

Still Water agreed, but a few miles later they began to spot definite signs of people living in the area.

Immediately, they became more wary.

Chapter 13

The first sign of other people nearby was the cultivated fields.

"Must be a farmhouse nearby," Ingor surmised. "Maybe more than one from the size of fields. Many men needed to do that much cutting."

"Listen," Still Water whispered, holding her hand up as a signal to stop and be silent.

"It's children," Ingor concluded. "From the laughter, they must be playing."

He stood in his stirrups and looked around. "I not see anything, but I think it time you either ride sidesaddle or here with me."

Still Water nodded, not putting up any argument. She knew only too well the consequences of being identified as an Indian woman traveling with a white man. Others she knew in that position were called bad names, spit upon and worse. She didn't want that to happen for Ingor's sake. He would jump into a fight to defend her and might not come out on top.

"If only this horse didn't have a saddle on, I could ride her barebacked and sit sideways," she volunteered.

"No sense thinking about it. No settler's wife that I ever see out here can ride bareback, much less sideways. And we need saddle to tie bundles on."

She nodded and slipped to the ground, as did Ingor. They untied the saddlebags and bags of food that had been hanging from Thor's saddle and tied them on the packhorse's saddle.

"I think we have to keep riding together all the way into Winnipeg," he said.

She nodded and waited while Ingor securely tied the reins of the packhorse to his saddle. "But I should ride behind you. Your legs not feel prickly, and you can get rifle out if you need it."

Ingor grinned. "You on my lap would make the journey much nicer."

"There be time for that when we not around other people."

"You right," he said, kissing her quickly.

He lifted her onto Thor's rump, and immediately tugged down her skirt over her legs. "I wish I ask Lissa to loan you her shoes. Those moccasins too visible, but there nothing we can do now unless you take them off. Too cold for that."

She tugged loose one of the deer hides they had just taken off and laid it over lap. "The apron and this leather will hide them."

Smiling, he climbed into the saddle, swinging his leg over the big horse's neck because Still Water sat behind him.

"Wrap your arms around me and hang on." A cluck of his tongue and Thor fell into a comfortable pace.

"How is it back there?" he asked over his shoulder.

"Not as good as in a saddle," she said, her voice jumping with every step that Thor took.

"No way to get away from bumps, but I be happy to massage you where you hurt tonight," he added with a laugh.

She poked his ribs and laughed, but quickly held on tight again. Though she'd ridden horses since she was a young child, she didn't feel secure sitting behind him.

"There they are," Ingor said quietly as a part wood and part sod farmhouse with four young children playing out front came into view.

He slowed the horses to a walk so he wouldn't frighten them and called out a hello. The children stopped their game in an instant and ran into the house. Seconds later, they came out again with a woman wiping her hands on her soiled apron in tow. She wore a yellow dress that had faded several shades lighter in years of washing. She was barefoot, too.

"Hello," Ingor called again.

"Hello, stranger. Where are you headed?" the woman called back, looking up at Ingor, his wife, and the sun beyond him. She shaded her eyes with her raised hand.

"Winnipeg to trade my furs."

"Might late in the season for that, isn't it?" the woman asked, eyeing the bundles of furs on the packhorse.

"Got leg caught in one of my traps, and it takes long time before I can ride again."

"Land sakes. It's a wonder you're alive. You new at trapping?"

Ingor laughed at the inference that only a new trapper could be so stupid as to trap his own leg. "No, but I should know better."

"Mama, that man talks funny," the oldest of the children said, tugging on his mother's apron. He wore worn pants that were too short for his fast growing legs and a shirt that was too big. It had been tucked in his pants, but the shirttails had worked their way out. He was barefoot and his hands and face were as dirty as his feet, as were the other children's.

"Hush now," she said with a swat that chased his hands off the apron she smoothed over her skirt. "Mind your manners."

The other boys were dressed in hand-me-downs that didn't quite fit, too. Only the girl, the second child judging by her size, was dressed in a dress that fit and had probably been made for her. The fabric matched the towel that her mother had tucked into the waistband of her apron.

"Don't mind the boy, mister. We don't see many folks passing this way this time of the year, and he likes to talk."

"He's no bother, ma'am." Ingor turned to the little boy and smiled.

"Where are you from, mister?" the boy asked, not willing to be shut up.

"I live in Norway before I come here two years ago."

"I was born in Canada," the boy said proudly.

Ingor chose not to reply. The boy didn't seem to expect it, and he took to staring at Still Water. Ingor didn't like that one bit. She lowered her face, but worried about what questions he might ask her.

"Why not come on down here and set? I'm just getting supper on the table. There's four families that eat together during planting and again during harvest. Tonight, dinner is here. You're welcome to join us. Course, I'd have to charge you."

"Thanks for the invite, ma'am, but we have little coin and a long way to go. We were just hoping to trade you for some bread and maybe some carrots or potatoes if you have extra."

"What are you trading?"

"Well," Ingor replied. "I have my furs.

The woman looked at the toddler sitting in the dirt and playing with a pile of rocks. "Would be nice to have a fur to wrap him in this winter. The boys wore out what they had or the mice ate it. I been putting patches over patches."

Ingor smiled and waited patiently while she made up her mind.

"Well, I wish my Tony was here to do the trading, but I reckon I could do that."

"Thank you, ma'am."

"Your wife want to sit on the porch while we get the vegetables from the root cellar?"

"Well, thank you for that, but she not understand a word we say. She come over on boat this summer. I think she happier staying right where she is."

"Suit yourself," the woman said with an indifferent shrug

as she stepped down off the side of the porch.

The children led the way to the root cellar that had been dug twenty feet or so from the house. Ingor grabbed the bag they had nearly emptied of food since they left the cabin and followed. He picked handfuls of small potatoes and carrots that he thought would cook better over a campfire than larger ones.

"I got a loaf of bread in the house that you can have," the farmer's wife said.

Ingor grinned. "I can smell it baking."

He hadn't eaten bread since leaving Lars and Lissa's home the end of May. Now that seemed like years ago.

With the bread set in on top of the root vegetables, Ingor tied the sack on the packhorse. "Thank you, ma'am." He pulled two muskrat furs from the bundle and handed them to her. "These a fair trade?"

"They're kinda scrawny," she said, eyeing her toddler.

Ingor pulled another from the bundle and put it on top of the other two in her hands. "Thank you again."

He didn't ask again if that made them even. He knew she had gotten the best of the deal, but he and Still Water would have fresh food to eat for the next several days.

Mounting Thor again, he was at the point of leaving when the inquisitive child spoke again. He'd been staring at Still Water since they came up the wooden steps that had led into the root cellar.

"Say, will you look at her shoes? They look like moccasins." He glanced at his mother. "What would a white woman want with moccasins, Ma?" Continuing to study Still Water's face, he asked, "Are you sure she ain't an Injun, mister?"

Ingor heard the little gasp from behind him just as the boy's mother swatted him on the back of his head. He quickly climbed into the saddle and put himself between his wife and their tormentor. He pressed his lips together to keep from saying all he wanted to in order to defend Still Water. Sliding a hand over hers as they circled his waist to hang on, he squeezed it gently.

"Now that is enough," the farm wife said. "I taught you better manners than that. No respectable man like this gentleman would be traveling with no dirty Injun squaw."

Still Water had adjusted the leather to cover her feet better before she wrapped her arms around his ribs for the ride out of the farmyard. Pulling up his shirt sleeve, he held his bared arm next to one of her hands and replied, "What an idea, boy. Her arm ain't no darker than mine."

He pulled off his hat to show his blond hair and stroked his blond beard. "You ever see an Indian with hair this light?" he asked to take his attention off Still Water.

The boy shook his head.

Not waiting for another word, he pulled the reins to the side of Thor's neck and the two horses cantered out of the farmyard. His heart was racing and it was all he could do not to nudge him into a gallop. He half expected the kids to pick up rocks and start pitching some at them. What happened to Canadians being more tolerant of Indians?

With no white women in the Territory yet, Ingor knew

other trappers who had taken Indian women to live with them. True, they had not had any wedding ceremony, but the men treated their women all right. He had seen them together in Winipeg trading their furs and no one bothered them. Maybe the tolerance would increase the further into Canada they rode. He just hated to hear anything bad said about Still Water. And he would give his life to protect her from harm.

Still Water said nothing, even after they were out of earshot of the family. He had just denied that she was an Indian to people he sincerely hoped he would never see again. He hoped she understood that he had done it to protect her and not because he didn't like that she was Indian.

"I am sorry they not…not nice," he said softly, laying his hand over hers for a time.

If an alert child could guess that she was an Indian, what would people in Winnipeg think? More importantly, what would they say or do? And if they did agree with the boy's assessment, would it matter?

Ingor had heard that people in Canada were more tolerant of Indians. Where had that tolerance gone just when they needed to find it?

Not taking any chances of the farm father or the other families running into them, they rode until the last light of day before they stopped for the night.

* * * *

Still Water tried not to think of what the farm family had thought of Indians, but she couldn't help it. It made her feel sad and she wanted to make it up to Ingor as if people not liking Indians would diminish him for marrying one. She was determined to follow the same routine at each camp that they had established when they started out. Wanting to do as much for him as she could, she made the fire while Ingor cared for the horses. Then she cooked the meal while Ingor walked a circle farther from the fire to gather enough firewood to last all night.

With no pots or frying pans, she buried several of the small potatoes in a hole in the ashes and pulled burning sticks and embers over them. Knowing she could fill the canteen in the Red River after dinner, she used much of the water to wash the soil from the carrots. They would eat those raw. With no fresh fish or meat, they would have to settle for sticks of jerky.

The best part of the meal would be the freshly baked bread. This was a white woman's bread recipe, but she had come to like it whenever she'd had a taste of it years before. She cut half the loaf into two thick slices for each of them, making sure Ingor's were thicker than hers.

"Too bad we don't have some bacon grease or fresh churned butter to spread over them," Ingor said when he returned to drop the firewood in a pile where it would be handy.

He'd startled her and she jumped, dropping the knife. She quickly picked it up and cleaned it on her apron without thinking that the soil would stain her white apron more.

"Now look what I've done," she muttered as she sheathed

the knife in her moccasin again and brushed at the soil mark.

The tears that she had kept at bay until then burned in her eyes, and she couldn't deny them. They overflowed down her cheeks though she batted at them with the backs of her hands.

"Honey, everything is going to work out."

She only had to look up at him and he gathered her into his arms and held her firmly against his chest.

"You not think about what that child say, do you?"

She shook her head. "It wasn't what the child said."

Ingor took a deep breath and released it as a sigh. "It was the nasty mother."

She nodded and tried to blink away her tears.

"You not let what people say, hurt you. You are beautiful niece to the Chief of a Sioux tribe. The white people not know you, but this is hard time. They may have very bad time with other Indians here. We not know what make her hate your people."

"I know, but it still hurts to be called names. Red Moon told me not to let the white people who say these bad things see how much they hurt me. Then their words lose their sharp edges and fall away useless like a blunt arrow with a worn tip."

"Your uncle is wise. That good idea. If they see they can hurt you, they try to hurt you more."

"I hide it, but it not easy to hide it when it hurts. In here," she said, tapping her chest over her heart.

He cradled her face in his hands and kissed her gently. "I

wish I could promise you that you never be hurt again. I not like to see you sad."

She sniffled and tried to smile at his concern. He wiped the tears from her cheeks with his thumbs. She smiled her thanks for the comfort he was giving her. "I think that they not hurt me as much if I was not still thinking about being taken from her people. Those men take me and hurt my body, but they hurt me in my heart, too. They say bad things about Still Water that not true."

"I think about them, too. I never kill a man before, and I hope I never have to again," he said. "But I do it again to protect you."

"I hit the boy choking you as hard as I could. And I would do it again too."

He wrapped his arms around her and held her close. Slowly rubbing circles on her back with one hand, he leaned his cheek on the top of her head. "I hope we never have to."

She nodded and they stood that way, watching the flickering flames in their campfire for several minutes until her tears had dried. The vows they had just said to each other were a manifestation of their deepening love for each other. Though they hoped they would never need to take extreme measures to protect each other again, the promises warmed their hearts.

"You must be hungry," she said, straightening and looking up at him, but not wanting to drop her arms from around his waist.

"Starved," he replied with a smile.

"Then let's not just stand here, let's eat."

With their hearts lighter, they pushed back the glowing embers and dug up the roasted potatoes.

* * * *

"We should get in and out of town fast to avoid trouble," Ingor explained a few evenings later as they sat by the fire after eating dinner. "But we must do what we came to do before we leave."

"Then we will go back to your cabin and rebuild it?"

Ingor shook his head and looked into the fire, hoping to find answers there. "I not know. I hope so."

He'd chosen their campsite so they could arrive in Winnipeg early the next morning. The earlier they went into the city, the fewer people they would meet, he thought.

"We'll sell the furs first. We'll have to trade food for most of them because we have little left. Sugar and coffee would be nice, but we will see."

Still Water nodded and went on unbraiding her hair. He loved it when it flowed down her back like a tall waterfall. She was finger combing it when he clasped her hand.

"Let me do it," he said softly.

She turned her back more to him and he combed it the same way he'd seen her do it.

"You have beautiful hair. You should have beautiful gold combs and I have none to give you."

She turned to him and he saw tears welling in her eyes.

"What the matter? Do I pull your hair? I'm sorry."

She shook her head. "No."

"What's wrong then?" He tipped her face up to his so that she had to meet his gaze. "Tell me."

"I weep for you. You are so good to me and I cause you so much trouble. I dress up in strange clothes, but you still must lie about me. Yet even a boy knows what I am. I cannot hide what I am."

"When we're back home, you won't have to." He drew her against his chest with his arm around her shoulders. "That child was guessing from your shoes. But it not matter to us what he think."

She nodded. "I didn't know what to say."

"But maybe not talking any is good idea even though you speak English better than me."

"I speak for my uncle when he talks to the white man."

"Yes, and he understand all that is said. I remember that."

They shared smiles, but they quickly disappeared.

"If I talk now, people will look at my face and know what I am. If they not like that…"

He backed up a bit on the log and their gazes locked. "I not care if they like it or not. But I want you safe. If problem comes, we tell folks you just come over on boat from Norway and don't speak English yet—like at the farm."

"What do I do with my moccasins?"

"You wear them. Everyone know trappers make friends with Indians. If someone asks, I say they were a gift to my bride."

He kissed her forehead and knelt down in front of her. After untying her moccasins, he slipped them off her feet.

"Did you make these?"

She nodded. "Every Sioux woman makes her own."

"I've never seen any better. I was sorry I cut off the fringe." He laid them carefully at the foot of her bedroll blanket that was between the fire and his.

"But they look more like high shoes now."

Nodding, he stepped around behind her and untied her apron. After shaking it out, he folded it and laid it on top of her moccasins.

"What are you doing?"

"I help you undress."

She thought about that a few moments. "Do white men often help their wives undress?"

He grinned. "Sometimes. I thought tonight would be a good time."

He took her hands and pulled her up from the log on which she'd been sitting. Beginning with the top button, he slowly undid each of the tiny buttons in the long row down the front of her dress.

Just past her waist a little ways, he stopped and took a big breath. His body was way ahead of him in the slow seduction of his wife that he had planned. He slid the backs of his bent fingers from her chest through her cleavage to her navel, and watched as her skin puckered into little bumps. Her nipples grew erect and pressed against the dress fabric, and he couldn't resist sliding his hands inside the bodice and cupping her breasts. He lifted them and squeezed them before toying with the hard pebbles her nipples had become.

Throwing her head back, she moaned. With a little wiggle of her torso, the too-large dress slipped from her shoulders and caught on her hips. It had been warmer that day and she had not worn the leather leggings under her dress.

Wanting to see all of her, Ingor undid the last two buttons and pushed the dress over her soft buttocks. It pooled on the ground around her feet.

Considerate of the fact that this was her only dress, he held her hand as she stepped out of it. He shook it and draped it over a nearby branch. He looked back at her and grinned.

"I bet you the only woman in these parts who ride naked under her dress."

"Lissa wanted to give me her…her shift, is it? And her petticoat, but I could not see that I needed anything else. And the dress feels better without anything under it on warm days. On cold days, my leggings and your leather cape keep me warm."

"And on cold nights, you not have to worry. I keep you very warm."

He pulled her into his arms and kissed her deeply. Their tongues entwined and stroked in and out erotically.

When they surfaced for air, his erection was straining against the button closure on his pants. He pressed her hips against it. "Do you feel what you do to me?" he asked, moving it side to side on her belly.

"Yes, and now it my turn to help you undress."

"I hope you say that."

"If this is the white man's way, I like it. We should do this often."

Ingor grinned. He was more than willing to go along with her plan.

Chapter 14

Still Water could make out the trees and finally the outline of some buildings when they rode into Winnipeg in the predawn light. Unable to sleep any later, they had broken camp in the dark. They rode at an easy walk and the horses managed to pick their way in the dim light without incident.

Her husband had told her he'd wanted to be on the city streets early before they got crowded. They had certainly arrived early enough for that. Only a few people moved about at that hour, and there were fewer wagons or men on horseback.

Locating the Trading Post was easy. It would have been even if Ingor hadn't been here before. The name was written in black letters high on the outside wall where they could see it from a long way off. While she could speak good English that she'd learned as she grew up, she could not read it. Her own language was all verbal. If they wrote anything down it was in pictures, generally painted on hides. Not learning to read and write wasn't unusual among many people who spoke

English. There were few books to read or other reasons to be literate. So seeing the letters on this building, she had to take Ingor's word for it that they said the name of the Trading Post.

They stopped in front of the entrance, and Still Water stayed on Thor while he walked up to the door. It was shut and locked.

"I not count on Trading Post not being open this early." He strode across the boardwalk to the rail where he'd tied Thor and she wondered what they would do next. Seeing a man walking toward them along the boardwalk, she ducked her head to the side so her bonnet would cover her face.

The man stopped a few feet from Ingor. "Store not open," Ingor told him.

"Not yet. Hector, he owns the Trading Post, well, he takes his breakfast over at Tillie's there each morning," the man told Ingor.

He pointed to a whitewashed building across the street with large multi-paned glass windows in front. Still Water thought it was a wonder to see so much glass in one building. Ingor's cabin hadn't even had one glass window, and this building had so many of them. Something was written over the door, but it was different than the words on the Trading Post wall. Only the very beginning looked at all the same.

"He opens up soon as he's done eating."

"Good. Thank you," Ingor said, taking hold of the rim of his hat in his fingers and tipping his head toward the man.

The man tipped his hat in the same polite manner at Still

Water. "Ma'am," he said with a smile, and then he walked on in the direction he had been going.

Ingor looked up at her and found her staring after the helpful man. He allowed himself to feel a bit relieved. They had passed the first test peacefully. Either the man hadn't noticed she was an Indian, or he had recognized that fact and didn't care. Either way, he felt good about it and thought she did, too.

"Slide into saddle and hang on. We go eat at Tillie's, too. I lead horses across street."

"No, we can't do that," she whispered rapidly in Sioux.

Ingor grabbed her thigh and squeezed it anxiously. "If you worried, you not talk, remember? And you not talk Sioux at all—not until we see how folks feel about us."

She barely nodded and lowered her face until her chin was on her chest.

"That's it. You be the shy, scared little wife, who not understand or speak English. We want to finish and get out of here without trouble."

"Ya," she said with a little smile, duplicating the sound of his word for yes.

He nodded and even smiled a little in return.

As he led the horses across the street to Tillie's, he was glad to see only two horses tied up out front. He hoped they could eat a quick breakfast that would go a long way to reviving their spirits and satisfying their stomachs.

Eggs. He wanted eggs and a beefsteak. He couldn't even remember the last time he'd eaten eggs or beef. His mouth watered just thinking about them with thick slabs of freshly baked bread or fresh baked biscuits with lots of gravy poured all over them. And coffee. It had been so long since he had coffee that he hardly remembered the taste. The lure of such special food led him to taking the chance of eating there.

At Tillie's hitching post, he tied the horses and lifted Still Water down from Thor's saddle. As they stepped up on the boardwalk, he patted his small bag of coins just to be sure it was still in his pocket. It wouldn't do to order meals that he couldn't pay for. At the door, he entered first and held it open for his wife behind him.

The waitress, who had people at three of the tables, poured a cup of coffee for Ingor and Still Water and took their order. She kept glancing at Still Water, who never said a word. Ingor ordered a steak and eggs for himself and for her, too, with plenty of biscuits or bread.

"My wife not speak English yet," he said when the waitress's gaze lingered again on Still Water.

"That must be tough. Why, she don't know what we're saying then, does she?"

"No, not unless I speak to her in the language of our homeland," Ingor explained further.

He said a few words to Still Water in Norwegian, which she couldn't understand at all, but the waitress didn't know that. His wife smiled at him and he nodded to encourage her.

"I just told her that now you will go fix the food and bring it back out to us. She hasn't eaten in a restaurant like this before. It is special treat for her."

"Well, ain't that nice of you to bring her in here. Your food will be ready in just a few minutes." Seeming to be satisfied, the waitress went off to the kitchen to turn their orders in.

Ingor noted the other customers were all men. He didn't know if a lady would take her hat off in a restaurant or not, but he was glad that Still Water had left hers on. The way she was sitting, the other men couldn't see her face.

Still Water sat with her head tipped down and her hands knotted on her lap. She couldn't remember feeling as frightened as she was now except when the two white men stole her away at the river. But this was a different kind of fear and in some ways it was even worse. What she felt now was the fear of the unknown, and she was not armed to fight it off. If she knew what was coming up, she would be able to face it. Not knowing was much harder.

She stole a glance at the other people eating at Tillie's and she knew that she didn't dare speak. Ingor was right in that. And keeping her face down allowed the sides of her silly bonnet to cover most of her face. She wished the food would come, but instead the waitress came back with just knives and forks.

Still Water had seen forks before and knew what they were called, but she had never eaten with one. While at Ingor's cabin, they ate with the wooden spoons that Ingor had whittled, and they each used their own hunting knife to cut their meat. She didn't know why she would need a fork when she could stab each cut piece of meat with the tip of the knife and pop it into her mouth. When should she use a fork? She glanced up at Ingor, but he was looking at the people who were seated at the other tables.

"The man with the big moustache is the owner of the Trading Post," he said quietly so only she could hear his words.

She stole another glance and picked out the man he'd referred to. He still had a good deal of food on his plate so he wouldn't be finishing right away.

The waitress interrupted her thoughts as she banged a huge plate on the table in front of each of them. Each held a steak that filled half of it, and three fried eggs. In the center of the table, she put a bowl of pale brown liquid and a spoon sitting in it. Another bowl beside it was mounded high with biscuits. Ingor thanked her and asked for more coffee.

"Coming right up," the waitress said. She came right back with the pot and filled Ingor's cup nearly to the brim. She looked at Still Water's cup, but saw that she hadn't touched it.

"Don't she like the coffee?" the waitress asked.

Before Still Water could even look up, Ingor answered her saying, "It too hot for her, but she like it fine."

"Oh, good," the woman said and bustled off to pour coffee for another diner, who had called to her.

Still Water looked down at her plate. So much food. She wondered why the lady was giving them each so much to eat. They could go for a whole day and not eat more than this. That woman with the apron that had ruffles all around it was truly kind and special. Was she so rich that she wanted to share her food with travelers? Still Water thought she was a very nice lady to do that.

Looking over at Ingor, she saw that he was eating already. He cut off big pieces of the beefsteak that looked so good. The thick layer of fat around the edge had been fried so it was crisp on the edges, just the way she thought it tasted best.

But the eggs were another matter. She'd eaten eggs before when they stole them from a duck's nests in the spring, but they were different that these. And she'd never seen eggs cooked with the yellow center staring up at her.

"Eat up," Ingor told her. "Trading Post be open any time now. He almost finished." He pointed with his fork toward the table where the owner sat. A piece of steak hung from the end of his fork as he spoke. Having made his point, he put the meat in his mouth and pulled it off the fork with his closed lips.

Ah, so it was the meat that she was to stab with the fork. She picked up the knife and fork, one in each hand, just as Ingor was doing. She held the meat still with her fork stabbed in the middle, and sliced off a long strip across the end. Stabbing that with her knife, she bit off the end. It tasted very good, much more tender and juicy than venison jerky she was used to eating. It sort of tasted like buffalo, but there was a lot more tasty fat on it.

Lost in her own thoughts again, she realized that Ingor was trying to get her attention. As she took another bite of the strip of steak, she looked over at him. He was pointing to his fork.

"Cut smaller pieces and pick each one up with your fork," he leaned over the table to whisper.

Her cheeks warmed with embarrassment and she almost choked on the steak she was trying to swallow. She was doing it wrong, but she knew no other way. She frowned.

"Here. Like this."

After watching him for a while, she got the hang of it. She cut the strip across the steak as before, but then cut it up into three or four bite-sized pieces. Then she stabbed them one at a time with her fork to eat them.

When her steak was gone, she looked at the eggs. Not wanting to make a mistake again, she watched Ingor some more. He stabbed the yellow part with his fork and mopped up the mess with a biscuit. He bit off the wet part and repeated what he had done. When the white part was left with only some yellow smears, he cut them in half, folded them over and forked each big piece into his mouth.

Still Water did her best to do the same. However, the first big bite of the white part just about gagged her. She couldn't take so much into her mouth at one time. He may not like it, but she just had to take smaller bites. She cut the eggs again and ate them one-quarter at a time.

"That's good," Ingor whispered over the table with a grin. "Ladies take smaller bites like that."

She smiled and her heart felt warmed. She had finally done something right. It was something that a white wife would have known to do, and she had figured it out all on her own.

As she finished the last egg, she watched Ingor take two biscuits and pour the brown liquid all over them. He ate them with relish. Willing to try anything that he found so good tasting, she prepared two on her dish the same way. With her first bite, she agreed that they were very good. She would have to find out how to make the brown juice that tasted so fine.

When her plate was empty and her stomach fuller than she could ever remember, she leaned back in her chair. Her knife and fork were still in her hands. Ingor pointed to his that he'd left on his dish and she did the same with hers. She had so much to learn to be able to live in the white man's world. And she would learn as quickly as she could. She didn't want her husband to be angry with her, or even disappointed.

She eyed the last two biscuits in the bowl.

"Go ahead. Take one if you want one," Ingor whispered in English.

Catching himself, he repeated it in the words she guessed were Norwegian. He glanced at the waitress, who was clearing a table nearby.

Still Water reached out and took one, but she didn't eat it. She slipped it into the deep pocket of her apron.

The waitress whisked away their empty plates and reached for the bowl with one biscuit left.

"You ain't gonna eat this lonesome critter?"

Ingor shook his head. "You filled me up without it."

Still Water couldn't bear to have the woman take the soft biscuit away. She grabbed it, knowing that it was not good manners to give back a gift that had been given to you.

The waitress laughed lightly and turned away to take the plates to the kitchen. When her back was turned, Still Water slipped the second biscuit into her apron pocket with the other one.

The men sitting at the other table rose to leave as the clock on the wall chimed eight times. Still Water had never seen a clock that large and never heard one chime. Startled at first, she stared at it and listened. It was beautiful. She wondered how a thing so small could make such loud music. It played a short song and at the end of the song, the rest wasn't much—just eight tones that had been all the same sound. Her tribe's storyteller could sing much better tunes than that. He used many different sounds even at the end of his stories.

"Come on," Ingor said, rising and putting some coins on the table.

She rose to stand close enough to ask, "Why you leave money when the lady was so nice to give us food?"

His eyebrows rose in a startled look. He recovered quickly and whispered, "I'll explain later."

He took her arm to lead her out of the restaurant. He untied Thor and led him and the packhorse, still tied to his saddle, across the street. He tied him up to the rail in front of the Trading Post. Still Water stood on the boardwalk beside him, waiting patiently.

"That was payment for our breakfast," he said first in

Norwegian, then repeating it in English as if he were teaching her English. "Tillie's is restaurant and you pay for food they give you," he added.

Then all that good food had not been a gift from the nice lady, Still Water thought. How odd this white man's world was. If a Sioux Indian traveled and went to another Sioux village, he would be invited into their teepees, and fed, and given a pallet and furs to sleep on. No money had to be given to get these kindnesses, though she knew gifts were often given in return.

Such kindnesses were given to others as brothers, even to the few whites like Ingor, who came into their village. As she walked beside Ingor to the Trading Post entrance, she concluded that whites just didn't consider each other as brothers as the Sioux did. No wonder they acted so differently and fought so often.

"Until we know what will happen, it best if you not speak inside where others hear you," Ingor, standing inches from Still Water, said in a low voice. She nodded.

"I trade the furs and get out of there fast as possible. Then we have one more stop to make in town, and we can head back south."

She welcomed his smile of reassurance. He held her bent elbow as he had at the restaurant, and opened the door. This time he waited so she could enter ahead of him.

Did he truly think she could not open doors and walk through them unaided?

Still Water's heart beat faster at seeing all the wondrous

things in the Trading Post. She had never been in such a place before. Ingor steered her aside from the entrance and released his arm.

"You wait here. I get furs."

Panicked at being left alone, she watched him walk out the door. But following her instinct to learn about her surroundings, she glanced around the store again. A white lady was at the counter paying for some fabric she had selected, but no one else, other then the clerk helping her, was there.

Feeling some relief at the store being so empty, she drew her attention immediately back to all the goods for sale. One section of the store held items for the white man's home. They even had a new wooden rocking chair tied up on the wall. There were two others sitting near the counter beside the pot-bellied stove. They appeared to be used, perhaps by the storeowner in the cold winter when he had time to sit by the fire.

Beside the counter were open barrels of ground wheat that Ingor had called flour, and dried corn, and a bigger barrel of dried beans. On shelves behind the counter were canned goods. Her uncle did not think it right to eat food that had come from a can. He only ate food that was fresh.

At the far end of the store, items for horses like bridles, ropes and even a saddle were hung on the wall. Several thick horse blankets were folded in neat piles on a table by the saddle.

On the other side of the front entrance near the window, where all the colors would stand out in the light of day, were two tables of folded fabric. On the tables near where she stood, Still Water saw dishes, both tin and thick ones that she knew broke when one dropped them. None of them were the baked clay bowls that her uncle used in his teepee.

There were coffeepots like in the restaurant and smaller ones too, and cooking pots stacked next to frying pans with the smaller ones nestled in the larger. She had never seen so many wondrous things in one place.

Her over-full stomach fluttered with excitement at seeing so much and she swallowed hard to settle it down. She'd never been in a city the size of Winnipeg, and she'd never been in such a big store before. Indians weren't allowed in such places, she'd heard, so she never would have come in alone. And here she was standing right in near the middle of it. So much new was happening to her in one day that she nearly felt lightheaded with it all.

Of all the goods, she was drawn to the colors of the fabrics. She took a few small steps toward the table displaying all the colors available.

She'd often dyed the leather from which she made her own clothes. Her tribe used the wild mustard seeds to make yellow. Brown came from boiling black walnut shells, and reds and blues from berries. The dyed leather faded quickly with age though. And never had she achieved so many bright colors together as she saw on the fabrics here.

Most of the colors decorating her usual leather clothes were from the tiny glass beads that the tribe traded for. She could make large beads by carving them from small tree branches. She dyed them in colors from nature, too. Drilling the hole in the center took the most time, but when it was done she could feed one of the leather strips in the fringe of her tunic through the hole. Then she would tie the strip with one knot so the bead would not fall off.

When she had tied on wooden beads all across the bottom of a tunic, the beads knocked together as she walked and made a merry sound. She liked wearing that tunic and wished she had thought to get it when Ingor took her back to Red Moon. She had many things that she wished she had remembered to take. She was lonely without them and didn't like to think that she would never see them again.

She looked down at the dress and apron she wore. The fabric was thin and not durable like leather. She could see advantages though. When it was hot outside, she could tell that the fabric would feel much cooler to wear. However, it was itchy where the seams were. The cut edges of the fabric rubbed against her skin, especially around her upper arm where the sleeve had been sewed on. She preferred her soft, more loose-fitting leather garments.

Thinking about it, she could see that it would be good to have clothes made of fabric in the summer and leather in the winter. But wait. She hadn't thought about what she would be wearing in a white man's home. Would Ingor expect her to dress like a white woman now that she was his wife? She would be sad if she had to give up her leather clothes. But Ingor had not been upset when she put on the leggings to keep warm during the storm. He would let her wear them again.

Remembering then, he already said that she could wear what she wanted in their home. She guessed dressing like a white woman would not be too bad when they went to see other white people.

The woman buying the pretty fabric walked past her to leave the store. She carried her paper wrapped bundle against her waist. A small bag gathered shut with a tie hung on a ribbon from her wrist. The color matched the dark blue of her dress. She wore a straw hat, not a white fabric bonnet like Still Water's. The ribbon holding the straw on her head was the same dark blue of the dress.

She tipped her head to Still Water and said, "Good morning," in a friendly sounding way.

Still Water froze. Her face turned down, she put her hands into her apron pockets. She was too frightened to look up. The woman didn't seem to mind though as she walked right out the door without stopping. Still Water released the breath she had been holding and tried to will her heart to slow down.

Watching through her lashes, Still Water saw the clerk push aside the roll of paper he'd used to wrap the woman's package. The string that he'd tied it with sat on a tall stand, ready for the next customer.

Next to them was the tall box with the buttons on the front that he pushed before he took the woman's coins. Little bells rang when he pushed the buttons and little numbers popped up in a narrow window on the top of the box. After pushing several of the buttons, a drawer slid out and he put the woman's coins in there and shut it. Still Water felt a little disappointed that the bells all sounded pretty much alike and hadn't played a nice melody, not even like at first on the clock.

"Can I help you, Ma'am? Was there something in particular you're looking for?" he said suddenly, looking up at her.

Still Water gasped with fear and dropped her head further until her chin was on her chest. He was talking to her and she didn't know what to do. Ingor had told her not to speak. She couldn't even shake her head because that would show him that she had understood what he had said.

She was so frightened she couldn't catch her breath. What should she do?

Chapter 15

The rain had stiffened the rope, and Ingor had a hard time untying the bundles of furs from the packhorse's saddle. Finally dropping them to the boardwalk, he took out the two hides they had used as ponchos in the freezing rain. He tucked those under the saddlebags. The chances of their needing them again were great. Picking up the bundles, he walked back into the Trading Post where he had left Still Water to wait.

In the spring when trappers normally brought up their furs to trade, there would be a special location outside of town where all the furs could be displayed and judged. The buyers could see furs from many trappers and compare their value. This late in the year, he was the only trapper with furs to trade. He wanted to think that would work to his advantage, but it might do just the opposite.

He stopped beside where Still Water stood. She met his gaze for a few seconds and looked down again. That's all the time he needed to see that she was very uncomfortable here.

He'd almost thought she looked frightened. Maybe he should have kept her with him instead of ushering her into the store to wait for him to untie the furs.

The trader remembered him and greeted him warmly. "Hello there. Not many trappers come all the way from Dakota Territory now. Why didn't you come in the spring like all the others?"

"I hurt leg and not come," Ingor replied as he walked to the counter and dropped the bundles of furs on top.

"And I see another reason you waited," he said, smiling and staring at Still Water. "Morning, ma'am."

She nodded but said nothing.

"My wife not speak English yet. She just come over on boat this summer. I teach her soon. By next year, she know how to speak English."

"Your wife is she?" The trader laughed. "Well, congratulations. I don't see many trappers with wives, you old son of a gun. She'll keep you warm this winter all right."

He continued to laugh a bit and shook his head as he helped untie the ropes from the furs. Rope being as scarce as it was, Ingor rolled it again and again around his palm. Taking off his wide brimmed hat, he stashed the rope coils in the crown and pulled it back on his head.

The trader lifted each fur and examined both sides. He ran his hands over the hair and even pulled at some to test that they were secure and not falling out. He found mouse holes from being stored in the barn rafters and sucked his tongue from the roof of his mouth to make little clacking sounds.

Ingor knew his furs could not match the good quality of those brought to trade in the spring. He still hoped to get a good price. He needed to get a good price for them. He had two mouths to feed now. It was not easy to stand still and watch the inspection.

Dust fell from the furs and he wished he had opened the bundles the night before and given them a good shake to get out the prairie dirt that had blown into them.

"You want to trade these now, huh. Who needs furs in the summer?" the trader said as he finished.

"Summer disappear fast. Ground will be covered with snow before you know it," Ingor insisted.

"But look. They are dusty and look here. There are mouse holes. A lady does not want a fur cape with a mouse hole in it."

"But it be good to cover her horse against the cold."

"Aacht," the trader said, showing he dismissed such an argument.

After a painful few moments of silence, the trader named a price for the whole bunch. Ingor's heart sank. What supplies could he buy for such a small amount? He countered with a higher amount. The trader waited a full minute before he came up a little and then wouldn't budge.

"If we take most of it in trade for food and…and cloth for new dress for my wife?" Ingor asked, hoping that trading for goods that cost the trader less than giving him cash would make him change his mind.

The trader looked at Still Water, who had been watching

through her lashes, her head still down and her hands in her apron pockets.

"Oh, all right," he said, agreeing to Ingor's higher price. "But you gotta take more than half in trade."

"Done," Ingor said with a grin. They sealed the deal with a handshake.

He followed the trader to the end of the counter where he made a list of the goods Ingor wanted. He made certain that coffee and two sweet cones of sugar were included. He also added a small cast-iron fry pan to use on the way home for cooking, plus two tin plates and two tin cups to eat and drink from. Hoping that the cast iron pots and pans at his cabin had survived the fire, he didn't want to buy more.

He and Still Water both had knives, so he only bought three spoons, one of them big enough to stir a pot of stew, and the other two the right size for eating it, plus two forks. He would wait to see what he could rescue from his cabin before he spent any more money on such things as these, too. They could always borrow things from Lars and Lissa and then get more in the spring when traders came to the fort with goods from the east.

For their trip back, he bought a canteen for Still Water to carry water on her saddle. They had been sharing his canteen the whole time, and they didn't always find a stream when it was empty and they were thirsty.

He had about finished dictating the list when Still Water walked closer behind him and tugged on his sleeve. He jerked his head around to see what was wrong. Seeing she was keeping silent as they agreed she should, he took her arm. She drew him over to where the fabric was displayed.

The trader thought she was pulling him there and laughed. "You know the wives. They always want something pretty, too," he said. He thought nothing of it and went on counting up the cost of the goods Ingor had ordered.

"What is it? What's wrong?" Ingor whispered.

"Needles. Thread—light and dark. I not sew your shirts with porcupine quills like for leather," she replied, barely loud enough for him to hear.

"Good." Happy that she had thought about what she would need, he grinned and led her back to the counter. He hadn't given a thought to what she might want him to buy.

"Ah, and we take some needles and thread. Different colors—white and black." He looked at her. She was looking at the rack that displayed all the colors available. "And some yellow and a blue," he added. "And green."

He turned to look back at the stacks of fabric they had been standing beside. He picked up a bolt and held it in front of her. He thought she looked pretty in it and the smile on her face said she liked it too, he hoped.

"And enough of this for a dress, the one with little yellow and blue flowers." Getting into the spirit of things but not considering that Still Water might not know how to sew clothes from fabric, he added, "And enough of that dark green for a shirt for me."

The trader nodded, retrieving the lengths of fabric and measuring out what Ingor had ordered. He placed the needles and thread inside the folds to keep them safe.

The most expensive purchase came next. Ingor looked at the wooden pole that was hung near the end of the counter. There were ready-made shirts, denim pants, dresses, and a few men's coats and women's capes.

"Fire at my cabin burn up our coats. In winter furs do fine job of keeping us warm, but on horse when it gets cold, we need coats."

"It was cool enough out this morning to need one." The trader went with him to the display. "This is the only one I have for your missus," he said as he held up a wool cape in dark brown.

Ingor waved Still Water over to his side and hung the cape on her shoulders. "Ya, that is good."

In the meantime the trader had picked out a wool jacket that he handed to Ingor when he turned back. He tried to put it on, but it was too tight over the shoulders. The trader took it back and gave him a larger sized one. This jacket wasn't as sturdy as the first one, but it fit him well. He raised his arms and swung them forward to make sure he had good room for moving around.

"Ya, this one fit better."

The trader nodded and returned to his counter where he added the costs of the coats to the long list. He added the whole list again to be certain it was correct.

Ingor turned to Still Water and found her lightly running her fingers down the front of her cape. He stepped closer and she looked up to meet his gaze.

"The cape, it is good?" he asked in Norwegian and then softer in English. She smiled and that's all he needed to know that she liked the cape.

"I never had one like this before," she whispered. He felt good and proud for being able to give it to her.

"Here's your total," the trader said, pointing to the figures on the paper. "You only get this much in cash."

Checking the numbers, Ingor was disappointed but not surprised. He could see that buying goods for two people was much more dear than for one.

"I threw in the coffee—sort of a wedding present for you."

Ingor grinned and thanked him. The owner rang up the goods in the cash register and gave Ingor the cash due him before he assembled the rest of their order. Ingor put the coins in his small leather bag, and returned it to his pocket.

The trader started a pile on the counter beside the fabric as he went down the rest of the list. The resulting pile on the counter was large enough to make Ingor wish he'd stopped sooner when it came to picking things out.

"You want me to wrap this all up in paper?" the clerk asked.

Surveying the pile, Ingor said, "Just sewing goods to keep them clean. I go get saddlebags and blanket for the rest."

He nodded to Still Water to be sure she understood he would be right back and ran out to the horses. Sleeping together under one blanket would be easy, and they would stay warmer. The second blanket would be put to better use holding the trade goods.

Putting what they would use on the trail like the frying pan and canteen in the saddlebags where they could get at them easily, he put the rest in the blanket. Using the rope that had held the furs, he bundled up everything securely. He didn't want anything to fall out on the long ride home.

Not expecting a woman to carry any of the heavy parcels, the trader took the saddlebags and followed Ingor, who carried the blanketed bundle, out the door. Still Water walked out behind them. She stood back a bit while they tied the saddlebags on.

Then the storeowner held the blanket bundle while Ingor tied it on the packhorse's saddle on each side. "That ought to do it," he said. "Thank you."

"We'll see you next spring, won't we?"

"Ya," Ingor said with a grin. "I have more beautiful furs than you ever see by then."

The trader laughed. "You be careful going home now. You never know when a snow storm can blow up and surprise you."

Another customer had passed them on the walk and entered the store, so he headed right back toward the door. "Good luck," he called over his shoulder.

"Our load is heavier now," Ingor said as he lifted Still Water onto Thor's rump. She had to bend her knees around the loaded saddlebags under her.

Ingor climbed into the saddle, lifting his right leg over Thor's neck. Leading the packhorse with her reins in his hand this time, he rode south toward the edge of town.

Her head close to his back, Still Water asked, "Did he know I was an Indian? He watch me a lot."

"Don't know if he swallowed story of you coming on boat or not. He not make trouble and that's all we need care about."

"I hope my uncle find people in Canada who don't make trouble for them here, too."

"That the way it should be."

Keeping Thor at a walk, heading up the main street, Ingor paused at the cross streets and looked left and right, trying to spot a small white clapboard building he knew was around this end of town somewhere. Thinking he recognized the next block, he turned down a side street and looked up and down one street over from the main road.

"What you looking for? Where are we going?" Still Water asked.

"I keep my promise."

They rode another block before he pulled up the reins and looked left and right again.

"There it is," he said brightly as he turned the horses in that direction and pointed.

"What is it?"

"That little church. See the sign out front? It is Methodist Church."

"What is Methodist Church?" she asked.

"I promise I marry you and get a paper that says we married in the way of the white man. This is house where the preacher is. I ask him to marry us."

He urged Thor toward the church and the packhorse plodded along beside them. His wife's grip tightened around his ribs. Was she as worried that the preacher would not marry them as he was?

* * * *

Still Water was filled with the wonder of seeing so many things she had never seen before today. Now she was entering another place she'd never been—a white man's church. This had to be where the white man's god stayed. She had never seen him before either. In fact she was worried and not a little frightened that the god would chase her out. She knew nothing of the white man's god except what the missionary had told her uncle's people. She had been young when he showed up in camp two summers in a row. She had learned little of his god, but he had been kind to her. She listened to what he said, to learn the words and because she didn't want to offend his gods. She certainly didn't want them to be angry at her now for going in their church to find the preacher who also stayed there.

For the most part, her uncle Red Moon had always tried to steer clear of white man and his ways. But now that she was married to one, Still Water could no longer do that. Happy that Ingor showed no hesitation in what they were doing, she tried to act as confident and followed close behind after they dismounted.

When they entered the church, her confidence fled. She prayed silently that the white man's god wouldn't strike her down. Still alive after taking several steps inside, she began to breathe more easily.

If this is where the white man got married, she couldn't help but wonder what his wedding would be like if he wasn't marrying an Indian. She wished she had asked Ingor about that. Maybe she would someday.

While she'd never seen a white man's wedding, he'd never seen the whole Indian wedding ceremony either. He could have if there had been time. It was not one of the ceremonies performed in her tribe that white men could not witness. Perhaps the Methodist Church was stricter and an Indian was not welcome. Then if they discovered what she was, there would be trouble.

But now there was just strange music coming from the front of the church. She had never heard such music before. Some of the notes made the same sound for a long time while others were shorter and changed more often. Though new to her, it was not unpleasant. She smiled as she listened and looked around.

The church was all white inside as it had been on the outside. She wondered at first why the people of the church had not wanted to write their history in pictures on the walls for all to see. Drawings on the white walls would look quite pleasant, she thought.

Several wide benches that would hold seven or eight people were lined up in two rows on either side of a center walkway. In front of the benches was a wooden raised part in the floor that held a tall wooden stand. Right in front of that stand there was a long narrow table with a white lacy tablecloth on it. She had seen no delicate cloth like that at the trader's post, but it would not do for a dress or curtains to cover a window. You could see right through it. That would not be warm at all in the winter.

Behind the raised platform, there was a tall narrow window and one more was on each side of the benches. The number of glass windows in the white men's buildings she had seen today was a wonder. She was delighted being able to see the trees and sky from inside. Could the white man's god slip out one of the windows when no one was looking?

As she got closer to the front, she could see a portly woman in her fifties poking white and black narrow bars that had been laid in a row in a high wooden box at which she sat. She had to be the one making the music because the sounds changed when she moved her hands. The woman stopped after a short time and smiled at them. "Good morning. If you're looking for the preacher, he should be here any minute. You're welcome to sit and wait for him."

"Thank you, ma'am," Ingor said, pulling off his wide-brimmed felt hat from his head and holding it in front of him in both hands. He'd told Still Water it was his summer hat. The wide brim protected him from sunburn. In the winter he wore one he'd fashioned out of furs, mostly fox. He'd put the fox's head on the front and said he liked thinking that the fox was looking out for where he was going, too. He'd worn a hat like that when her people found him nearly frozen. The fox wasn't working for him then.

The woman went back to making music and seemed to think nothing of their being there. That made Still Water feel a bit more at ease, but they still had to find the preacher. They didn't know what he or his god would say about them being there.

Ingor took Still Water's elbow to usher her toward the front, and though she was still frightened, she didn't dare put up a fuss. She didn't want to call any attention to herself.

They stopped when a side door near the front of the church, which Still Water hadn't noticed before, opened and a tall man dressed all in black came through it. He wore the same long robe as the missionary who had visited her tribe. She hoped this man was as nice as the robed man she had known.

"Good morning, Ruth," the man said as he walked over and laid a piece of paper on the wooden box where she sat. "Here's the list of hymns for Sunday's service."

"Thank you, Reverend Marks. You have some visitors," Ruth said, raising her hand toward Still Water and Ingor.

He turned back and spotted the couple. "Well, so I do." He smiled broadly and directed his steps to where Still Water and Ingor were standing in the center aisle. He extended his hand to Ingor.

"Good morning. What brings you here this fine day?"

"I come here with my wife to get married," Ingor said without preamble.

"But if she is your wife, why…"

"No, you see, her uncle Red Moon, Chief of the Sioux,

married us. I want us to be married in the white man's way."

Still Water gasped at his easy confession that she was an Indian. Now would be a good time for Mother Earth to open a big hole and swallow her whole.

Her beautiful new cape that she still wore around her shoulders made her much warmer than she wanted to be. Her face felt hot, but she didn't dare remove the covering now. At the same time her legs felt wobbly and she wished very much that she could sit down. There were all the empty benches beside her, but she didn't dare sit in any of them.

"You want to be married in the way of the white man," the man said.

"Ya." Ingor nodded and pulled her closer to his side and wrapped his arm around her waist.

Still Water looked up and felt the penetrating gaze of the preacher on her face and that made her feel even warmer. She swallowed against the lump of fear that had stuck in her throat and tipped her head down. She wanted to hide inside her hat.

"I understand now what you want, but ah…she doesn't seem too excited by the idea," the Reverend said with a little nervous laugh.

Though she wanted to, Still Water couldn't even move to run from the building as they both stared at her.

Chapter 16

Ingor looked at Still Water. She looked so nice in her new cape that he was proud to have bought for her. She didn't raise her face to look at him so he took her hand in his. It felt cold so he wrapped his other hand around it too. She looked up then and he saw the frightened look back on her face. He smiled to put her at ease.

He asked her in Sioux if she wanted to marry him and be his wife all the rest of his days. Without turning in his direction, he told the preacher in English what he had said.

"Yes," the preacher said. "I understand a bit of the Sioux language. Does she speak English?"

"Ya, she speak English better than me," Ingor said with a laugh.

The preacher turned to Still Water then and asked her again in English, "Do you wish to marry this man before God and to be his wife?"

She dared a little smile and replied in Sioux, "Yes, with all my being."

"Good. Then I see no reason not to go ahead," the Reverend said with a broad smile.

"How you understand Sioux?" Ingor asked.

"I was a missionary to several tribes for ten years before the church assigned me here."

Still Water dared to meet the preacher's gaze again. He had been a missionary, too. He had to be a nice man like the missionary she knew. "Then you will marry us?" she asked in Sioux.

"As long as you truly want me to make you man and wife," he replied in English.

"Oh, yes," she replied breathlessly, speaking English as well.

The preacher turned to stand in front of the platform and opened the small black book he'd pulled from his pocket. "Ruth, we're going to have a wedding here now. I need you and Etienne as witnesses. Could you call him please?"

"Right away."

Smiling broadly, Ruth left the little round stool on which she had been sitting, and opened the side door of the church through which the preacher had entered. She hollered out Etienne's name and waved her arm to signal him to come inside. He arrived at a run in a minute or so. "We need you as a witness," she told him as she shut the door behind him. "We're going to have a wedding."

Etienne grinned and walked with Ruth to stand beside the preacher. Reverend Marks introduced them to Still Water and Ingor, getting their names at the same time. He wrote them near the back of the book he'd carried in. Still Water looked at the writing and wondered which was her name. Learning to write it in the white man's way would be a good thing to do, she thought.

From there things happened fast and in somewhat of a blur to Still Water. When the ceremony began, the preacher had a strange way of talking that made understanding his English hard for her. His voice was louder and deeper, and he changed pitch often. It was not at all like the monotone chanting in a Sioux ceremony. Maybe the white man's god couldn't hear what he said unless he talked that way and yelled most of the time.

But Ingor seemed to know what was going on and when she couldn't understand the question, he prompted her when to say, "I do." He said it soon after and then there was a moment when the ceremony stopped. The preacher asked Ingor for a ring and he had none.

"What he want ring for?" she whispered to Ingor, not understanding the problem.

The preacher explained briefly that the groom should have a ring for his wife to wear on her finger to show that she was married. Still Water looked at her hands and thought of all the duties they would perform. A ring would only get in the way. And more importantly, she didn't need to wear a symbol of their union.

"I don't need a ring," she said softly with a smile for Ingor. "All will know we are man and wife from what is in my heart, not what is on my finger."

Thankfully, the preacher seemed to accept that and he went on to pronounce them man and wife. His voice was not so strange after he started again and she had understood all he said for that part.

She looked at the tall handsome man beside her who was now considered her husband by the white man, too. Taking her hands in his, he looked down at her and smiled as sweetly as she had ever seen. Her heart was full and she knew she would remember this moment the rest of her life.

"*Jeg elsker deg*," he said softly in Norwegian. "I love you," he added in a whisper.

"You may kiss the bride," the preacher said, as Ruth returned to her wooden box and made more music come out.

She felt uncomfortable kissing Ingor where others could see them. Grinning, Ingor looked embarrassed too, but he leaned forward and kissed her cheek. The men all shook hands and then congratulated her, too. She had thought it a little odd that Etienne had hung back, but didn't get a chance to figure out why. He hadn't said a word to anyone.

"Well, you're Mr. and Mrs. Oleson now," the preacher said. "Ah, it is customary for the groom to give a small monetary gift to the church for the wedding." He was back to his loud and deep voice that he'd used for the ceremony.

"Monetary?" Ingor asked, not understanding. "What that mean?"

"Ah, money. You know. For the church in a way of a thank you."

"Oh, and we need the piece of paper that says we legally

man and wife, all proper by white man preacher."

"Of course. If you're going back to Dakota Territory, I can see that would be important." He looked at Still Water and she knew he understood the difficulties they were having.

Ingor dug his leather bag of coins out of his pocket and picked out a couple. Still Water didn't know the value of the coins, but she saw a happy smile on the preacher's face when he thanked Ingor for what he had put in the palm of his hand. Whatever the amount was, she hoped that being married to her turned out to be worth that much.

Now that the wedding ceremony was done, Still Water actually felt more at ease. Surely this meant that she couldn't be taken away from her husband and relocated by the Army. It would not stop some white people from not liking her because she was an Indian, but she knew Ingor loved her and that was all that was truly important.

"Etienne, show Mr. and Mrs. Oleson over to the Courthouse, if you please," Preacher Marks said. "You tell them that I just married these folks, and they need a Certificate of Marriage from the civil registry 'cause I have no certificates left here in the church. But I put their names in the record book here if anyone wants to see it."

Etienne nodded and turned to walk down the aisle and out the door. The man still had never said a word, but he obviously understood the preacher. Still Water and Ingor ran a few steps to catch up.

"Is it far?" Ingor asked once outside.

Etienne shook his head and pointed across the street.

"Then we leave the horses here."

They soon entered the Courthouse. Inside, he led them into one of the offices. A woman behind the desk watched him as, using his hands, he managed to tell her what they wanted.

Still Water understood better now why Etienne had never spoken. She didn't think he could speak.

A thin woman behind a large desk, that made her look even smaller than she was, greeted Ingor and Still Water. Etienne pointed to a large book bound in brown leather and then pointed to the wedded couple.

Ingor had not realized that Etienne had already requested the Certificate of Marriage by his motions because he told the clerk what they had come for, too.

"Yes. That's what Etienne just told me," she said with a smile, apparently used to the situation.

Still Water smiled at Ingor's confused look but covered it with her hand. She was used to sign language used among tribes. While they might not speak each other's tongue, they all knew sign language. She glanced at Ingor's big brimmed hat and knew the sign for white man was a good one. With the hand flat and palm down at the forehead, one would pass the hand in that horizontal plane around to the side of the head. The sign was mimicking the wide brims on Army hats and most trappers' hats that kept the sun off their faces and ears.

The clerk pulled a formal looking certificate out of a file and handed it to Ingor after filling parts out and signing it.

"Take this back to Reverend Marks. That'll be fifty cents."

Startled at the amount, he paid it nonetheless. Rolling the paper to protect it, he took Still Water's hand, and they followed Etienne out of the courthouse and back across the dirt street to the church.

Still Water was relieved that it didn't take long for the minister to fill out the form with the wedding date and place. Ruth and Etienne signed as witnesses, and then Reverend Marks signed his own name. Turning it to them, he asked them to sign it. He handed the quill pen to Ingor to sign and then when he was finished, he looked expectantly at Still Water.

She took the pen, but didn't know how to write her name. Embarrassed, she looked up helplessly at Ingor, who didn't move to help her. It was the preacher who came to her aide. He guided her hand so she could write Still Water on the curling piece of paper. She had to re-dip the quill in the ink well, but they finished the words with only two little dots where the black ink had spattered.

"Is that my name?" she asked in Sioux when they finished.

Preacher Marks nodded.

Fortified by his support and friendliness, Still Water switched to English. With a smile she said to Ingor, "When we get home, I want to learn to write my name."

The preacher laughed. "You got a right smart wife here, Mr. Oleson. I hope you two will be very happy."

Ingor knew he had a smart wife, but she didn't know how ignorant he was. He could write his name and speak enough English to get by most of the time, but he couldn't read English. He'd had some schooling in Norway before he had to work fulltime as a teenager. However, here in English, everything was new. He didn't know words, but he knew places from looking for them. He didn't know the name of the place where he traded his furs, but he knew where to find it because he'd been there before.

He hadn't been able to help his wife write her name because he didn't know how to spell it, and this time, how he wished he did. It had been a blow to have the preacher do what he should have been able to do.

Once the ink was dry, the preacher rolled up the paper and handed it to him. He could only pray that the paper said what he thought it did because he couldn't even read the big long words across the top. Not even when their lives depended on it.

But no one made any special note of this shortcoming and right quickly they were saying their goodbyes. Ingor made a point to thank Etienne for his help getting the paper at the courthouse and got a nod in return.

Etienne signed something to the preacher and then pointed to the door.

"Yes, you go back to work. And thank you," the preacher said as Etienne scurried to the side door. There he turned and looked back at Still Water for a few moments. Then he turned and ran out the door.

Still Water felt uneasy from the look she'd seen on his face, and didn't know what to make of it. The preacher,

Ruth, and Etienne all had known right away that she was an Indian. Maybe all the people in the restaurant and the store had too. They had been friendly and helpful. The tension she felt at being discovered seemed to melt away. But why had Etienne stopped and seemed to glare at her as he did?

"In case you're wondering," the preacher said as if he had read her mind, "I think that when you said you were from Red Moon's band, he felt relieved. But still… You see, though he's forgiven them in the Lord's name, it was other Lakotas who cut out his tongue when they tortured him and left him for dead three years ago."

Still Water felt cold all over. There was nothing that either of them could say to that.

With a nod to the preacher, Ingor took her elbow and they walked out to the horses. White men and Indians had a bad and murderous history fighting against each other. With the recent news of the Great White Father insisting that the Indians move off the lands that had been theirs for all time, she could only imagine it would get worse. Braves like Tall Cloud crossing the Territory with murderous intent and whites who thought the only good Indian is a dead Indian would make it worse.

Would her husband come to hate her too? The furs gone, he lifted her onto the packhorse saddle. She bent a leg over his neck and Ingor helped adjust her skirt and apron to cover her legs. Her leather boots showed, but he didn't seem to care. Now that they were married by the white preacher, could she be an Indian again? Or did she still have to pretend she was white? She wasn't certain what he wanted of her now, but she didn't know how long she could keep playing the role of a white woman.

* * * *

Mr. and Mrs. Oleson rode in a thoughtful silence as they left Winnipeg and headed south. Ingor wondered if their experience there was only one of many meetings with people mistreated by the Indians. He was thankful that Etienne had not transferred all his hate, which he had a right to have, into his actions toward Still Water. Most people like the farmer's wife, with the boy who knew she was an Indian, hung onto their hate and acted on it.

With the Certificate of Marriage tucked inside his hat for safekeeping, Ingor put a knot in the ties that he normally tucked inside and let them hang down on his chest. In case there was a wind or low tree, he didn't want to lose the hat. His only worry was rain. He would have to figure another hiding place then to keep the precious paper dry.

Once clear of Winipeg, Ingor followed a game path that riders had widened. It was farther from the Red River than the route they had traveled on going north. He didn't want to pass the same family-group farms on the way back, though he wasn't as worried now. Even though being married wouldn't stop people from hating his Indian wife, he was confident that if they ran into the Army, they wouldn't have any trouble with the soldiers taking her away. He took great comfort in the fact that they had been married by a white preacher, and he had the paper to prove it.

They found another trading post built where several farmers lived fairly close together and traded the goods they grew, made, or hunted. Families came from the whole area for their goods. Ingor hoped the family with the inquisitive boy didn't show up while they were there. He wanted no more of the boy's questions for Still Water's ease of mind, even though everyone could see her as the Indian that she was.

Tempted to go on past without stopping, Ingor wanted to meet the men running the post. They might be interested in some of his furs next spring. If he could sell them here without having to go all the way to the gathering in Winnipeg, it would be better.

The dogs running loose outside the post set to barking as they approached. A tall dark-haired man came out and shouted at the dogs. They ran off and then he turned to greet the couple as they approached more closely.

"Hello," Ingor called. "You mind if we stop and look at your goods? This is my wife. I do trapping down in Dakota Territory two years now."

"You're welcome. Come on in," the man called.

"I come by this way last spring and not see you," Ingor said as he lifted Still Water down to the ground. He still did that as long as she had on the dress that made it hard for her to dismount. They tied their horses to the post by the front porch.

"Just started to build it all last spring. We got four families working together here, so the buildings went up pretty fast."

"That explain it," Ingor replied with a grin.

"We're just about to have supper. If you want to join us, it'll just cost you fifty cents for the two of ya. We got fresh pike from the Red and lots of fresh vegetables we've been harvesting."

Ingor's stomach growled at that moment, making up his mind for him. Laughing, he accepted the offer and they followed the man inside. There, he turned back to Ingor and introduced everyone.

"I'm Ian Bruce and that's my wife. Them's our children. It's our night to run the post and fix supper for travelers."

"Thank you kindly, Mr. Bruce," Ingor told him and then he introduced himself and his wife but without using her name.

"You're about the third trapper we've met this year who's got himself a squaw," the man said in his same conversational tone.

Ingor straightened, not because he cared if they knew she was an Indian, but because he did not like the term *squaw* used in reference to Still Water. "Mrs. Oleson is niece of Red Moon," he explained to establish that she was not what he thought the man had meant by "squaw".

"Say, I heard tell they were settling in west of here. I guess there's more than enough trouble for them down in Dakota Territory. But I sure hope they steer clear of us."

"Come and get it if you want it hot," Mrs. Bruce urged. Her children ran to sit at the long benches on each side of the table. Mr. Bruce pulled up a chair at one end of the table.

Ingor seated Still Water on the bench next to one of the children, and then sat between her and the end of the table. Mrs. Bruce moved along the table giving each of them a big slab of golden fried pike that she took from two big cast-iron fry pans she had cooking on the blackened wood stove.

Bowls of plump kernels of corn cut from the cobs, green beans, and carrots boiled together, and a large bowl of mashed potatoes were already lined up down the middle of the table. Each diner took the bowl nearest them and started passing after helping themselves. Slices of homemade bread with apple butter followed.

"This is the first apple butter of the season," Mrs. Bruce said proudly. "My Jonny here just started picking them apples today."

"It's very good, ma'am," Ingor said politely. He looked at Still Water, and she nodded her agreement.

Their hostess smiled and managed to eat a bite or two before she went back to the stove to turn the next batch of pike filets.

"How come you got your hat on?" the child next to Still Water asked her.

"Now don't you pester her, Lily," Mrs. Bruce ordered.

"But, Mama, you said it was bad manners to wear a hat to the table," the child insisted.

"You just hush up now and finish your supper."

Ingor was thankful the child's questions about Still Water had been halted. He hadn't even known a woman should take off her bonnet inside. He'd been telling Still Water to keep it on. She wasn't a white wife, and he didn't expect her to know how to act as one.

Maybe his brother's wife Lissa would be amenable to helping Still Water learn all that she needed to know to be around white women without them pointing out what were mistakes in their eyes.

There weren't a lot of people in the Territory yet, but there would be soon with the offer of free land. Once she knew what to do and how to do it, they could blend in and live their lives without being marked for special treatment, good or bad. That's all they wanted, just to be left alone to live their lives together.

After dinner, Ingor and Still Water couldn't tarry. He paid for their meal, and they were going to leave when Mr. Bruce insisted they stay the night. "We built on a room to rent," he said with a grin. "It's not like a fancy hotel, but it's got a clean bed and I'll bring you warm water to wash up."

"He's right. It's pitch black out there. Your horse could break a leg before you saw the hole he stepped in," Mrs. Bruce chimed in.

"I'll give you the room and breakfast to boot for only twenty-five cents more for the two of you."

Ingor decided easily that the loss of another twenty-five cents was less of a danger to them than the possible injury to their horses. He saw no objections in Still Water's face, so he got their bedrolls and saddlebags and brought them inside after taking care of the horses. One of the boys showed him where to put them up for the night and helped unsaddle them and stack their trade goods on the saddle in the corner of Thor's stall. Thor wouldn't step on them, but he would protect them and not let anyone get past him to take them.

Left in the house alone, Still Water wanted to help. Their hosts had been kind, and she appreciated that even if it did cost them a great deal of money from what she knew of its value. She helped carry the plates to the kitchen where Mrs. Bruce washed them in a wide tin pan.

"I'll dry them and stack them there on the table again," her hostess told her. "We'll need 'em soon enough in the morning."

Still Water had been afraid that she would drop one of the slippery wet dishes, so she was just as happy she didn't want her help. She stood patiently and watched as she washed and dried the forks and knives and spoons next, laying them beside the plates.

"I'm sorry my girl was pestering you about your hat."

Still Water was nonplussed and didn't know what to say. She decided honesty with this kind woman was the best policy. "I didn't know it was not good to wear the hat at the table."

"I don't imagine you see a lot of white folks in Dakota Territory to know how we live."

"No."

"How long you known your husband?"

"I know him for two years. We first met when he came into Red Moon's camp."

"Doesn't that beat all? He just rode into Red Moon's

camp? That took a lotta guts. Other men have done that and never lived to tell the tale."

Still Water's delight in the admiration this woman had expressed for her brave husband had been quickly crushed by what she said about men dying in her uncle's camp.

"My husband was nearly frozen and my people saved his life. He stayed with us many weeks until he got well again."

"I never heard of such a thing." Mrs. Bruce walked to the door to toss out the pans of wash and rinse water. She dried them before she hung them on the wall over the dry sink. "That about does it."

Still Water didn't know where to go or what to do next. She was relieved the men returned from the barn just then, saving her from any wrong choice of her own.

"I finished cleaning up just in time," Mrs. Bruce announced. She showed them to the room they rented and filled the pitcher on the little table with warm water she'd carried in from the stove.

"Thank you," Ingor said as she left. "Good night," he added as he closed their door.

Still Water hung their coats on the pegs on the wall while he set their saddlebags and his revolver on the table in the corner. He leaned the rifle against the wall right next to where he would sleep.

He was moving around and settling in and leaving her as if she knew what to do. She had wanted to go with him to care for the horses so that she wouldn't be left alone. In camp they always worked together to settle horses and get the fire started. Expecting to help him again, she watched him leave without saying a word about what she was to do. Though she knew all there was to do to care for the horses, she was not asked to help. Was it bad manners for a woman to help with horses, too? She had so much to learn and no idea how she would learn it.

Releasing some frustration, she yanked at the bow under her chin and pulled off her bonnet. Remembering how precious they were, she was careful to take out the few pins she had left that Lissa had given her. Her twisted braid tumbled down her back. That is why she hadn't wanted to take her hat off. She didn't have enough pins left to keep it tight against her head. Her hair was straight and thick, and she wished there was another way of holding it up.

Sitting on the edge of the bed, she began to untie her moccasins when she noticed the door opening slowly. Alarmed, she rose and silently stepped into the corner of the room so that the dresser was between her and the door. Calling his name softly to alert Ingor, she looked over the polished surface to see who was coming in.

Chapter 17

Leaning over to see who was outside the opening door to their bedroom, Still Water saw the blonde head of the little girl who had sat next to her at the table. Just as she was about to move where she could talk to the child, her mother's hand grabbed her upper arm and yanked her out of the doorway.

"I told you to stay away from that woman. It was bad enough you had to sit by her at dinner. You never know what she might have that you would catch," Mrs. Bruce whispered loud enough for Still Water to hear every word from her position close behind the door. The door shut and their voices were too muffled to understand anymore, but she had heard too much already.

She glanced at Ingor, who was on the other side of the bed, pulling off his boots after watching the door move. She felt numb. Their hosts had been polite as long as they were paying guests for dinner or the guestroom. Now she knew in her heart that without payment, they wouldn't hand out even a drink of water to an Indian dying of thirst. She was almost surprised that they even allowed her sleep in the bed. Did they have something planned like robbing them in the night?

Her husband dropped his second boot and rose to gather her into his arms. "People not always like they seem to be."

Still Water blinked away the tears that burned at the backs of her eyes. "Are the horses safe?"

"I left the packs in the stall with Thor. He not let anyone mess with them."

"Good. I almost wish we hadn't stayed the night."

"I know, but as long as we have a bed to sleep in, let's enjoy it."

He kissed her and turned away, unbuttoning his shirt. He undressed quickly and so did she. Their clothes kept handy beside the bed, they climbed between the clean sheets on the soft straw mattress. At Ingor's cabin she had lain on a pallet and had a quilt over her. Sleeping between clean sheets that smelled sweet from being dried in sunshine was a treat she had never experienced.

"Enjoy the bed while you can. It will be some time before I can rebuild our cabin and make a bed and all the furniture again."

She snuggled up next to him and welcomed his arms when he wrapped them around her. "I will help."

"That be good. We must have fire for cooking and to keep warm and fire too dangerous in barn unless we build a rock fireplace and chimney on the end."

"And I can go with you to check your traplines?"

"You want to keep me warm at night?" he asked with a grin.

"I think I like that."

"Then between trips we have to take care of fur."

"I can help tan the hides."

He kissed her. "You always so willing to help."

"All the wives I know in Red Moon's camp work very hard to help their husbands."

"Yes, I guess you right. And out here white husbands take all the help they can get, too, but I think some get no help. At the fort I see wives who hate it here in this lonely territory."

They lay quietly for a few minutes.

"I wonder if Red Moon is far away," she asked. "The man say he settle to west of here. I wonder how far."

"You're worried about him."

She nodded, her cheek rubbing against his bare chest. "He raised me and I love him. I have much to thank him for. He protected me from Tall Cloud when I told him I not want to be his wife. Yes, I worry. They are my family and I want them safe."

"When we come through here with our furs next spring, we can take the time after we sell them and find where he is. Maybe we could stay at his camp for a time."

Pleased at the happy prospect, she stretched up and kissed him hard. At the same time, she slid her hand over his flat stomach. He quickly lifted her hand and held it on his chest.

"Tomorrow night you can do that all you want. But tonight we have to get sleep so we can leave with the dawn."

"Then you don't want me to do this?" she teased, kissing

him as her thigh pressed against him.

"You know I love it when you do," he groaned into her mouth. "But the sheets. We might stain them," he said, breaking off the kiss.

"That doesn't matter," she said with a perceptive smile. "I know that Mrs. Bruce will wash them very carefully after we leave. She will probably boil them after I sleep on them."

"Well, in that case..."

* * * *

At the river that flowed into the Red near to the border, they knew they had crossed out of Canada. While they still might be taking a chance going back, Ingor felt a good deal happier and less worried than before they were married in Canada. He was confident now that the Army could not relocate Still Water. And if they tried, they would have him to deal with.

Beyond the Army, he knew, there would always be people who didn't want the Indians around. He wanted to protect Still Water from meeting up with them, but he knew that was unrealistic.

What he did have to worry about now was the questionable disappearance of the two vermin who had mistreated her. That and the huge matter of rebuilding his cabin or at least some shelter before winter set in.

A heavy rain somewhere to the west had widened the tributary a good deal more. As on their trip north, they had to find a safer place to cross where the river was narrower and not so deep. They rode west along the north bank.

"Looks like we can cross here," Ingor said finally.

His wife was riding the packhorse astride despite wearing a skirt. They'd decided there were few enough people around not to worry about meeting them.

He wasn't certain what the river bottom was like here because the rain-fed rush had kicked up the mud and made the water a cloudy brown. He waited until Still Water's horse was next to his.

"Hang on," he said. "Take us across, big fella," he coaxed with pats on the horse's neck as Thor stepped into the swiftly moving water.

Shy of the water, the packhorse resisted being ordered into it. After Still Water kicked her sides, she finally entered with a little burst of speed that splashed water all over everything and everyone. Halfway across, Thor stepped on what must have been a large rock. His foot slid off and he had to catch himself with several small sidesteps.

Frightened by him coming closer, the packhorse pulled away. Ingor tried to grab the reins, but he couldn't reach them to help. While Still Water talked to her to calm her, the packhorse had turned sideways to Thor and her head hit his neck. Thor took strong exception to the contact and screamed as he rose up on his hind legs and pawed the air with his front legs.

Frightened, Still Water's horse leapt sideways to get away and lost her footing. Her front leg bent and her shoulder went down into the water. Still Water's moccasin slid out of the stirrup. Her horse surged upwards again with a scream.

Unable to hold onto the bucking horse, she slid into the rushing river. Free of her load, the packhorse splashed on to the bank and climbed out of the water.

Putting out a hand for Still Water, Ingor pulled down the reins to stop Thor. But afraid Thor might step on her as she fought to get to her feet, he dug his heels into his side and got him to the south bank as quickly as possible.

Looping Thor's reins over a sturdy branch a couple of yards away from the river, he rushed back to help Still Water.

Sucked under the water by the weight of her white-woman's dress, she could not manage to stand in the water that looked about waist-high here. Instead, she tried to swim to shore, but her feet, tangled in her skirt and apron, were ineffective. For every foot she gained toward the shore, she lost two going downstream.

Ingor pulled his hat on tight to protect the precious marriage certificate, and ran along the bank to get ahead of her. Finding a tree that had fallen from the bank into the water, he walked into the water upstream of the trunk.

"Catch the tree," he shouted. "I get you from here."

Still Water, a good swimmer, pulled hard with her arms and could only hope that the kicking she did was helping her and not hindering her. She grunted when her hip hit a large rock, but it actually slowed her progress downstream and turned her closer to shore. She was able, with a few more strokes, to grab the tree where Ingor stood reaching for her. Rotted in the water, the branch broke away, but she'd gotten enough momentum from grabbing it, to catch hold of the trunk. From there, Ingor pulled her onto her feet. Clinging to each other, they made it to shore.

"You not hurt?" he asked.

Panting as the shock of what had happened settled in, she shook her head but didn't try to talk.

Nearly dark by then, the temperature was falling fast. Still Water was shivering more by the time they reached the horses. Thankful the packhorse had not wandered far, he tied her reins to Thor's saddle.

Ingor pulled off her dripping cape and helped her into his jacket. She clutched at the front to double it over as he pulled a deer-hide cover over each of them for warmth.

"We'll find a place to camp right away so you can get rest of wet clothes off," he said. She nodded. "Let me help you up on Thor."

"N-n-no," she stuttered with cold. "I w-walk to g-get warm."

He gathered up Thor's reins and they walked along the north edge of the trees that ran along the river. Finding an open area where the trees thinned out, they stopped to set up camp. Ingor immediately started a big fire to warm Still Water. There was plenty of deadfall, but it was wet from the rain the night before. It took extra time to get the flame going.

As he worked, Still Water took off her soaking wet bonnet, cape, apron, and dress. Naked except for her tall moccasins, she draped the clothes over a nearby scrub bush to dry in the heat from the fire. Turning back to the warming flames, she stood as close as she could to dry off and to get warm.

"How tempting you are," Ingor said with a smile as he walked up with another armload of wood for the fire that was finally burning. He dropped it in the pile he'd made and reached under the leather covering to unbuttoned his shirt. "But you'd better put this on so you don't catch a fever from the cold."

Her hands shook so badly that he had to button the shirt for her. It hung down to her thighs and afforded her a little warmth but not much. He tugged her close to kiss her when he had finished.

"It is shame to cover one so beautiful," a deep voice said from behind him.

Ingor reached for his revolver, but before he could aim it, two Indians grabbed him and pulled him away from Still Water. His revolver that he'd barely gotten free from his hip holster sailed into the bushes. Two other braves yanked Still Water's arms back and pulled her to the far side of the fire.

He should have been watching his captors that dragged him back instead of her. He might have tightened his stomach muscles to lessen the blow when one sent his fist into his gut. He doubled over, though his upper arms were held high behind him. A brave jerked his hat off and tossed it beyond the tree.

Ingor could only see that it had landed with the crown up so the white paper inside was not visible. He saw no more before a brave jerked his hair up and hit him squarely on the nose. The pain shot throughout his head, and he tasted blood as it ran down his throat and into his moustache and beard.

Whooping with the fun of beating him, two others kicked at him, but with his feet free, Ingor bent a knee up and twisted away from them. Their kicks missed his groin where they had been aimed and hit his thighs.

"Stop them. Stop it!" Still Water screamed in Sioux as she struggled to be free to come to his aid. "Do not hurt my husband."

With a grunt from somewhere, the men stopped. Ingor looked up to see Tall Cloud seated on his horse, smiling down, but it wasn't an expression of happiness. He was looking at Still Water with an evil smile that said he had plans to get even with her, too.

He slid to the ground and walked past the fire to face her. He grabbed the front of Ingor's shirt that she wore and hauled her up until her face was inches from his.

"Whore!" he shouted in Sioux. "You don't tell me what to do. You struggle to be free to run back to your white bastard. When we finish with him, he will not have any skin left on his body. I will tear a piece off for every time he has touched you. Then you will not want him."

He shoved her away, but the braves holding her arms held her up so she didn't fall.

"Is this the Sioux way to treat your chief's daughter's husband? I must struggle to be free of my brothers who do not know the proper way to treat their sister."

"You should be *my* wife," Tall Cloud shouted louder, his face turning darker. "And now you are this white man's whore."

"I am no man's whore. I am his wife. You saw that Red Moon married us in front of our people before he left for Canada."

"Yes, and I told him he was a fool. He said it was what he wished for his niece, but it was not what I wished. I never should have waited so many years for you. I should have taken you the first year your body grew ripe. Then he would have to give you to me."

He took a rope from his saddle and tossed it to the men holding Ingor. "Tie him to that tree. We will see what kind of a man Still Water has wed," he said, still speaking in Sioux.

Ingor had understood most of it, enough to make his blood run cold. If he had any chance to survive and rescue Still Water, it was not going to be tied to a tree. "You need all these braves and a rope to hold me, Tall Cloud?" he asked insolently.

One of the braves whipped out a long bladed knife and held the blade to his throat. He said something that sounded threatening, and Ingor didn't dare move his head. "If you have dispute with me, Tall Cloud, then we settle it man to man," Ingor shouted in English with much more strength than he felt. "Do not tell these boys to do it for you."

"Well, the yellow hair thinks he is man enough to fight Tall Cloud," the brave said more slowly so Ingor got every word.

"You let my wife go and promise to leave her alone. Then I will fight you. You argue with me, not her," Ingor shouted. With his movement talking, he felt the knife, held rock steady by the brave, cut into his neck under his chin. His warm blood trickled downward.

"You not tell me what to do," Tall Cloud yelled. "I kill you one inch at a time and then you tell no one what to do." He motioned the brave with the knife to step back.

"I kill him. Then his yellow hair is mine," the brave wielding the knife insisted with a laugh.

"Then we go kill other white men," another brave shouted excitedly.

"We kill all the white men west of the Red River," yet another chimed in with a wide wave of his arm. "And their women and children, too. Then we have many scalps to count and no one is left to steal our land."

"No, no, you can't," Still Water called. "Let my husband go. Please! You can't do this."

"No one tells me what to do. I decide!" Tall Cloud shouted, pounding a fist on his chest.

Ingor knew Tall Cloud was angry beyond reason, and there was nothing he could do to make him see reason. The braves had tied him tightly to the tree with his hands still tied behind his back. He pulled at the rope around his wrists and rubbed it on the rough bark, trying to slip his hand out of the loops. As he moved, the bark dug into his skin.

"You will not touch him, Tall Cloud," Still Water shouted. "My uncle is the Chief Red Moon, and it will not go well with you if you kill his niece's husband."

Tall Cloud spat on the ground. "Red Moon is old. He takes his people and runs from the Blue Coats. He should stand and fight like Tall Cloud."

"Stand and be killed, you mean. The great white father send more white soldiers every new moon. My uncle says that the Great War in the East is ended. Now soldiers all come west to fight the Indian. Soon there will be more white men in the territory than quills on a porcupine's back."

"Tall Cloud fight them all. I would rather die than live where white man send me."

Ingor wished there was something, anything that he could do. But he could only watch Still Water gather her strength and stand up as straight and proud as she could with the two men holding her arms.

"Tall Cloud, I thought once that you were an honorable man, but I can see I was wrong. I have seen you cheat and pick on your weaker brothers to win in contests. Now you do a greater dishonor. You dishonor your chief's niece by your treatment of her and killing her husband, the father of her unborn child."

She paused a moment to let that sink in and felt the grips of the braves that held her soften a bit.

"Do you and your braves remember nothing of honor among The People? Mother Earth will not look kindly on you when the time comes and your life's blood is shed. She will know that you dishonored me and my husband. And my child will know. I will teach him to speak of the dishonor that Tall Cloud had for us. It will not go well with you then. Your memory will be as the wind and The People will not speak of you any more. There will be no songs to herald your bravery.

The men will only sing of the coward who harmed his sister's husband." She stopped her tirade and stood erect, panting, staring at Tall Cloud.

Ingor was trying hard to translate the rapid Sioux. He thought it was something about being Mother Earth's child and Tall Cloud being dishonored with no songs. The Indian didn't like the idea of traveling into the afterlife without all the glories afforded a brave Sioux warrior who had counted coup many times. No Indian wanted to die without being remembered. There was more he couldn't translate, but whatever she'd said, he could tell Still Water had hit home. He saw a look on Tall Cloud's face that gave Ingor hope that he might see another sunrise.

"To horse," he ordered his men. The men who held Still Water dropped her and she fell to the ground. They scrambled to mount their ponies and stood in a circle around the camp, awaiting Tall Cloud's next order.

With great dignity, Still Water stood and pulled the shirt closed to cover her nakedness. Without speaking, she looked up at Tall Cloud, her face and stance a perfect picture of defiance.

After staring at Still Water for several seconds, Tall Cloud spit at her. "I will shun you, and I will not give you or your child the power to deny me a warrior's rewards now or when I join Mother Earth. My name will be great and remembered for many kills." He jerked his reins over his mount's neck and the whole band disappeared into the trees in seconds.

Even as the sounds of their hooves were swallowed by the winds from the west, Still Water ran to Ingor and untied him. He slumped into her arms, and they stood clinging to each other.

"I thought they would kill you," she said, tears wetting her cheeks. "I couldn't let him kill you."

"I hate to think what would have happened if you had not saved us. A man must protect his wife, but I could not."

"Together, we save each other." Wiping away her tears with the sleeve of his shirt that she wore, she helped him nearer the fire where he could lie on his blanket.

Bent over and clutching his stomach, he hated feeling helpless. He hated more knowing now that he could never have fought Tall Cloud. The beating he had taken already made him too weak. He could hardly stand. He had almost lost her and there had been nothing he could have done to stop them. It made him realize all the more how vulnerable they were in the wilderness that was the Dakota Territory. And it made him realize how lucky he was to have such a wife—a wife that had saved his life now more than once.

"My hat," he said suddenly. "They knock it off my head." He was relieved when Still Water quickly found it and returned it to him. "We not want to lose this." He tried to raise his hands to put it on his head, but grunted with the pain in his midsection.

She took the hat and looked inside. "The paper still there," she told him as she placed it squarely on his head.

When she lowered her arms, he said, "No. Tighter.

It must be tight."

She pulled on the hat until he approved of the tightness. She was doing so much, but he had to do more. Pay more attention to their surroundings. Don't camp without looking around the area first for signs of others. Listen to what is happening around you. Be alert. Whatever rule for safer living he came up with, he could come up with an exception he'd made tonight.

He'd built the big fire to warm Still Water and to dry their clothes quickly after her fall into the cold water. But the fire had been an invitation to anyone within miles to come see them and what they were doing. He hadn't taken time to look around, nor had he listened because he'd concentrated on getting her warm before she took sick.

And he'd failed her. He hadn't protected her. She had been the one who saved his life—again. He curled on his side and brought up his knees, hoping to make his stomach feel better.

"I'm sorry," he said once he was settled. "I wasn't as careful as I should have been, but what you said saved us."

Without looking at him, she asked, "Did you understand what I said to him?"

"You were talking fast and with his yelling at you that way…" He shook his head. "No, I didn't get it all."

She smiled. "That's all right. They're gone. You don't have to worry now. If The People want to find me, they will find me. No matter what we do. But Tall Cloud gone now. He does not live in the ways of Red Moon. He will always be riding outside the tribe."

"I hope he is gone for good. I not want to lose you, Still Water."

She smiled. "Me too," she said as she dug out her leather clothes and got dressed so Ingor could have his shirt back. He could hardly straighten and raise his arms to put them into the sleeves. As she buttoned it for him, he folded his arms back over his stomach and asked for her help in taking off his belt to make him more comfortable.

Drawing her lower lip into her mouth, she bit on it and worried that the punches and kicks he'd taken had done more damage than could be seen on the outside.

Had she been able to stop the beating in time? Or had irreparable damage already been done?

Chapter 18

Still Water slept little that night. She pressed a folded cloth under Ingor's injured nose until the blood stopped flowing. Then she'd cleaned the blood from his face and beard. His nose swelled quickly and she couldn't tell if it was broken or not, but suspected it was. He had to breathe through his mouth. She knew the braves knew exactly how to hit a man to hurt him the most. Ingor was lucky he had been quick enough to deflect some of their blows.

As he slept, his legs relaxed and she took another look at his stomach. The corner of his fancy, flat metal buckle had cut the flesh, but softened many of the blows. No wonder he'd wanted it taken off. The skin beneath it was turning dark. Other bruises were darkening on his upper thighs where the kicks had barely missed his manhood.

She hated that braves from her own tribe had harmed her husband. She didn't want her husband hurt, and she didn't want the braves to act so dishonorably. Indians made war on their enemies, and they hated the white man for pushing them out of their own land. But her own tribal brothers had no right to fight with her and Ingor. She could not like them for what they had done. She saw how easily a white person could hate Indians when their own had been hurt or killed. But she had never harmed a white person. Could she expect to be treated differently than those who had?

During the night, Ingor woke and wanted a drink. She held the canteen for him and knew what pain it was costing him to sit up enough to swallow. He insisted that she curl up with him under the blanket then. He curled one arm around her. Only then was she able to get a little sleep.

By the next morning, more dark bruises had surfaced on his stomach, back, thighs, and hips like purple and red war paint. Both his eyes were surrounded with deep color and his jaw could be seen to be dark even through his beard. His nose looked fairly straight, but a swollen ridge had grown across it, and he still couldn't breathe through it.

She laid her hand on his forehead and thankfully could feel no rise in his temperature. That was the best sign yet that nothing was terribly wrong inside where she couldn't see it.

Her clothes were dry by then, so she dressed again like a white woman though she left on her leggings and would have preferred to be dressed all in leather. Her thick cape, dripping wet the night before, was still damp. She turned out the other side to the warmth of the fire, in hopes of driving out the remaining dampness. Until then she would wear her leather tunic for warmth.

She went back to the river to hunt for leeches to draw

out the pooled blood under Ingor's skin, but the water yielded none. It was too muddy to see them. The bruises would have to run their natural course.

"I'm hungry," he said when she returned to the fire circle.

"That's a good sign," she said with a smile.

Using the fry pan they'd bought in Winnipeg, she boiled some jerky in water to make a hot broth for him. She didn't know if his stomach should hold solid food yet, and felt they should test it slowly as he had for her.

When he insisted he was still hungry when that was gone, she fried two of their potatoes in the pan. They each ate some and Ingor quickly fell back asleep.

She could tell that they would do no traveling today. She set some jerky in water to soften over the fire. Retracing her path to the river, she gathered some wild onions and parsley and cut them up into the pan along with potatoes, carrots, and the softened jerky. She added water as it cooked and stirred it occasionally. She didn't want it to go dry or burn. They couldn't afford to waste any food.

Ingor ate a little when he woke and slept again that afternoon. She was worried about him and kept watch at his side. Later that evening, when Ingor awoke after sunset, she served him some of the jerky stew. He ate it right down, and she felt good that his appetite was getting better. That had to be a good sign.

She reached to take the tin plate from him, but he didn't release it. She had rolled up her sleeves while working and he saw the dark bruises on her arms where the braves had held her as she struggled to be free.

"They hurt you. Are there other bruises too?"

She shook her head. "Not where you could see it. They hurt me in here," she said tapping her chest over her heart.

He set the plate down and took her hand in his. "Tall Cloud not bother us again."

She sighed. "I don't think so, but he will make big trouble for all other white men wherever he can. He's had much hate in his heart for a long time. He was always picking on his tribal brothers as a child. Now he has changed his target to the white man. I fear for what he might do now to take out the anger for us that he swallowed."

"I very glad you say no to him all those years when he want you."

She smiled. "I am too. And I am thankful that my wise uncle did not press me to be Tall Cloud's woman." She leaned over to kiss him lightly and then picked up the plate to clean it at the water's edge.

"It's going to rain tonight," she said, returning to the camp. "This afternoon, I started to build a shelter." She pointed to the branches she had gathered to make a lean-to roof on the north side of the fire that they could both lie under.

"Good. I should help. It's getting cold fast."

She pressed her lips between her teeth to keep from saying he should stay on the blanket. "You are feeling better?" she asked as she helped him up.

"Yes, thanks to you. I hurt all over, but I can do this."

Bent over and limping, Ingor moved to sit on a thick log the other side of the fire. He cut the small leafy branches the right length with his knife from the branches Still Water had set in a pile. She laid them over a slender tree trunk she'd propped up on two Y-shaped branches stuck in the ground. Every few branches she pulled loose a strip of bark from a young branch and used it to tie them to the support trunk. Creating the open side toward the fire to catch the heat, they laid the branches on the far side until they were thick enough to give them the maximum protection from the weather.

"Have you ever been east of Red River?" he asked as they worked.

"No," she said. "My people move north and south and sometimes west, but not east. We have all we need here."

"In Minnesota to the east, there are many pines. They grow straight and tall toward heaven. Their branches make better protection than these from the rain and snow, but few grow here on the open prairie."

He waited while she tied the last few branches to the trunk and then handed her another one.

"There are many lakes there and land not so flat. It is pretty country."

"I would like to see this Minnesota some day. Do you ever go there to set your traps?"

"No, but we go there to get more logs if we want to build a cabin like one I had."

She nodded. "My people send young men to cut the poles

for their teepees there, but women not go with them. Other times, they cut them in Canada. But the poles last many years, so we don't need to go often."

Once their shelter was judged thick enough to stop the rain, they put the saddlebags topped with their fur wraps at one end to use as pillows, and spread out their blankets. They piled some of the firewood at the other end to break the wind and to keep the wood dry for during the night and in the morning.

An icy rain began to fall as Still Water was adding more large logs to the fire, and Ingor was checking that the horses were tied securely. They ducked into the lean-to and sat facing the fire. She drew a blanket around their shoulders and leaned against him, his arm around her waist.

"If this keeps up, I know a trapper who live farther to the west and close to the border. It out of our way, but we could go there until it lets up. He is closer than burned cabin."

Still Water looked up and smiled. "We can wait and see if it keeps raining."

He nodded. With his tangled beard covering his face, his hat on, his eyes blackened, and his nose swollen, he didn't look like Ingor.

"How is your nose?"

"It not work and hurt if I touch it." He leaned down to kiss her and knocked his nose on her cheek. "Ouch," he said, ending the kiss and gingerly pressing on his nose.

"No kissing until it better," she guessed.

"But there's other things we could do." He reached over

to cup her breast in his hand but squeezed it harder than he intended when a pain shot up his side. He grunted and straightened.

"You wait until feel better," she said, and then laughed at his complaining groan.

"I hate to say it, but I think you're right."

They curled up together, facing the flames. The fire sizzled as the rain hit, but the flames kept going. Physically and emotionally spent, they soon fell asleep.

Twice during the night, Still Water slipped out of the lean-to and added some of the dry wood to the fire. It sparked and caught as she ran and climbed back under the shelter. She was glad she had put her leather leggings on under her dress. They and her leather tunic over the dress kept her much warmer than without them.

By morning the rain had stopped, but the air was cold enough to see their breath clearly as they spoke. Frost had frozen on the ground overnight.

"Winter come quick," Ingor said as he ate the wheat pancakes and bacon Still Water had fried in the new pan.

Not having a big enough pan for it all, she'd fried his first and then her own after she'd served him. By the time hers was ready to eat, Ingor had managed to saddle the horses, with her help lifting them, and was ready to leave. He spread the burning embers and kicked dirt on the remaining fire while Still Water placed her bacon between wheat cakes and stuck them in her apron pocket. She would eat as they rode so that she didn't delay their departure.

Though it had gotten very dirty, she was discovering that an apron was very handy. They had enjoyed the biscuits from the restaurant that she'd hidden in the pocket, and now she could carry her breakfast until she could eat it. When she lifted the hem, she could carry wood to the fire or wild greens to wash in the river. She had to admit, though, she didn't think she could get it as white or as smooth as when Lissa had given it to her.

The cooking pan and plates stored, she rolled up the bedrolls and tied them in place. This morning she helped Ingor onto Thor before he had a chance to object. She could see the pain that he still felt etched on his face as he moved. Managing to pull his hat down good and fasten the leather tie below his chin so no wind could fly away with it and the Certificate of Marriage, he leaned on the pommel. It took him a full minute to get over the pains that shot through him at that exertion.

"What is it? What's wrong?" she asked.

"I not sure. Maybe have cracked rib to remind me of run-in with Tall Cloud. Maybe just hurt from blows." He smiled. "Instead of feeling bad about pain, I feel good about coming away from fight still alive."

"I try not to squeeze you too hard," she offered. "But I ride behind you and hold you."

"You think I sleep more on Thor's back?"

"You should not do too much." She smiled as she wrapped her cape around her shoulders. "And you block the wind and keep me warm."

Liking that she wanted to care for him, he took his foot

out of the left stirrup, and she mounted with a little help from tugging on the back of the saddle.

"I not want to pull on you," she explained when he reached a hand out to help.

Relinquishing the stirrup to him again, she settled as comfortably as she could behind him and tugged her skirt down. It didn't move far and she left it. Her leggings covered her legs to her high moccasins and would keep her warm and modest. She liked her soft leather garments and felt more like herself dressed in them even with the dress layered in there.

He smiled and gently patted her arm that was resting on the side of his waist. She didn't wrap them around to his stomach where all the bruising was.

As they made the way west with Thor at a smooth walk and the packhorse not far beside them, she finally broke her fast.

* * * *

Ingor and Still Water rode steadily, but the sky was dark and cloudy with another coming storm. It was difficult to be certain of their exact direction without the sun. To make matters worse, it began to snow. They stopped long enough to unpack the leather ponchos that he'd made and slip them over their heads on top of their coats as they rode. The hides would protect from the wet much better than the coat and cape.

"You warm enough?" he asked.

"Yes. I learn a second thing this silly hat is good for."

"What's that?"

"It keeps off the sun and now it keeps the wind and snow off my cheeks."

Ingor breathed a sigh of relief when he finally recognized some landmarks. Using these, he knew that the snow was coming on a northwest wind. The wind gave him a good sense of direction. He just hoped the snow wouldn't come down any harder. It was very easy to get lost in a heavy blizzard when seeing landmarks was impossible. At least they shouldn't have to worry about extremely low temperatures this early in the winter. He hoped the early snow was no more than an annoyance they would try to avoid.

"We not far from trapper's place. I meet him at the fort last year. I come by here one time, but I not find him home so I go on. Cabin not much and he not very friendly at fort, but I think we stop."

"I hope the snow will stop by morning."

"Yes, but we'll be warm and dry until it does," Ingor said. "His soddy not too far."

They rode another hour in the miserable weather before he caught a good sign. "I smell smoke," he said. "That must be trapper's cabin. No one else live out here."

Built into the side of a hill on a tree line near a stream they forded to get to it, the soddy was half the size that Ingor's cabin had been. The back was cut into the hill, but the sides and front were rough-hewn planks over base layers of sod bricks. Light was visible between the horizontal planks and he knew that if light could get out, wind could get in. Not finished, or not well made, he wondered.

"Hello in the cabin," he shouted.

In seconds the door flew open and a skinny man stepped out, holding a rifle trained on the riders. "That's fer enough," he shouted.

Ingor pulled up on the reins. "No need to fear us, Archer." He used the only name he'd ever heard for the trapper. He didn't know if it was his first name or last. Everyone at the fort just referred to him as Archer. "I'm Ingor Oleson and this my wife. Can you give us shelter for the night? We get cold in snow."

"Ride over here so's I can get a good look attcha."

Ingor clucked at Thor and he walked toward the front door. With no front porch, the man was standing in his shirt-sleeves on the path in front of his cabin and getting snowed on.

"Take your hat off, mister. Let me get a look attcha," the settler ordered Ingor.

Ingor removed his hat and held it against his chest so the snow wouldn't blow inside and get the Certificate wet. "I see you a year ago at the fort. You said you were just starting the cabin back then."

"Yup, I reckon I remember you with all that yeller hair." He stepped to the side, looking at Still Water. "What's the matter with your wife? She deaf?"

"No, she not deaf," Ingor assured him, not knowing why he asked.

"Well, why she ain't taken off her hat? I said to take off your hats so's I could get a good look."

"A lady don't take her hat off just 'cause you're wielding a rifle."

The man stepped closer and grabbed the front of Still Water's hat, jerking it back off her head. The ties instantly tightened around her neck and snapped her head back. The hat caught her pinned up braid roll and painfully ripped the pins from her hair. Her long black braid fell down her back.

"She ain't no wife. She's a dirty Indian squaw," the man yelled as he dropped a shell into the chamber of the rifle.

"She's my married wife, mister, and I won't have you talking about her that way."

"Git! Go on, get out of here," the man shouted, the gun aimed at Still Water. "You want to live with a dirty red pig and call her your wife, that's up to you. But you ain't welcome here, not now, not ever."

Ingor felt her grip tighten at his waist. He knew that there was no talking back to a loaded gun, but he would remember this treatment. As he tugged the reins over Thor's neck to leave, he saw the settler's gaunt wife appear in the doorway. She looked as unkempt as he did and though the light from their fire inside was low, he could easily make out the bruises on her face. Indians weren't the only ones who had suffered the brunt of his unreasonable anger.

Before moving out here and building the cabin, Ingor had heard that Archer stayed a time at the fort. Coming out to the Dakota Territory, they had run into renegades who had attacked their wagon. Their young son had wanted to help to protect them in the attack and had taken his father's pistol while his mother was busy loading the one long gun while Archer shot the other.

Instead of staying in the wagon as his father had ordered him to do, the young boy tucked the pistol into the front of his belt and climbed down the back to help. His knees bent and ready to jump from the wheel, the trigger caught on his belt. The pistol went off, shooting him in the upper thigh, splitting the artery. He fell to the ground just as the Indians had decided the little food they might have wasn't worth all the gunfire. Helping their wounded, they road off. But by the time Archer and his wife got to their son to tend his wound, he had bled to death.

Ingor couldn't imagine the pain of losing a son. The boy shooting himself while trying to help shoot renegades had made Archer hate all Indians just as Tall Cloud hated all white men. So much hate.

"You all right?" Ingor asked after they were out of earshot of the cabin.

"Yes," she said softly.

"I'm sorry, Still Water."

"No, my husband, you cannot be sorry for every white man that hates Indians."

Ingor sighed and nodded, but he still felt inadequate again at not being able to protect his wife.

"I think he get over it, but do you want to know why he hate them?"

"Tell me."

As they rode toward his cabin site again, he told her the

story as he learned it at the fort. He kept the horses moving at a steady gate. He would get them home as soon as possible.

Still Water loosened the ties on her bonnet pulled tight by the man's violence and rubbed her sore neck. She twisted her braid up and started to replace the bonnet over it but paused. As she released the braid, it fell down her back, the familiar weight comforting to her as she retied the bonnet over it with shaking hands while she listened to his story.

"We'll just have to lie that much closer together tonight to keep warm," Ingor noted after a long silence followed his story.

"That's good. We will keep warm. You will see."

She sounded like she was trying to be cheerful, but he could hear the catch in her voice.

* * * *

The next morning after bedding down under the protective low branches of a huge tree, Ingor wanted to do something for Still Water to make up for the rude treatment she'd gotten at the trapper's house. Sure there were bad Indians. Tall Cloud and his friends would be at the top of the list in his book. But he couldn't hate all Indians because of them. That trapper who had chased them away at gunpoint seemed to be unable to see beyond the loss of his son and he blamed all Indians for the disobedient actions of his son. There were many whites who wanted the Indians out of the area or at least forced to live on reservations. But the Indians didn't want to leave their land. The situation couldn't help but lead to more hatred and more trouble.

Living in the midst of it with an Indian wife wouldn't be easy. It wouldn't be easy for her either. During the night, each time the pain of his bruises woke him when he moved, she was awake. He didn't think she had been able to get much sleep at all after hearing the story he told.

There were a good four inches of snow on everything when they rose. He brushed off the horses and shook out their blankets before he smoothed them over their backs again. He fed them a good measure of oats. The sack was nearly empty so he could use it for feeding instead of his hat. The horses would need the extra measure for energy and warmth today. He'd have to make certain their camp that night had grazing grass to supplement their feed.

Surprised that Still Water hadn't stirred yet despite not sleeping well, he set about as quietly as possible to fix their breakfast. Normally, she'd done all the cooking while he cared for the horses each time they stopped. But he'd been cooking for himself for over a year, so working past how stiff he felt, it was no trouble to throw a little sliced bacon in the pan. He inhaled the smoky aroma and was started when Still Water suddenly leapt up and ran into the woods without a word. Moments later, he could hear her retching.

When she came back, she looked pale. She clutched her stomach as she curled up again under the blanket. Worried she was ill or had eaten something bad for her, he rose and went to her.

"What wrong? Did you eat some bad jerky?"

She groaned and shook her head. "Don't speak of food to me."

"Don't you want something to eat before we start out? Maybe that would make your stomach feel better. We not have much for supper last night."

She shook her head again. "You eat now. I eat later when stomach feel better." She smiled at him and he had to take her word for it that she was doing the right thing by not eating now.

"If you want anything, you ask me." She nodded and rolled over with her back to the fire.

Not knowing what else to do for her, Ingor cut up a potato into the bacon fat and a carrot that happened to be within reach in the sack. While they cooked, he packed up the rest of the food in the saddlebags. The only good about seeing how much less food they had was the fact that the bags were lighter for the horse to carry.

Getting a winter storm this early was the last thing he needed. He'd have to count on the heat from the horses to keep their food from freezing if the temperature fell any more.

As he ate, he looked at Still Water. He'd never known her to stay in bed after waking, except for the mornings they made love, that is, when they both stayed there together. She was always quick to rise and get started on the work to be done before they could eat and move on. He hoped she wasn't getting seriously ill. He didn't know what he should do for her then. Fixing up wounds and watching for a fever was one thing. Knowing what to do if someone was sick from something on the inside was another.

She was asleep, if her even breathing was a true judge, when he'd cleaned up the pan in snow and packed away the last of their things. He had only Still Water's bedroll left to tie on the horse and they would be ready to ride out.

Because of the cabin fire, he had only the clothes on his back with him. Still Water had the dress and apron plus her leather outfit. Yesterday, she had put on the slit-front tunic like a jacket, and worn it day and night over her dress to keep her warmer. The new cape, which she clutched around her on top of that, was close to useless without sleeves. If she loosened her grip, the wind would take it and the tie would choke her as it blew out like a sail.

Wearing the same outfits for the whole trip meant their clothes were all dirty and wrinkled. He smiled thinking of his late mother back in Norway. She would be embarrassed to see her son dress so poorly. Clothes didn't need to be fancy for her, but they needed to be clean. He wondered if she would understand there was no way to keep them clean on the trail.

"We'll clean them when we have something else to change into," he murmured.

Still Water rolled over and opened her eyes. "What did you say?"

He grinned and squatted at her side. "Nothing. How do you feel?"

"Better." She looked around and saw the horses saddled and packed, patiently waiting to leave. She sat up and pushed off the quilt. "I will be ready quick," she said, rising to go into the woods to answer nature's call.

"Here. Put this on your shoulders. It cold this morning." He helped her by swinging her cape around her and tying it under her chin. Grasping her shoulders, he kissed her lightly. "You're sure you want to travel now?"

"Yes. I feel much better already."

Ingor let her go and was glad he didn't hear her get sick in the woods this time. When she returned, he was seated in Thor's saddle. As she walked toward him, he slipped way to the back of the saddle. He had folded her bedroll and laid it over the front of the saddle and the pommel like a pillow.

"You ride here where I can hold you today," he said. "Step in the stirrup and I lift you up."

With his hand to steady her, she stepped on a log and then into the stirrup. From there he swung her up to sit sideways in front of him. Once she was settled with the cape doubled over in front of her, he wrapped his arms around her and picked up the reins he had left crossed over Thor's neck.

"Can you ride that way?" he asked.

"I think the blanket will slide off the saddle and me with it," she admitted. "I have nothing to hold onto but Thor's mane."

Ingor chuckled. "You not fall with me holding you."

Just to be certain though, he tucked her tight against him. The front of her bonnet poked him in the face. She remedied the situation by folding the fabric back. Her face was exposed more, but the hat was out of his way.

"This is warmer too. You break the wind for me," he added with a laugh.

Thinking of the patient way she had worn the white woman's clothes to try to make their way easier, he asked, "Want to take the hat off?"

She thought a moment and shrugged as she shook her head. Looking up at him with a grin, she said, "It keeps my ears warmer." They shared a laugh.

A touch of his heels and Thor headed for home. When they broke out of the trees where they had camped, the sun was shining brightly and had begun to melt the snow.

Ingor could only hope again that this had been an unusually early snow. There had to be weeks yet before the cold weather of winter set in. He needed that much time, and more, to build onto the barn or to build a cabin. They needed some place safe to stay until spring.

Chapter 19

Still Water felt better as the day progressed, as she knew she would. She hated to see the worried frown on Ingor's face each time she looked at him. She would have to tell him tonight that he had nothing to worry about. She was pregnant, not ill.

Very excited about the prospect of having a baby, she was thankful that the women in Red Moon's band had been very forthcoming with all their knowledge about the process. She knew what to expect during her pregnancy, and what to do when her time came early next summer.

Being Ingor's wife, she had it a lot easier than it was for her friends, married or unmarried, still traveling with Red Moon. They had no release from all their work during their pregnancy. Their husbands did not help with cooking or making bedding smooth as Ingor had as they traveled.

Because the women's time of the month didn't come any more while they were pregnant, they didn't even get the few days off each month to stay with the other women also having that time of the month. It was bad medicine to be with a man during those days, so the women were restricted to their own lodge on the edge of camp away from the men. Still Water remembered it was a good rest and a very educational time.

Spending time in that lodge had taught her all the details she needed to know about men and about babies now. The pains would come and tell her when it was time. If she were with the People, there would be herb teas to drink to help. She had none of those with her but knew they had to be picked fresh and dried by the fire. If they found Red Moon next spring when they took the furs to Winnipeg, she could get some from them then, she realized. That made her feel better because the tea might be important to drink.

When the baby came, she knew to tie the cord two times with a strip of leather and then cut it free between the two, or bite it off if she didn't have a knife close by.

Where would she be? Would she have a knife? Who would help her if the birthing took a long time, and she was too weak to do it alone as sometimes happened? That was no job for a man. She heard Lissa say that a woman had come from the fort to help her when her baby was due.

She sighed and leaned against Ingor's chest more heavily. She was an Indian. Would anyone come from the fort to help her? Not likely. She thought they wouldn't want to help birth a half-breed. She would be on her own for the birth. Realizing that, the prospect of the potential danger to her baby and to herself frightened her. Her heart sped up even as she thought of it. She didn't want anything bad to happen to her baby. She tightened her arms around her waist. The child was the most precious gift that Ingor had given her. She couldn't let anything happen to him.

"Snow's starting again," Ingor said, bringing her out of her reverie. He pulled the deer hide covers from under the rope on the packhorse and they pulled them on over their heads. They wanted to keep as dry as possible for as long as possible. They would stay much warmer that way.

"It is not time yet for snow. It should stop," she said.

"Tell that to clouds that make sky all gray," he replied with a laugh.

"Sometimes the sky wants to fool us with a taste of snow before the winter is here."

"I hope that is it. I not want to think that winter this soon."

Wanting to get home and out of the snow, they only stopped to rest the horses. They ate their noon meal of jerky and raw potatoes on horseback as they rode. Still the snow didn't let up. The flakes were large and stuck to everything, even them and the horses as they moved.

"We not making very good time. I hope we be home by now, but I know place where deadfall pile up in spring floods of the river ahead. I pulled out some of the logs and made shelter last winter when storm caught me. If we stay there tonight, we only have half-day's ride to cabin tomorrow. Maybe the snow be gone by then."

Still Water nodded. "Even sleeping in barn will be warmer than out on the prairie."

"And the horses will be out of the snow."

They had been on horseback for more days than she could remember to count. She would welcome stopping early today and having only a few hours' ride in the morning.

"There it is," Ingor announced.

Looking along the river, she couldn't help but laugh when they saw the pile of deadfall on the opposite bank of a creek. "It looks like a big beaver dam," she replied, making him laugh too.

"Tonight we will be beavers."

She slipped her hand out of the cape and fluffed his beard to knock off the snow. "You already look like a snowy beaver," she said, still grinning.

"I have never seen a beaver this color," he insisted. "Such a pelt would be rare and worth much." The uneasy thought of how close he had come to possibly losing his pale scalp sent a shiver down his back.

They crossed the small stream easily to reach it. The packhorse didn't even object to walking in water this time when it was much shallower. She seemed to want to get past the water because she would be that much closer to home, too.

The snow on top of the pile of branches acted like a thick white roof. The grayed branches and trunks from the trees piled there were so tightly knotted together that no snow reached the ground in the cave-like opening Ingor had cleared the year before.

"This is good," she told him. "My own tribal brothers

could not build a better shelter. Maybe there is Indian blood flowing in your veins too." She laughed and shook her head. "No, not with that yellow hair." After all they had gone through, it felt very good to laugh.

After tying up the horses and removing their packs and saddles, Still Water tied on the horse's blankets to keep the animals warmer. She wished there was a way to dry them from the sweat of the day's ride, but the snow would soon make them wet again. Ingor gave them the last of the grain and treated each to one of their carrots.

While Still Water took on the task of starting the fire and getting supper, Ingor pulled out the loose branches and debris that had caught in the wooden cave floor during the last flood. He swept the dirt clear with one of the branches and broke the dry wood up and set it aside for their fire.

Still Water got a fire going and set their small pan filled with snow by the flames to melt. She added more snow as it turned to water until the pan was nearly filled with simmering water. She added a few cut-up strips of venison jerky. As that softened and boiled down, she spread out the bedroll they would share. By the time the jerky had softened, she added a few chopped carrots and the one wild onion left that she had tucked in the food bag. Two potatoes were nearly baked in the ground under the coals.

Meanwhile, Ingor had added to the wall to protect them from the wind by dragging deadfall into a long pile at the end of their beaver dam to the northwest of their fire. An added benefit was that the flames quickly calmed when the wind could no longer reach them directly.

"I think you still have some pain when you bend over to pick up the wood," she said softly.

"You are seeing what I am trying to forget," he told her.

"But it is no worse?"

He shook his head and that made Still Water feel better. However, where it took effort for him to stand up straight, she knew the long day on horseback had been hard on him.

"I'm glad you remembered this place to camp," she said to take his mind off his pains.

"It's good except when the river floods, but I not think there's enough snow to make that happen overnight."

The year before Ingor had set a wide but short log nearer the fire and now they could sit on it to eat, too. She watched as he sat down and stretched his legs out. The old wound in his leg ached too much to squat the way she could, she had noticed. The new aches were only making moving harder for him. She wished she had some of the tea she had given him when she cared for him to relieve his pain.

When the potatoes were done, they each took a tin plate and smashed the roasted potato over the bottom. Still Water used their new large spool to ladle on the liquid with the carrots and pieces of softened jerky.

"A meal fit for the King of Norway," he joked.

"What is King of Norway?"

"He is Chief in country where I live as boy. Norway is across big ocean of water that took my ship more than a whole moon to cross."

"I cannot imagine a water that is so big. Do you miss Norway?"

He chewed his mouthful and thought a minute. "I miss my family—my brothers, my uncle. 'I never see them again' was all I can think when I walk up the gangplank to ship that brought me over ocean."

She covered his hand with hers. "But now you have your brother Lars with you here."

Smiling, he looked at her. "And now I have you, my wife, to keep me company. I very happy about that."

Still Water almost told him then that he would have even more company, but she decided to wait a little longer.

Ingor was of the opinion that Still Water had been very worried much of the day. Perhaps it was just that she didn't feel well. As he added wood to the fire for the evening, he was glad to see her moving about the camp, doing the work that she usually did. He hoped that meant she no longer felt ill as she had that morning.

The bad treatment they had gotten from the trapper must have bothered her a great deal. Ingor couldn't begin to imagine what it felt like to be refused safe refuge by a family just because you were born an Indian. He wished he could make it up to her, and would do anything for her, but what could he do?

"I hope the bad things the trapper say last night not make you upset and not well this day," Ingor said.

She shook her head. "I think there will be more men like him who do not want me near. To have a child die is a hard thing."

He nodded. "But if Army not want you here, they can't take you away from me now," he said, tapping his hat. "But still, I think you right about other people."

"There is nothing I can do then. I cannot change who I am," she insisted.

"No, and I not ask you to. But we will meet people who not like Indians. Then we keep away from them. We can find a good life without them."

She smiled and nodded.

After the dishes were washed and packed away, and the campfire was built up, they climbed under the blankets and lay spoon-style as usual, facing the fire. Still Water was toying with the quilt over them, running her fingers around all the little squares that made up the colorful pattern. What was she thinking about?

"My mother made that for me in Norway," he offered. "She made one for each of her children to use in their own homes one day."

"She made many tiny stitches."

"You have needles and thread now. You will make stitches that small, too."

"I only know how to make hole with quill and push the thread or leather ribbon through."

"Lissa could show you how to sew on the white man's cloth—if you want to learn."

"Yes, that would be good. We will visit her?" she asked in a more excited voice.

He nodded. "After I fix up place for us to stay in the barn

that will be warm and dry, I must ride there to borrow their tools to build the cabin. Even if mine in fire are still good, I will have no handles. Even staying in the barn where the horses help keep us warm, there is much to do to shore up the walls against the cold. And…and we must have a place for a fire that we can cook on."

"I help too."

"Then you're feeling better?" He slid his hand to lie over her stomach.

She laid her hand over his and held it there. "In the morning my stomach feels upside down, but it go away by afternoon."

"Do you think you ate some bad jerky?"

She giggled and Ingor had to laugh. He couldn't remember ever hearing her giggle before. But then they hadn't had a lot to laugh about.

"Is bad jerky something funny?" he asked.

"No, it not the jerky." She turned to lie on her back and lifted her head to kiss him. "But I thank you for the worry you have for me."

"Then there is something wrong?" he asked, more alarmed.

She shook her head. "No, nothing is wrong. Only right."

"I don't understand. What you mean—everything right when you not feel good?" Ingor asked.

She pressed against his hand on her belly. With a smile she said, "I have baby inside here now. It turns my stomach upside down each morning."

"A baby?" he cried, jerking his hand back as if he'd been burned.

She looked startled. "Are you angry that baby comes when you did much to make him?"

"Angry? Well, no. It just that I not think about baby coming so soon. We have no cabin to live in. We lost food I stored in the root cellar. We...we don't even know if we have a coffeepot we can use."

She laughed. "Baby will not care. He doesn't like coffee so he will come anyway."

"When? When will he come?" Ingor asked eagerly.

"Early next summer, I think," she answered with a serene smile.

"A baby."

He laid his hand back on her stomach and kept it there for some time. She tried to move it to her breast, he thought as an invitation, but he didn't think they should make love now, not with the baby coming. He might do something that would hurt the child, and he wouldn't want to do that.

She eventually gave up trying to arouse him and they fell asleep.

In the morning he was the first to rise. He knew she didn't like to eat right away, so he packed everything up and saddled the horses. He would wait to eat also.

When she did get up, he slipped the cape and fur poncho over her and handed the bonnet to her.

"Don't want you to get cold," he told her.

She frowned, but stepped away from the campsite to get

ready to leave. The second she returned to camp, he took her hand and seated her on the log by the fire.

"You sit here. We almost ready to go. I just need few minutes more."

Seeing the blankets needed to be folded to fit over the saddle for her seat if she was to ride with him again, she rose. He took hold of her shoulders and gently pushed her back down to her seat.

"I'll do everything. You sit and rest."

"I just woke up from resting. I can work. I not sick," she insisted. "I didn't smell food this morning, so I didn't get my stomach upside down."

He ignored her explanation and took care of the blankets himself. Having uncovered the saddlebags they used as pillows, he tied them on the packhorse. When she rose to hand him a tin cup he'd left by the fire, he ran back to stop her.

"No, no. You sit. I do all work."

She made fists of her hands and planted them on her hips. "Why?" she said in a voice that sounded to him as if she were angry.

He frowned. "You not work. You having baby."

She groaned loudly and dropped her hands to her sides. "Do you know any other woman who has a baby?"

"Well, of course. I know my brother's wife Lissa. She had baby this spring. Cute boy but so tiny. I not remember that babies came in such small size."

"And did Lissa do any work before the baby comes?"

He grinned. "They had so much to do helping me. She

cooked and cleaned my cabin while Lars and Wally help me with trapline and tanning hides. Lissa sewed fur coats for them, too, like mine so they not be too cold," he replied easily with a smile, remembering their winter together.

"Ahhh," she said, dragging out the word. "So Lissa is allowed to work, but I am not."

Looking at her, he frowned suddenly and then looked away. She walked over to stand close to him.

"I not want you to overdo it," he explained.

She slid her hands around his waist. "You are a good man, my husband. That is why I love you. But I am not a piece of pottery. I not break."

"But the baby."

"The baby grows inside me. I know what is happening in my body and I am not worried. You don't need to worry. I take care of everything."

Wrapping his arms around her, he hugged her against him. "I am very lucky man."

"You *lucky*?" she asked incredulously. She leaned her head back so she could meet his gaze. "You nearly freeze to death; your leg catches in trap; two men try to kill us; your cabin burns to ground; and you forced to marry Indian. You get little for furs and the wife you not want now having your baby so you must build a home quick. Oh, yes. You are very lucky," she said, nodding and looking like she didn't believe it at all.

He laughed suddenly, so loudly that he startled her. "No, no. You think wrong. I *very* lucky. When I nearly freeze to death, a beautiful woman I now love saves me; I make friends with her uncle, the Chief of her people; my brother and his wife, who is a good healer, arrive just in time to save my leg. My cabin burned but fire saved us from the two men trying to kill us, so they no danger anymore. I got something for my furs, but the best reason for trip to Winnipeg was to have preacher marry you and me. We married and I have proof in my hat. Now I am very lucky man because my wife tell me she loves me; I am lucky most of all because we have made a baby."

He squeezed her and kissed her hard. "I very lucky to find you. I love you, Still Water, and I proud to be father of our child that you make grow." He kissed her again and it was several minutes before he straightened again.

"And last night? You didn't want to be with me," she reminded him softly.

"Oh, no. I wanted to make love with you with all my heart, but I not want to hurt baby now."

She grinned and shook her head. "We will not hurt baby that way. Baby will grow happy with loving parents."

"You mean it? We can..."

"Yes, my husband, we can. And I want to, very much."

Kissing her again, he quickly decided to postpone the start of their journey home.

If they had not postponed their start, they might have missed the trouble that was riding their way.

****

Ingor could not mistake the column of men in blue that

he saw coming toward them in the distance. Still Water was dozing in his arms so he woke her. When she saw them too, he heard her small gasp as her body tensed within arms on Thor's back.

He was certain the Army had seen them too. It made no sense to try to ride off toward the river to escape their scrutiny. It would mean they would have to hide the rest of their lives. He didn't want that.

Ingor thought of the Certificate of Marriage hidden in his hat. He had to trust that the preacher was right—that once he showed the certificate, no one could doubt they were married. Ingor would let no one take away his lawful wife. He kept Thor at a steady walk to where their paths would intersect.

But should he have believed what the preacher told them? Neither of them could read the words. If it didn't show they were legally married in a white man's church, they would be victims again, and this time, outnumbered as he was, he stood a good chance of losing Still Water forever.

The sergeant raised his arm to halt the patrol column. He called out no greeting, but he seemed relaxed. He looked like the same officer who had stopped at the cabin, looking for Indians. Ingor hoped he hadn't learned that he had sent the patrol in the wrong direction so they would miss finding Red Moon's band.

Within a few yards of the sergeant's horse, Ingor reined in Thor and called a greeting.

"I thought I recognized your horses, but I didn't expect

you to be riding double. I didn't know if it was you or a couple of horse thieves," he finished with a laugh.

A few men around him laughed too. Instead of staying in the column formation, some of the men had ridden closer to the sergeant to see what was going on.

Ingor could feel Still Water's spine straighten even though she kept her face down. He guessed she wished the sides of her hat were covering her cheeks instead of being pushed back so they wouldn't poke his face.

"I ride double going home with...with my new wife," Ingor said, trying to keep an even voice. Now the test was in front of them. There was no way to hide that Still Water was an Indian.

"Your wife?" the sergeant asked as if he didn't believe it. He laughed loudly and turned to the others who laughed too.

"A squaw? That's not what I would call it," he muttered. The men around him laughed again.

Ingor felt anger surge through his body. Attuned to his rider, Thor sidestepped nervously.

"Still Water is my wife," he said louder and slower than before. "We were married in Canada, and we come home to live at peace."

"You really married her? A preacher and all?"

"Yes, and I have paper to prove it."

A couple soldiers reined their horses to the side and rode around Ingor and Still Water. They looked at her closely and then at him before they laughed again. Ingor had taken about all he was going to take, even from the Army. And then he thought of the trouble they could make for her. He thought of his life without her in it everyday. He took a deep breath and gritted his teeth until they ached to control his rising temper.

"I'd better see that paper," the sergeant told him, moving his horse to stand right next to Thor. "Get back where you belong," he ordered the soldiers watching from a closer vantage point.

Ingor handed the reins to Still Water and pulled his hat off. Taking out the certificate, he unrolled it and turned it toward the sergeant. His heart was beating fast and hard. He had a hard time holding his hands still, but he didn't want to just pass it over. He didn't trust what might happen to it.

His wife had raised her face and now looked directly at the sergeant too. They each sat silently waiting while the sergeant read the paper. So much would depend on what the soldier said next, but he didn't speak. He finished reading and just looked at her.

"You meet my wife. Her name is Still Water."

"Well, I'll be damned," the man in blue finally said. "You really did get married. If that don't beat all." He laughed and turned his horse back toward his men. "They're really married."

"What would he want to do that for?" the man who had been riding beside him asked. "There's plenty of squaws waiting for a white man to take 'em whenever they want. They is camped all around the fort."

"You insult my wife?" Ingor put in, staring at the soldier who had spoken.

"That's enough, Tyler," the sergeant barked. The soldier who had slandered female Indians sat more erect and glared at the sergeant, but he said no more.

"If you think I'm gonna say 'congratulations', you are wrong," the sergeant told Ingor. "But now that you've gone and married her, I reckon I should leave her with you."

Ingor rolled up the certificate and put it back into his hat. "Just say you tell Army we are man and wife. Tell Army to leave us alone. My wife stay with me, and we bother no one."

The sergeant stared at them a few moments and then nodded once. Without another word, he swung his arm out as a signal to the patrol to follow and he reined his horse past Thor and headed west.

Ingor pulled his hat on firmly and took the reins, keeping Thor standing there as the column passed. He sat erect and proud and met each hateful or curious gaze as they fell on him and his wife. When the men in blue had passed, he tapped his heels and Thor started out in a walk.

He relaxed his spine and squeezed his wife. "We safe now," he said softly. "No one take you from me now."

He heard her take deep breaths after the fast shallow ones while the Army rode near. His own heart began to beat more normally. He had prayed that they would be safe, and now he was confident that they were.

"We safe now," he repeated to her.

She relaxed against him. "From the Army."

Flipping her cape open, she raised her foot and replaced her knife back in its holder in her moccasin top. Calmly, she lifted the cover flap over it so it wouldn't fall out as she moved. After lowering her foot, she flipped the cape back over her lap and held it with both hands inside.

"Still Water?" he asked softly.

She looked up at him, her clear gaze meeting his. "I told you. I won't let them take me away."

****

"You warm enough?" Ingor asked Still Water an hour later on the final leg of their journey. He thought they should make it to the cabin site by afternoon.

"Yes. Very warm close to you. There's not so much snow here as to the northwest and in Canada."

"No. We have easier time looking through the ashes for anything worth saving in the cabin. If I can't rescue a saw blade and an ax head, I must borrow them from Lars before we can begin work."

"Then we will travel to where the tall pines grow to cut the logs?" she asked with a smile of anticipation. "I would like to see Minnesota."

"I not have enough money left to buy logs from the farmer who deliver them in his wagon. I must cut them and let the horses drag them back to the cabin. That will take several trips to get enough, but it is only half day away. Then each one has to be notched to fit."

"I'm good with an ax. I cut fire wood all the time for my uncle."

"No, you just rest and…"

She laid a finger across his lips. "I won't break, remember? I will be fine and our baby will be fine. If I sit and do nothing, it will be harder on me."

Her comment shut him up, but he still didn't want her working too hard.

"You are amazing wife. You can do so much and you speak more English than me, too. The missionary taught you well. Did he do much good for The People?"

She lowered her head for a few moments and then slowly shook her head. "I learned English from the missionary before my parents died. He stayed two summers with us to teach us the white man's religion. Some of the people liked that, but most did not."

"How did you learn the English so good just listening to him?"

"Chief Red Moon ask me to speak for him to the missionary and to white men who came into camp to trade."

Ingor nodded. "When summer over, then the missionary moved on?"

"Yes, he said he was going to Minnesota, to a big city there."

"Minneapolis?"

She shrugged. "That could be it. I not remember. He wanted to talk to people in church there to get blankets and iron pots and other things to bring back to Red Moon and his people the next summer. To help us."

After she had remained silent for a time without continuing the story, Ingor asked, "And did he come back?"

"Yes," she said, nodding. "He came back the next spring."

She took a deep breath and let it out slowly. "He had spent the winter gathering these things for us. Some people bought new blankets and gave them to him for us." She looked down at where her hands clutched at her cape. "Others gave him blankets they...they no longer needed."

She lapsed into silence again and Ingor didn't understand why. He wanted to hear more of what happened. It made the miles pass more quickly to be talking. "And he bring these blankets to your tribe?"

"Yes, and more. Along with the blankets and a few iron pots, he...he brought the fever."

"How could he do that?" he asked with surprise.

"Some of the blankets must have been used by people who died of the fever. Instead of burning them, their families give them away and he brought them to Red Moon's people."

"That not right."

"I don't think he knew the blankets were bad medicine because he was one of the first to get sick. My mother and my father became ill soon after he did because he had been eating his meals and sleeping with my family."

She shook her head and looked off across the prairie. "My mother and father had been generous enough to invite him into our teepee, and they died for it."

"What did you do then? Were you sick?"

"No, I never get the fever. I helped cook and serve them food, but I not sit wrapped in his blanket and eat with them. When my parents got sick, they sent me to live in Red Moon's teepee because I was too young to stay by myself.

And I was too young to take care of them. I always feel sad about that. I could do nothing to save them."

"You were child," he said, giving her what he hoped was a comforting hug. She nodded, but he could see the sparkle of unshed tears in her eyes.

"Others who came to talk with the missionary about his god became ill next. Before it was all over and the fever went away, almost everyone who had talked to that white man and taken one of his blankets had died. But not me. I had talked with him, but I never slept on his gift blanket. I did not need blanket in summer, and I would not give up my soft fox fur that I slept on."

"That all very hard on little girl."

She nodded. "Red Moon insist that I live with him after my parents were gone. He ordered that my family's teepee be burned along with those that the other sick people had lived in. Then we moved on to Canada quickly instead of waiting. We never went back to that place again."

"Good to stay away from the fever."

"A white man had come into our camp and he killed many of our people."

"I not blame you if you grow up and hate all white men," Ingor told her.

"Like so many white men hate all Indians for what one did?"

Ingor squeezed her gently. "Just like that, but I glad you not hate them. You would not have saved my life when I came frozen into your camp."

She shook her head. "They not think you live. Otherwise, they not let me take care of you."

"See? I am lucky man."

A few minutes later, he added, "You think you can teach me more good English?"

"Red Moon ask me to speak whenever white man come to camp. In Canada when he went to trade goods with farmer, he ask me to do the trades in English." She shrugged. "I use English every year in Canada, but not so much in Dakota Territory where there are few white men except in forts. We stayed away from forts." She looked up at him. "But I can teach you." She paused and then went on. "Yes, and you teach me something, too."

"What you want to learn from me?"

"I want to learn to learn the ways of a white woman so I know what to do when we are in same place." She looked down at her hands that had crumpled the front of her cape. "And I want to write and to read. The only book the missionary had was his Bible and he never let that out of his sight. So I never had a book of my own. I can speak English, but I cannot read or write any."

Ingor sighed. The truth embarrassed him, but it had to come out now. "Oh, Still Water, I wish I could, but I can't."

"What do you mean?"

"First, I know little of what white woman here should do. I lived with just brothers after our parents die in Norway and here I live alone. I only see white women when I go to fort to have horse shoe fixed or to trade." His face brightened.

"But Lissa help you with the ways of white ladies. I know she will."

"Good," she replied with a grin. "Then you only teach me to read and write in English."

He shook his head, his smile gone. "I not do that either."

"You not want a wife to read and write, but you don't need to worry. I not change after I learn. I start the fire and cook for you. I will be a good wife and mother to your children, so you can teach me."

"No, I mean I can read and write in Norway but not here in English. I never learn either."

She laughed. "Then we both must find someone to teach us so we can teach our baby. A person can do much more here if they know how to read and write. I want that for our child. I not want him, or her," she amended. "I not want him to be a victim of others because he not know what papers say."

He looked down at her and kissed her. "We learn so our baby will have better life. I think Lissa teach us both."

Chapter 20

The miles left for the morning ride passed quickly as they compared stories of how they grew up and what they remembered from their childhood. Ingor had been raised in the house that his family had lived in for generations. He had a hard time understanding what it would be like to move from one place to another so often as Red Moon and his people had done. The tribe lived as hunters and gatherers, and he knew Still Water had taken for granted that they would move when the food supply was gone or the season changed. They followed the herd of buffalo to have a constant supply of meat, and raised their teepees where nature's bounty of fruits and nuts were available in late summer and fall. They had never stayed in one place long enough to cultivate any crops. They only harvested what Mother Earth provided.

When Ingor described his life in the hills overlooking the fjords in Norway, she could not imagine what Norway looked like with its high mountains and deep valleys. She already admitted to not understanding how an ocean could be so big that it would take over a moon to cross it. Picturing the steep cliffs that plunged straight down into such a big water was impossible for her.

Finally, they were following the tree line by the river to his homestead. Knowing how close they were to resting, the horses walked faster. Suddenly, Ingor pulled up the horses and held up his hand in a sign of silence.

In the distance to the south, they heard tapping—sometimes slow and sometimes fast.

"What that?" Still Water whispered. "It's not like any woodpecker I ever heard."

"No, I bet it made by two-legged animal."

They rode for several hundred more yards in silence and stopped right next to the river where the trees, dead from the floods and some still alive, were thick. After listening again for a time, he directed Thor to cross the water to the south bank there where he knew it would be safe to ford. Once on the other side, they stopped.

"You stay here with the horses," he said in a low voice. "Whatever noise is, it where my cabin used to be. I go on ahead to see what is there. I won't stand for another settler walking in and thinking he can build there and use my barn."

He dismounted and lifted her down, thankful that he wasn't feeling much from the effects of Tall Cloud's beating any more. "Can you water the horses and then tie them to that log where there's grass?"

Nodding, she took the reins. He lifted the rifle from the saddle and swung his revolver forward a little on his hip where he could reach it faster.

"Watch yourself," she said softly.

Looking back, he smiled. It felt good to have someone worried about him. He stepped back to her and kissed her, a good deal more briefly than he would have liked.

"I'll be back as quick as I can."

Bent over to stay hidden as long as possible, he wove through the trees. When he could see through the remaining trees to the cabin site, he straightened and just stared.

A hundred feet beyond a pile of burned rubble a new cabin was partially built. The log walls had nearly reached roof height. A large stone fireplace was growing in height along with the walls. Looking more carefully, he realized that they had taken the blackened stones from his old fireplace to build the new one. Someone was making himself at home in his home.

His blood began to boil. Not only had some settler taken his spot, they had taken the stones that he had laboriously gathered from riverbeds and lakes. They were using his barn, too. Someone else was building a cabin on his homestead, all right, and they were more than halfway done. They must have started immediately after he left for Canada before the ashes were even cold. Perhaps it was even the smoke rising high from the fire that day that brought them there.

Over toward the barn two people worked at cutting the small branches and bark off the next log, making it smooth the whole length, while a third wielded his ax to cut out a notch near the end to fit into the one already in place in the wall.

Ingor frowned. He leaned forward and squinted to be certain that he was seeing right.

With a broad grin, he suddenly turned and ran back toward the river where Still Water was waiting for him.

"What is the noise?" she asked as he ran toward her, heedless of the noise he was making.

He barked a laugh. "Come on and see for yourself. You not going to believe it."

He lifted her up into the saddle and swung up behind her.

"You're smiling, not angry. What *is* the noise?"

"No, I not angry. I lucky, just like I tell you. Only now I have more proof for you."

Digging his heels into Thor's flanks, they rode directly to the cabin. Jumping down, he lifted Still Water to the ground and left the horses to find their way to the barn where they knew they would find food and water. He would remove their burdens, but he had something else to do first.

"Ingor! You're home," Lars shouted as he, Wally and Lissa stopped working and ran to greet them.

Once the hugs and handshakes were over, Ingor turned to look at the new cabin. "You must have been working day and night to get much done in time we are gone."

"Actually, we had a lot of help," Wally admitted.

"Help? Who help you? No one else is around except for a couple other trappers, and they stay west or north of here."

"Not a trapper," Lars said. "The United States Army come here after they couldn't catch Red Moon before he escaped into Canada."

Still Water cried out in joy and then quickly covered her mouth. “Then my uncle Red Moon is safe in Canada?” she asked softly.

“As far as we know, he is,” Lars told her. “The Lieutenant suspected they’d had some warning, but I insisted it wasn’t any of us or you. We were all too busy fighting the fire. Then I told him you took your furs to Winnipeg to get supplies.”

“And the Lieutenant? Did he look around the fire?” Ingor asked, looking straight at Lars.

“No, he didn’t want to get his uniform dirty from soot and ashes,” Lars said with a wry laugh.

“But how did the Army help build the cabin?” Still Water asked. “I never heard of soldiers doing that.”

“Well, they camped here because Wally had just shot a deer and we invited them to eat venison steaks with us,” Lissa explained. “There were so many of them that there wasn’t much of the deer left.”

“In the morning, I think the Lieutenant was looking for an excuse to stall going back to the fort to say they couldn’t find Red Moon. He said it would be good exercise for the men to help cut a little wood. They rode west of here to a stand of tall pines in Minnesota. They cut them and tied them between their horses and dragged them back here,” Lars said. “With all their horses to drag them, they brought nearly all we needed.”

“That what I tell Still Water we have to do as soon as we get here,” Ingor said. “And they already did it.”

“We’re not done yet,” Wally put in. “But we sure appreciated the help that we got. The Lieutenant had to get back to the fort, but he was going to get someone else to go hunt for Indians to move. I pity the lesser officer who got the job."

"We took the wagon and went back for more logs after the patrol went on to the fort," Lars explained. "We cut shorter lengths and carried some back in wagon, and dragged the rest. With all the horses we had, we got enough to finish."

Ingor's gaze leapt to Lars. "Horses," he said, thinking of the two extra ones there since the fire. "Army not talk of horses here?"

Lars shook his head. "No, you not even know those horses. Wally got them cleaned up good."

"Feeding them right sure filled them out too," Wally added.

Ingor slumped with relief.

"You can see the pile of logs we have, so we're making the new cabin a little bigger than the old one. This one has a smaller room on each side of the big center one," Wally said proudly. "Now you'll have lots of room for us to come visit and stay overnight," he added with a laugh.

"We not finish the roof or fireplace yet, but we can do it before the snow comes now that you back to work with us," Lars concluded.

"You do so much for me. How can I thank you?" Ingor said softly, his gratefulness choking his voice.

"You led the way here, my brother. We wouldn't be here if you not the bold one to come here from Norway alone and make a life here."

Still Water laid her hand on Ingor's arm. "You are right. You are very lucky man," she said softly.

"You have to watch for another patrol around here now," Lars put in.

Ingor nodded. "We meet him to the west coming here."

"You met up with the Army patrol? But what did he say about Still Water?"

"He not have much to say." He smiled and put his arm around her. "I tell him that we get married in little church in Canada. A lady played organ and the preacher signed paper for us." He pulled off his hat and showed the Certificate of Marriage to Lars and Lissa.

"The lady played the organ? Is that what you call it that makes the music?" Still Water asked.

"Yes," Ingor said, pulling her against his side. "You push the white and black keys and it makes music. We have those in Norway too."

Besides Wally, Lissa was the only one who could read all the words on the certificate in English. The brothers prompted her to read it out loud, which she did solemnly. When she had finished, she rolled the paper carefully and handed it back to Ingor.

"No one can doubt that you are married now," she said with a smile. "Congratulations."

"That good because we have baby coming," Ingor said with a laugh. "We got to get working on cabin fast. Baby will need roof over his head."

They laughed and Lars and Wally slapped Ingor on the

back with good wishes for the new father.

Still Water felt as if her heart were full to bursting. Her new family around her was happy that she had become Ingor's wife. This was not her Indian family in Red Moon's camp, but she knew now that this was a family where she could be happy. And she could be an Indian.

Lissa stepped close and hugged her. "I'm so happy for you," Lissa told her.

"I have so much to thank you for, Lissa, but I have made your apron and hat dirty beyond getting clean."

Lissa brushed aside her worry with a sweep of her hand. "The Dakota sun will do much to getting them white again."

"Good. But I still want to ask you for a big favor."

"What is it?" Lissa asked, the smile still on her face.

Still Water felt her cheeks warm as she decided how to say what she wanted. She could think of no way better than using the direct approach. "I want you to teach me and Ingor how to read and write the English."

"Oh, is that all?" Lissa asked with a laugh. "That will be something we can start in the evenings by firelight while we are still here. I even have a book with me that I read while I feed the baby. I'll leave it with you and give you others each time we visit each other. I brought a whole box of them from Philadelphia."

"It will be hard to learn. The words all look so different."

"It won't be hard for you. Since you speak English so well, learning to read and write will be easy."

"Thank you," Still Water said, daring a quick hug. She

ran to Ingor to tell him the good news.

After the horses were unsaddled and their food stowed, they all got to work. Building a log cabin was hard work, and it took the five of them several days to finish the walls. The fireplace grew with the walls and then they put up the roof supports. Over those strong logs they laid much more slender ones. When open spaces had been filled with thick branches, they covered the roof with thick sod blocks the way they had in Lars' sod house. Packing the squared pieces tightly together, they were confident that neither rain nor snow could get through.

"We have house but no furniture," Ingor lamented.

"But it warmer than sleeping on ground in the barn. We will be fine," Still Water insisted.

"I wish our soddy was closer. We could get the planks we have left and Wally could make you some," Lissa offered.

"Say, if you want, I could get them and stay with you for a few weeks to make some furniture for your new cabin," Wally offered.

"That would be good," Ingor agreed with a grin.

Ingor turned to Lars and Lissa. "You not mind if Wally stays here?"

"No, and he can help with the reading and writing lessons after I leave," Lissa said.

"Aw, that would be like going back to school," Wally complained.

"But now you will be the teacher," Lissa pointed out.

"Oh, yeah. I didn't think of that," the boy who had become a man over the past year replied with a grin. He caught his thumbs in his suspenders and strutted to the cabin.

"It would be good to have a bed up off the cold ground," Ingor put in. "I not want my baby born on the ground."

"And I could even make a cradle for the baby," Wally turned back to suggest.

"Oh, yes. He made a beautiful one for me," Lissa said, pausing as a big smile filled her face. "Eric loves it when I rock him to sleep in it."

"This calls for a festive dinner," Lissa announced. "You get the door to the front porch hung so we can close it to-night, and Still Water and I will cook the food."

They all had a good deal to celebrate besides the new cabin for the newlyweds: Ingor and Still Water's marriage that meant Still Water could stay with him, and their baby on the way, plus the important fact that Still Water and Ingor were going to learn to read and write English while Wally played being the teacher as well as furniture maker for them.

They all feasted on venison that Lars had shot after the Army ate the other one. The women also had cooked carrots and potatoes, and fresh sourdough bread that Lissa showed Still Water how to bake in a small box oven they built into the new fireplace. Enjoying an after-dinner cup of hot coffee from the grounds the Trading Post owner had given him as a wedding gift, Ingor wrapped his arm around his wife and held her against his side.

"It would be good if our family in Norway could celebrate with us. I wish they know how happy we all are," he said.

"We must write them a letter," Lars proposed.

"They be happy we have found good wives," Ingor said.

They all clapped in agreement. Lars and Ingor reminisced about the old country that seemed so far removed from their happy new homes in Dakota Territory.

* * * *

And on that same October night, another celebratory dinner was taking place in Ingor and Lars' uncle Ole's house in Norway. Their uncle announced to the family and friends gathered around him that he had made his mind up. He had picked the two local young women who would go to America to marry his nephews.

He would send the young ladies to America on the first ship due to leave the following spring. From New York they would travel by train as much of the way as possible by then, though Ole wasn't certain how far that was. From there they would take a horse-drawn coach and arrive in Dakota Territory before winter.

There they would meet their new husbands-to-be, the brothers Ingor and Lars Oleson.

ABOUT THE AUTHOR

Lois Carroll has been writing since her childhood when she received a daily diary as a gift. With a bachelor's degree in English Literature and a master's in Theater, she began her professional writing and editing career working at a publishing company. Now a wife, mother, and grandmother, she lives in Arizona and writes full time. You can read about her books and email her through her web site at: http://loiscarrollbooks.com/

She loves hearing from her readers.